CRIMSON MADNESS

A Paul Isaac Vampire Series

JAMES C. GILLEN

Hydra
Publications

ISBN: 978-1-942212-95-9

Hydra Publications
Goshen, Kentucky 40026
www.hydrapublications.com

To my mom and dad.
All the love and support I could ask for.

CHAPTER ONE

I looked at the three undead figures far off in the ink black night. They stood as still as statues, never breathing, never moving. That's the creepy thing about the undead. They truly are nothing more than animated death. Corpses with fangs. Walking maggot farms. Coffin bait.

Each one of them looked at me as I pulled the stake out of the heart of their fellow vein weasel and wiped away the slime on my jeans. Death and I had somehow synonymously become one. I pulled the large Bowie knife from its sheath on my belt and cut the bleeding heart from the dead maggot's chest. I held in my hand and showed it to others in the distance as though I was the wicked witch offering them a poison apple.

Cockroaches. There was no other word for what they were. Those a little more politically correct than I am call them vampires, but when it comes down to it, they are nothing more than cockroaches.

It took the work of the bleeding hearts in this country, known as the Knights of the Night, to turn them from the killer monsters they really are, to legal citizens with rights and protection. The cockroaches are now seen as historical artifacts that can no longer be killed unless they were turned after the laws went into effect. They crawl through our cities, spread their nasty diseases, live on the filth of humanity. Take it from me, simply killing these four is not enough. The only solace will be in total genocide of the species.

All this compromises what I do for a living. You see, I'm Paul Isaac, vampire executioner. It's dangerous and has very few rewards other than knowing that you are ridding the world of one more bloodsucker. Some say I have a hidden agenda in what I do and I don't deny it. They killed my parents and still roamed the street with no fear.

I threw the muscle into the swamp and stood again. I was about to change all of that.

All four of these coffin sleepers had been given death warrants by the police department. Seems they were having a little too much fun with a freak, or willing blood donor, and drained her dry. Shame, but death warrants are the only way I'm able to kill the monsters anymore without retribution from the new laws and the Cockroach Nation. Unfortunately for them, I usually don't let a little thing like the law get in the way of what I do.

We moved further into the cypress swamp, filled with all the creepy crawlies I could handle. Spanish moss hung from the branches like grotesque bats, glowing in the moonlight. The darkness was working for the blood slurpers better than it was for me. I stopped to listen for any sounds that I could hear. My eyes searched for any movement. Shadows ahead of me in phantom form.

I lit a cigar and got ready for the only thing worth living for. With my right hand I pulled out the Magnum filled with ultra violet bullets from my shoulder holster and began to move. My leather trench coat pulled away so I could get to my other arsenal if needed. That was the good thing about the coat. It had plenty of pockets and places to keep things such as holy water, crucifixes, and extra weapons.

The big one saw me and began to move away from the other two. He climbed in a tall cypress, trying to hide among the endless branches. I pulled the Magnum up and held my breath, waiting for a clean shot to present itself. Being younger daisy pushers, they weren't as quick and strong. But at least they were smart enough to know they weren't a match for me and my playground of firepower.

Our eyes met for only a brief second. His filled with fear, mine with joy. Finger touched the trigger. An explosion filled the emptiness of the desolate night. My bullet found its mark, turning the monster into cinder, showering the swamp below in unholy ash.

In the darkness I could hear the other two moving fast. Branches gave way to speed. Feet struggled to make distance.

I exhaled the cigar smoke from my lungs and began to move through the dark maze again. The last thing I wanted to do was gloat over my kills while the other two escaped in this mosquito filled hellhole.

My boots were slick with wet mud as I began to pursue the two monsters that remained. Sweat rolled off my clean shaved head and threatened to go into my eyes. Even on an October night in Florida, the temperature can be an issue. Being a chain smoker and out of shape didn't help either. Go figure.

I stopped from time to time and listened. I followed the sounds and kept my eyes open for a sneak attack. Remember, two monsters remained. Playing fair was not something that vampires were known for. Especially when they knew they were in a life or death situation. I looked in every direction, including up. Cockroaches could levitate if powerful enough. Yeah, I said they weren't that powerful, but I wasn't about to find out I was wrong the hard way.

Silence.

Nothing.

Not even the frogs were making a sound. It was as if death had taken over everything in the swamp. A silence so thick it became an entity all its own.

I turned in circles trying to see or hear anything I could. My breath and heart the only sounds. Shadows of branches the only sight. I kept the Magnum up and ready, knowing somewhere nearby two cockroaches were waiting for me to make the next move. My breath became shallow sniffs.

From the right I was hit with the force of a freight train. Spinning in circles, I landed on the soggy swamp bottom, mud mixing with stagnant water on my skin. Cigar shooting from my mouth. Still, luck was on my side for the moment. I ended up on top of the cockroach with my Magnum still in hand. Unfortunately for me, it was pointed away, harmless to the monster. Resisting hands trying to pry it free.

I looked down at the cockroach and noticed it was the female monster. Gleaming white fangs inches from my throat. I used every bit of human strength I had to keep my body on top of hers. If she got free before I killed her, she would have the advantage. Even newly turned roaches have far more strength than humans. To win in these situations, I had to fight as dirty as I could. Just because I was fighting with a bitch dirt napper wasn't going to change that.

A knee jammed between my legs, knocking me off the monster and on my back. Instant nausea. I guess it's safe to say bitch cockroaches know how to fight dirty too. I tried my best to catch my breath as the bloodsucker scratched me across the face, bringing with it instant pain and blood. Now I was simply pissed and about to show it.

I never had time to react when the second cockroach joined in the fight. He landed on me with an incredible force, shoving out what little air I still had in me. Long fingernails dug deep into my skin. I saw the female monster move toward me. A sinister smile rose on her lips.

With every ounce of strength I had, I turned the Magnum on the male blood junkie and pulled the trigger. Demonic music filled the quiet night as blood rushed from the wound, followed by smoke, then fire. Ultra violet light spread through him like a foul disease. Evil fireworks shot from the wound and reflected on the swamp water.

I tried to fire a second shot at the female fang head but there wasn't enough time. She was back on me. Determined to either kill me or really piss me off. The result would be determined by whether or not I got an advantage.

Her hands wrapped around my throat like a vice, cutting off all air. I moved the Magnum in her direction, only to feel a foot crush my wrist and pin it in the inches of muck underneath me.

I fired the shot anyway, hoping that I'd get lucky. Hoping that it scared her enough that I might be able to regain some ground. Tonight wasn't looking like my night for that sort of luck. The gun went off with a violent growl but the bullet missed everything but the sky.

I felt one hand loosen from around my neck and grab the wrist with the Magnum. With a quick aggressive move, my wrist met with a cypress stump. I heard a sickening snap of bone and the Magnum fell harmlessly next to the water. Pain flooded into my hand, spider webbing to numbness.

Nothing says panic like a broken wrist *and* losing the best fire-power you have on you in the middle of a life and death struggle with a cockroach. With my remaining good hand, I reached into my trench coat pocket and blindly searched for any of my other weapons that might do the job. Fingers found a crucifix. Christianity never felt so good.

She laughed. "Tonight you die, Avenger."

Sucks when the monsters might be right. No pun intended.

She began to drag me deeper into the God forsaken muck and water. Undead hands pushed forcefully on my throat. My face plunged under the water.

Now, a minute ago, I was thinking nothing says panic like a broken wrist and losing my Magnum, but I was wrong. There was suddenly another factor coming in to play. A broken wrist. Losing my Magnum. *And drowning.* That was a true triple threat of panic for me.

I had to give that one to her. At least she was more creative than most other roaches I came across. Still, drowning or bleeding meant the same thing right now. Death. The only saving grace drowning had was in the fact that I wouldn't rise as a blood sucker.

But I wasn't in the mood to die just yet.

From under the water, I could see her emotionless face staring back at me with dead eyes. Most people can't look a roach in the eyes without the monster gaining control, but I was able to do it with the less powerful ones.

My lungs burned, deprived of oxygen. It felt as though my head was caving in. I wanted to fight back with the broken wrist enough that I could get my head back above water, but the pain was way too much. Chances were, I was going to die, but I wasn't about to die without leaving a little reminder for her.

I jammed the crucifix in her right eye and twisted it with as much pressure as I could. Streams of clear liquid mixed with crimson blood as I burst the eyeball like a ripe grape. From under the water, I could hear her hellish screams and it made everything all right again.

Wrong.

She grabbed me out of the water, hands still firmly around my neck. The crucifix still dangled in the eyeball, bouncing on her cheek.

I gasped for air. It was the most incredible sensation I had ever had. Teetering on erotic. You never know how wonderful a set of lungs full of air can be until you've been under water for who knows how long.

She lifted me up to her fangs. I knew what this was going to feel like. I had had a cockroach bite me before. It hurts like a son-of-a-bitch. A sensation I'd be damned if I would repeat.

I drove my fist into her temple, repeatedly. I could feel the flesh on my knuckles ripping with each drive, but so far it was less painful than having fangs pierce my jugular.

Her head twisted toward mine and I caught the crucifix and eyeball with my hand. I pulled them both free from the socket, then drove them into the gaping mouth at my throat. Dark screams bellowed out of her. I could hear and see the destruction the object was doing.

Without warning, she began to shove me back under the water again. She pounded my head on the sediment on the bottom. Again and again. I fought to remain conscious. But with each smash of my skull, it looked more and more like a losing effort.

I saw colors forming in my eyes as I began to pass out. Was it from the concussion or from drowning? Did it matter? One thing was for sure, I wasn't going to go towards some damn light if things faded to black.

Then the unexpected happened.

Her hands released my throat. Weight lifted off of me. One minute full on, the next non-existent.

Lifting my head back above water, I looked over at the fang mouthed bitch and saw her face down in the water. Floating. Shit, that's not right. To be face down, she'd have to have a head.

I wiped the mud and water from my eyes as I continued to gasp for breath. Skin crawled. Knowing I couldn't have been lucky enough not to have at least some cockroach blood on me. My lungs felt as though they were on fire. I gagged and puked, not from the headless monster, but from the water I strangled on. I wasn't going to die from a vampire. I was going to die from some microscopic entity I just swallowed. Ameba City, here I come.

Only steps away from me, I saw the Magnum lying on the ground at the water's edge. I stumbled the few feet and picked it up.

Something told me I was far from out of danger. Vein weasels don't pop their heads off like this. And even if she swallowed the crucifix and eyeball, it wouldn't have done this much damage. Im-freaking-possible.

I pointed the Magnum in every direction with my left hand. I wasn't as dangerous with it as I was with the right, but I did what I had to in these situations. My eyes tried to focus as I continued to catch my breath.

Only trickles of light from the large moon overhead gave me any source of sight painting the swamp with different shades of darkness. When dealing with monsters like these, I wanted as much light as I could get.

The big question was a simple one. What the hell took the head off the cockroach that had been on top of me? The first thing that came to mind was maybe there had been five roaches frolicking in the woods with me, but that didn't make any sense. Given the choice between me and their fellow living dead, they would choose me to lose my head. Next thought was werewolf. They definitely had the strength to do it. And their alliance with the cockroaches weren't all that tight.

I made sure I still had the 9mm in the hip holster just to be safe. It was filled with silver nitrate bullets. There was nothing I could put my finger on, but something told me that this attack wasn't from a fur ball. They usually move in packs, make a lot of noise and eat what they kill.

Power.

Like electricity, it moved over my skin, raising the hair on my arms and along the back of my neck. Mystery solved. Somewhere very close by was an extremely old and powerful cockroach.

CHAPTER TWO

I turned as quickly as I could and came face to face with the source of the power. My Magnum now pressed against what I had planned on being its temple, but I found the barrel closer to his chest. He was easily the tallest and widest monster I had ever known. Add the amount of power falling off of him, and I knew I was in deep trouble.

Before I knew it, I had taken a large step backwards. "You make one wrong move and I swear I'll put this bullet through you blood sucking head." Might as well act as though I wasn't scared. I wasn't even sure I could convince myself of that.

He smiled and turned his head down to look at the gun. "You must be quite a marksman to shoot me in the heart and have the bullet go through my...blood sucking head."

I kept the Magnum on him. "I'm not kidding. You blink and you're ash."

"I would have expected much more gratitude from you after what I have just done." The corners of his lips began to curl into a smile.

"What the hell do you want, Asa?" That's right. I knew this oversized piece of bat dung. He was the master of what are known as the pure blood cockroaches. Ones that were born roaches instead of rising as one. All being said and done, he was far more powerful and dangerous than anything I had ever come across before. Ageless and menacing.

"Perhaps not much different from what you want, my friend." His dark skin looked nearly purple in the thin light. A voice so deep it vibrated my bones. Or perhaps it was my fear that was vibrating in me. Jamaican accent, I assumed. Either way, I didn't like my newfound situation much better than the last.

"Let me guess, you want to see the world rid of all the walking dead too." I tightened the muscles in my legs to keep my knees from knocking.

He laughed. "Precisely."

"So pulling the trigger is okay with you?"

"I understand your sarcasm and appreciate the wit behind it, but I am not one of the living dead. I do believe you have missed that very important key point."

"And you never seem to get to one." I took a breath as I looked at him. The smirk on his face made me want to hit him, but it also told me he was far from being intimidated by me. That sucks. "You've been here the whole time haven't you?" I began to move out of the swamp water, feeling and smelling the wetness sticking to me like a film. I spat the remaining water from my mouth.

He gave a simple nod. "Simply watching you kill. I find it quite fascinating actually. A work of true art if I may say so myself." He looked at my wrist. "It seems as though the young vampire has broken your wrist. I fear you may need a doctor." For the first time since coming face to face with him, he moved. Just short of pacing.

"I know killing you would make the pain go away."

"Ahh," he said and smiled revealing those menacing damn fangs. "Will this no doubt help you and your nightmares?"

"Killing you? Warm and fuzzy all over."

He seemed to look me over from head to toe. I could tell the wheels were turning but I wasn't sure why. Then again I hadn't figured out why I hadn't just pulled the trigger and left him for whatever lived in this living hell. Chances were really good I'd be able to get away with it.

He took in a deep breath and put his index finger to his nose. Yes, those born a plasma parasite breathe. "Rumors in the night. Facts or fiction?"

"About?"

"The disease running through your veins. Neither vampire nor lycan." His eyebrows rose as if asking the question. "I smell it and it is very intoxicating. Powerful. Tempting."

"I don't know what you're talking about."

He shrugged. "I hear rumors you were injected with a poison meant to kill you and turn you into a vampire by Quinn Rubio, master vampire of the undead. Rumor also has it you were bitten by a werewolf along the same time. The combination left you with traces of both, but so far, no symptoms. Outwardly, anyway. Actually, I envy the dilemma." He kept his eyes on the Magnum. "I never knew you were so hard to kill."

"And I never knew you were so full of bullshit."

He smiled again and nodded. "Do you deny it?"

"That you're full of bullshit? No."

He howled with laughter. "Come now, we both know I talk of the attacks."

"What if I do?"

His eyes grew wide. "Time will tell if the rumors are true. If they are, the wrist in question will be healed within twenty-four hours. Your very own body will give away the secret if it in fact exists." He looked back to the Magnum once again. "Now do you plan on shooting me or not, Mr. Isaac?"

"You'll be the first to know." He had graduated from being just a simple pain in the ass to a full-blown threat to my disease. I still hadn't come to terms with it yet. I think it's called denial and I was its poster child. To think I had the very same virus running through me that he did made me want to put the first bullet to my very own head.

"It is just that if you plan to hold that weapon on me you should shoot. Otherwise, pointing it at me is merely pointless do you not think?" He leaned against a cypress tree as if posing for GQ.

He had a point. I lowered it, but kept it in hand.

"Why did you kill the bitch instead of me?"

"Doing my part to save humanity."

"Are you really going to make me waste my breath and say bull-shit again?"

"Did you not just say it anyway?" He pushed away from the tree and floated toward me again.

God, how do you match wits with something that is over a thou-sand years old? "Damn it Asa, enough with the endless riddles. Tell me what you want or I'll kill you here and now. No one would ever question it and we both know it." I spat more swamp from my mouth.

"Same thing as you do." His shadow dwarfed me.

"To see yourself crumble into a pile of ash at my feet, I doubt that, but go on." I picked leaves and twigs from my skin that had formed a bond with the drying pond water.

"A repeal of the Vampire Laws." Moonlight glowed off the top of his shaved head. Between his baldhead and mine, we were prob-ably a potent light source in the thick darkness.

"You think that's why I'm here? I'm not here to repeal any damn cockroach laws. Simply killing a few monsters that sucked off more than they could chew. Cockroach laws had nothing to do with it."

"No, I am not quite that presumptuous. I am aware that your motive is far darker. I am not asking you about your desires simply for tonight, but more long term. If the laws were to be repealed, I think we would be equally satisfied with the results they gave, would we not?"

"Meaning I could kill you and not have all the paperwork to fill out. No laws, all joy."

This made him laugh. "Something like that I suppose."

"It all sounds great to me, Asa, but that perfect little world doesn't exist. Now if you don't mind, I have to go." My wrist was throbbing, but letting him know that wasn't an option. And regardless of what ran through my veins, seeing a doctor seemed like a real good idea. Morphine to the max.

He bowed with a swooping motion of his hand. "As you wish, but keep in mind that the tide of necessity may already be in motion. I am not here to stop you from killing the commercial vampires. In fact, I encourage the act. But there are those around you, those you trust, that seem to be hiding a great deal from you in the form of distraction."

"Bull…"

He stopped me with a raise of his hand. "You have heard of the Knights of the Night have you not?"

"Yeah, an extreme group of human cockroach supporters that goes around spreading the good word of cockroach legalization. The ones responsible for making all of you protected beings. Protected as living artifacts. Fanatics as twisted to my kind as PETA is to meat eaters."

"So you are aware that certain high level members of their society have gone missing over the last few weeks."

I walked back toward the cockroach in front of me. In the moonlight I could see his well-tailored purple velvet jacket. White pants interrupted by shiny black cropping boots. He was dressed like something straight out of the eighteenth century. Funny thing about cockroaches I have never been able to figure out. They've claimed to be around for thousands of years, yet their fashion sense stopped in 1750. I just didn't get it.

"More than missing, Asa. They're dead."

"Tragic, I am sure. And do tell. How did they die?"

"Michelle Kevington was killed in an automobile accident. George Hernandez committed suicide."

"Are you sure of this?"

"Why would I question it?"

"Some presume they were killed by the hand of vampires."

A laugh escaped before I could stop it. "Really. And how do you know about that?"

"A great cover up exists. The police department does not want the news to be leaked to the press. You know as well as I that any bad press against the commercial vampires will not be tolerated. Far too much money would be lost. That is why you are here tonight. The police do not wish for you to know the truth."

"What truth?" I waited for the punch line.

"The two humans were killed by vampires."

"And you are nothing but a liar." Even though I didn't believe him, I was already making mental notes to ask Kansas.

He shrugged. "There is an easy way to find the truth if you truly wish to seek it."

"Meaning check the bodies myself," I answered.

"Precisely."

"You know something about the deaths?"

"Only that they exist. I assure you I have had nothing to do with them."

My mind began to play games with me. Was I truly standing in the middle of a Florida swamp, getting eaten alive by mosquitoes and falling for this? Part of me was. Kansas had been acting a little secretive lately. I took a deep breath. There was no way the police would know of vampire killings in the city and not tell me. They wouldn't take that kind of a chance. "Then why bring them up?" I asked.

"To protect the vampires loyal to me. I wish no harm to be brought to them by you or the police. There is a wave of revolution among the true vampires. For centuries, we have lived by our own creed and law. Now, thanks to the human laws, the Knights of the Night, and commercial vampires like Quinn Rubio who embrace the laws and the status it brings, true vampires like myself have been compromised."

"So you think by telling me this keeps you from being on my radar screen?"

For some reason, this brought another smile. "I am simply telling you there is an undercurrent going on in this city that is reaching epidemic proportions. In the centuries past, we monitored the human deaths that occurred and corrected the problems that are prevalent today. We never allowed the carcass to rise as a true vampire. We sever the heads after feeding, so they would never become a nightwalker. It was a way of keeping our race pure and strong."

"Humanitarians to the end aren't you."

He gave a quick shrug of the shoulders. "Call it what you will."

"Tell me something I don't know."

"You were sent here on a...what is it you call it..." He tapped his finger on his chin while looking upward in a bad attempt of thought. "A wild goose chase."

"A wild goose chase," I repeated.

"Precisely. It was the only way Detective Kansas could keep you from interfering."

"What do you mean, interfering?"

"He sent you here tonight to kill the four vampires so they could cover up a more prominent murder under your nose. With you out of the way, they will be able to make yet another killing go away. The press cannot report on something they do not know. You cannot hunt and kill what they wish to remain silent. It would appear as though your friend Detective Kansas has aligned himself with the commercial vampires and compromised the very oath he stands for. We must work together for a common goal." He walked back into the shadows. "The vampires like you killed tonight, feed off the human freaks, filled with disease. Bottom feeders. They are the true, as you say, cockroaches. Quinn and the police are trying to keep you occupied while they frolic in the world of death until they can use you. If you attack too soon, their justification will not be welcomed."

Why is it that anytime there is something evil, twisted and nasty in this city, the name Quinn Rubio comes up? "What are you talking about?"

A deep grunt came from his throat. I think it was laughter, but I wasn't sure. His voice so deep even Barry White would be impressed. "You were brought here to kill insignificant vampires while the police destroy the evidence of a vampire attack."

"What attack?"

"Another member of the Knights of the Night. A killer is taking them out one by one."

"Who?" My hand gripped the Magnum again. Was this the confessions of a killer? I tried to slow my breathing and remain as calm as I could. Not something I was sure I could do.

"Of this I am not certain."

"Why do you care? I thought they were your enemy anyway. Last time I heard, you wanted them all dead."

"And still do." He looked up at the full moon and basked in it as if it were the sun. "I am not looking for justice for them, I am looking for protection for my kind. Expose the killings and we both move closer to our ultimate goals. There is an old saying, the enemy of my enemy is my friend."

"There's also an old saying of don't bullshit a bullshitter so don't start with another riddle."

He put his hand up to silence me again. "I do not wish to...as you say...bullshit you. I am asking for your help and protection of my coven. We have had nothing to do with the killings, yet the police and those loyal to Quinn Rubio are plotting to frame the murders on us in order to save grace with the human sentiment."

"Why would a cockroach loyal to Rubio be killing members of the Knights of the Night?"

"Of this, I am not sure. I care even less. For us it has golden rewards and for me much more."

"Do tell."

"Retribution."

"Retribution?"

"Yes. If we work together, we can rid this place of the impureness that is like a plague among my kind as well as yours. Death has an uncommon way of waking the slumber of ignorance. Sooner or later, questions will surface about the deaths of the members of the Knights of the Night. I, along with the pure vampires under me, will be blamed for the attacks. We would be hunted, arrested and killed, needlessly. If we are successful in repealing the vampire laws, then you and I will be able to settle our differences without involving the laws of the humans. Together we will be able to kill the commercial vampires. We will gain purity in our species, you will once again be able to go on a killing spree. True retribution for us all."

"And what exactly is it that you think I'm going to do to help in this?"

"Expose the deaths for what they really are and the die shall be cast on its own." Asa stepped back into the moonlight. "Turn your back on this and you will only be turning it on the victims and their families in the killer's wake."

"For someone that knows nothing about the killer or the killings, you sure have a lot of theories on it."

"I have seen the bodies before they were taken to the morgue.

You're killer is killing for the sake of the act, not for nourishment. That alone should make you afraid."

And it did. "What if I chose to do nothing? After all, aren't they doing us both a favor by killing the activists?"

"The authorities will place the blame on my kind and the true killer continues to walk free. For you and the rest of the humans, the deaths will not stop. Visit the morgue if you fear I may be trying to deceive you." He tried to catch my eyes. I lowered them in time. "If you do not warn the humans of the massacre, more will die. Expose the secrets and expose the vampires as nothing more than dangerous beings that must be hunted and killed."

I had to laugh. "Let me get this straight. You actually want me to warn the members of the Knights of the Night, tell the press, confront the police, all so the public will turn against your kind."

"Nay, not my kind, but the commercial kind. I am counting on the fact that the human's fears and hatred will overturn the human laws with the vampire nation. If that happens, both you and I will be able to live the way we wish. No more sneaking around and killing only when a judge tells us we can."

I moved past him and began to walk away. "You're a nut case Asa. Fight this battle on your own. I'm sure the cockroach nation would love to hear this theory."

"Does the name Susannah Metzgar sound familiar?"

"Yeah, she's one of the movers and shakers for the Knights, why?"

"She is the latest victim of our killer. Killed like the ones before her."

"Why do you think even if her death is fang related that I just won't kill all of you? You're no better than the commercial vampires, just a little more elusive. Kill each other for all I care." I continued to walk.

He stopped me again. "The Vampire Nation is vast and complicated. You can ignore it, analyze it all you want, or you can be a part of it and expose the truth. The choice is really up to you." He started to move away from me in large steps. "I must go now. Make your choice. Your actions will align you with Quinn Rubio and the commercial vampires or the true nightwalkers like myself. Either way, death shall rise again."

"Sounds like…"

Again, he raised his hand. "All you have to do is visit the morgue. If there is no sign of a vampire attack then you shall have your proof that I am, as you so eloquently put it, a bullshit artist."

"I don't need a corpse to prove that, Asa. You are a bullshit artist."

CHAPTER THREE

I had stopped by the emergency room and had my wrist set and placed in a cast. Deep inside, I hoped that I didn't heal quickly. The more pain and the more therapy it took to heal, the better. As crazy as it sounds, it proved to me I was still more human than monster.

The conversation with Asa still ran through my head like a bad movie. No matter how much I told myself that it was all lies, I kept coming back to it. I could call and confront Kansas, but that wouldn't do any good. If Asa's story was true, the detective would simply deny it. But there was a golden opportunity that I knew I couldn't pass up. The body of Susannah Metzgar should still be in the morgue. All I had to do was go down there and see it for myself. If the victim had died of natural causes rather than a victim of a cockroach bite, I'd be able to tell. Especially if she had been killed old school style, meaning the head was cut off.

I stood and looked at the morgue door with my body shaking and numb. There were a million emotions running through me and I wasn't sure how to process them all. I was scared, angry, and confused. The thoughts of a serial killing cockroach roaming the streets once again was bad enough. Throw in the questionable fact that Kansas and the police were involved in the cover up made me sick. When your only informant is a thousand year old master vein lover, there's reason to be skeptical. If they involved you, you could rest assured that it benefited them in some way.

Tonight was the first time I had been to the morgue since Dr. Montgomery was found with a bullet hole in her head. She used to be the doctor down here at night until she got caught up with a very evil roach that loved to amputate and torture his victims. As twisted as it was, I still missed her in a way. Take away the fang freak connection and she had been kind of cool. But as I always say, mess with the monsters and you'll end up six feet under. That went for me too, by the way.

I punched in the code, took a deep breath and opened the door quickly. There was no other way to do it. If I stood any longer, I'd lose my nerve and walk away.

The room looked very different from the last time I had been there. On that night, I had found myself face to face with a newly turned bloodsucker. It killed one woman and threatened to kill everyone in the hospital. I had to shoot it with ultra violet bullets. Several times.

Now, there were no signs of the killings. No blood on the floors and walls. No bullet holes. Only fresh paint and tile. The morgue looked as though nothing had happened here at all. As if death itself was now absent.

A man with a long brown ponytail looked up from a microscope to greet me. "What are you doing here?" He looked confused. His pale skin let me know right away, this one didn't get out much. The kind of guy that masturbated to any movie with a spaceship in it.

I had scared him. It was just one of those things you can tell by the look on the other person's face. It made me laugh to myself. "I'm Paul Isaac. Where's Susannah Metzgar's body?"

"I didn't ask you who you were. I asked you what you were doing here?" Angry eyes looked into mine as he stood. He tried to be intimidating, but it came across as desperate and sad. I could tell by his quick movements he was searching for something to hit me with. Big mistake.

He looked past me to the door I had just come through. "Didn't the security guard stop you out there?"

I looked behind me and shrugged my shoulders. "What security guard?"

The man walked back toward a small desk, holding his first finger up. "Just hold on. I'll get to the bottom of this. You're not supposed to be here." With the other hand, he reached for the phone. "I was given very strict orders not to let you in here." He began to dial the phone.

"By who?"

"That's none of your business."

I pulled the phone from his hands and smashed it against the wall. He crumpled on the desk, melted, and cowered to the floor. I could feel anger rush through me at lightning speed. Not at the seventies throw back on the floor, but the fact that everyone was in on the murders but me.

"They said not to let you in here. It was a police matter," he finished.

"Why would a woman that died of natural causes be a matter for the police? Or need a security guard at the door? What are they covering up?"

"How did you even find out about this? They said you wouldn't even be here. That there was nothing to be worried about." He paced in small spurts. His eyes darted between the door and phone. I wasn't going to let him get to either.

"Well as you can see, they lied. Now where's the body? This is bigger than just a police matter. It's a matter of human security." My eyes searched the room. Hoping to find a body, fearing I'd find an undead sun crispy. "I have reason to believe Susannah Metzgar was killed by a blood sucker. Surely you heard what happened the last time a neck biter rose in here."

"Yeah, you shot the place to hell, one person was killed and they had to practically rebuild the morgue."

"And I'm about to do it again, Dr..." I searched him for a name. Might as well use my intimidation to get what I wanted. With a bend of my arm, I allowed the Magnum to show. I had no intention of using it, but he didn't know that. That was the good thing about having a reputation like mine. I pulled him to me by his credentials. "Doctor Zusack?"

"Please don't kill me. I just did what I was told." He gasped for air like a goldfish out of water. As well he should. Being no more than a hundred twenty pounds wet, I'd have a field day with his spine if he gave me any reason to relocate it.

"And what was that?"

"Not to tell you anything. They said you weren't to know about the bodies." He pushed against me, but I held tight.

"Know what about the bodies?"

He looked at me through trembling hands. Eyes glassy with formed tears. I opened the trench coat enough that he could see the Magnum, again. He swallowed hard. "Cause of death."

"Which bodies and what cause of death."

"All of them. I was told if you came poking around here asking questions, not to tell you how they died. I was to call Detective Kansas immediately."

I lifted him to my eye level. It was one of those questions you know you have to ask, but are already afraid of the answer you know you'll get. Like with bad medicine, the quicker you take it, the better. "Well Dr. Zusack, I *am* here and I *am* poking around asking questions. How did they die?"

"Please God, don't make me say it. They'll kill me."

"They're the police, doctor. They're not going to kill you. I on the other hand just might."

With a quick jerk, he looked me in the eyes again. There was no doubt, he thought I was serious. "Not the police you asshole. Them!"

"You mean the fang heads." I dropped him, but still didn't allow him any room to move away.

He closed his eyes tight and shook his head. "God, I'm a dead man."

"Where's the body of Susannah Metzgar?"

"She's not here. She was taken to the funeral home already by the family."

I patted the Magnum with my bandaged hand. "I'm a very desperate man. I won't think twice about killing you. Like you said, the last time I was here I killed a lot of things and messed up a lot of paint. Some even think I might have been the one that put the bullet in Montgomery's skull. According to my therapist, I'm known to be unstable, ruthless, and a loaded gun, so don't become another statistic simply because you lied to me. Just tell me where she is and I won't kill you no matter how hard you beg."

"In there," he quickly nodded to a room I knew well. It was a holding room for roach victims. In the event that they turned early, they were locked in the room with ultra violet light and crucifixes. It was here that I normally would behead the victim and remove the heart. A gruesome task, but somebody had to do it.

I moved past the doctor and opened the door to the room, expecting to find the remains of Susannah Metzgar, but instead I saw nothing. No gurney. No body. Simply four walls.

The blow to my back came quick and violent. I slid across the floor and landed on the cast with my face. Confusion set in at first, then anger. Ideas were already blossomed in my mind about how I'd beat him to a pulp.

As I rose to face him, I heard the door slam shut, felt the distant purr of power. I cursed under my breath, realizing I had been tricked by this punk doctor barely out of med school. There was no doubt in my mind the door was locked, but I tried it all the same. I had to get out. I was sure I felt power lurking somewhere in the darkness.

"When the vampires get here, we'll see how cocky you are," I heard him shout.

I was standing in total darkness. Black in every direction. I kept moving, trusting in the invisible rays of ultra violet light. Until I knew the source of the power I wouldn't stop bobbing and weaving.

"What do you want?" I heard him say. "Please don't hurt me. I'm just doing what they told me to do! I just did what I was told. I didn't tell him anything." Movement. A soft voice. I couldn't make out the words.

"Who are you talking to?" The power grew. Shit, I had to get out of this abyss.

I could hear a light struggle. Whimpers. Silence. Okay, now would be a damn good time to panic, but I had to remain calm or I'd be a lot less juicy in a few minutes.

With my ear against the door, I strained to listen. Something was really wrong. Death was in the room. Not like the corpses, but a living death.

"Doctor? You alright?" A part of me hoped he wasn't. I was still too angry to care all that much. No, the real truth was, if he was going to die, I wanted first dibs on him. I placed my ear to the door and listened. "Doctor, answer me."

I tried to remain calm, but feared the worst. Silence was never a good sign in a situation like this. Chances were, the cockroach on the other side of the door was here to protect his little secret. I was trapped like a rat, and Dr. Zusack was about to be a hot meal.

Stepping away from the door, I reached up and grabbed the Magnum with my left hand. It felt awkward, but if it kept me alive, so be it. There was no way I'd get off a good shot with the cast on the right hand. I pointed it at the door ready to kill anything that came through.

I could hear the blood run through my ears. A powerful combination of silence and the unknown waited for me on the other side.
To my advantage, the cockroach would not be able to attack me in
the room. There were just too many artifacts that worked against it.
Ultra violet light alone would stop it in its tracks. I knew all of this
in the back of my mind, but I wasn't willing to count on it. If the
coffin sleepers had gone to this much trouble to hide the corpse, I
was sure they had all the crucifixes removed from the rooms. They
may be ugly and smelly, but they were very thorough.

The door opened and I rushed it. My shoulder hit hard. Feet
continued to dig for ground. The Magnum searched for its target.
My body rolled to the floor as I over compensated the resistance.
My nose smashed against polished leather. As my thoughts gathered, I noticed I was at the heels of the boots rather than the toes.
The cockroach wasn't even facing me. I moved with as much speed
as I could. Turning over on my back, I pointed the Magnum
between his spread legs. The barrel snug against his balls. The dark
roach towered over me like a building. I stopped just short of
pulling the trigger.

"Would you be so kind as to shut the door, Mr. Isaac?" the low
soft voice asked, still looking away from me. I wasn't even sure he
knew I had the weapon on him.

"Asa?"

"Please, the door." He covered himself with a large blanket.
Even his face was behind it.

"Still a little early for Trick or Treat isn't it?"

"Please Avenger, the door. Then we will converse on your lack
of humor."

It hit me. The ultra violet from the room was washing out into
the morgue. Something told me to keep it open and keep Asa as
powerless as possible, but I ignored it. He seemed hell bent on
undermining Quinn Rubio and the commercial roaches, so ride this
wave as long as it went.

"Not until you answer a few questions."

"I will answer them all once the door is shut."

"What are you doing here?" I asked as I shut the door with more than a little reluctance. I kept the Magnum where I could use it. Being left handed now, was going to slow me down. Finding an advantage against it was a must.

"Thank you." He turned to me. "It looks as though rescuing you." A grin sprouted in the corner of his mouth.

I looked over to see Dr. Zusack, deep in a magical trance. "I was holding my own."

Asa followed my eyes. "I can see that. I have no doubt you were simply allowing the doctor to have an edge in your game of wits. Good thing I did the same with the guard before you got here or who knows where you would be locked up."

"You still haven't answered my question. Why are you here?"

"To tell you there is no body to be found here." His fangs caught the light in the room.

"Duh." I kept my eyes on Zusack.

"And to help you find your way out."

"Thanks for the concern, but all is under control."

"So you had locked yourself in the room so you could search each nook and cranny. Keeping the good doctor at bay until you could finish the investigation." He shook his head in agreement. "I apologize for my intrusion. It appeared as though you had been outwitted by your young adversary. A small, weak, dim-witted adversary."

"You're such a condescending jack ass, you know it?"

He bowed low. "At your service."

"You better have a real good reason for me not finding a body here."

Again, a slow nod. "I can, but it will no longer give you the proof you seek."

"Why not?"

"I have come from the funeral home."

"And?"

"The body has been cremated. It was merely ash. Someone is going to great lengths to sweep the dust under the rug. And no offense, but I don't think the humans involved are smart enough to think that far in advance. But their fears have made them very dangerous."

"Something you could have told me before I came rushing in here."

"True, but you would not have believed me. I knew you would torture the young doctor until he told you the truth. It would be unlike you to take the word of a vampire holding nothing but ash. You may be dangerous, but you are also very predictable." He stepped over the doctor. "I hope this one has told you enough that you now believe me. Before being locked away in the vampire room, that is."

I slowly put the Magnum back in the holster and turned to face the bloodsucker in front of me. "Without a body, I still have no proof that it was murder. For all I know it's you that's causing all the distraction. Probably put her in the furnace yourself. According to Dr. Zusack, it was a blood gluten that killed them. That doesn't rule you out by a long shot."

He shrugged. "Not to worry. Stick your head in the sand and soon enough there will be another victim. Or you could try and save the unfortunate soul while he or she is still alive. I thought saving the humans and killing the vampires was your specialty. I guess I was mistaken. Perhaps your reputation is exaggerated."

I wanted to say something rude, but he was right. Believing the word of a roach was going to take some getting used to. I looked back to Dr. Zusack. "What about him. From what he told me, I think he's helping cover everything up for the fang heads."

He shrugged. "Well, I have not fed tonight. Perhaps…"

The morgue door opened with violent force. Detective Kansas

entered with several other officers. He looked at me as though I had just licked the icing off his cake. His eyes shot to Asa, to me, to the doctor. Back to Asa. "What did you do to him?"

Asa never responded. Kansas looked to me. "And you, what do you think you're doing down here?"

Unlike Asa, I wasn't able to hold my tongue. "As if you don't know." I began to walk to the detective. "How long did you think you could keep this off everybody's radar? And an even bigger question, why?"

"I don't answer to you, Isaac. Now again, what happened to the doctor?" He nearly jumped as he looked at my new cast. "And what happened to you?"

"Cut myself shaving. Now, who do you answer to?"

Kansas looked back to Asa. "Arrest him." Asa made no attempt to move as officer placed him under arrest. The large fang head looked to me as if I was supposed to choose sides.

"For what?" I asked.

"Again, I don't answer to you."

"How much money is Quinn giving you to make all this go away?"

"You have no idea what this thing has done," he said as he looked up to Asa.

"Try me. Tell me why he's the only one not giving me bull in all this." I balled my fists to keep from punching the detective in the face. "Tell me you didn't send me on wild goose chases so you and your henchmen could cover up the murders of Michelle Covington and George Hernandez. And now Susannah Metzgar."

"Wild goose chases? I didn't do anything of the kind. They were legitimate vampires that had an order of execution. If you don't like what you do, find another job. As for a cover up, we've been trailing Asa for weeks, waiting for the right time to nail him. Looks like that time is now." He took a deep breath, but never looked me in the eyes. "Besides, when did you start listening to the lies of vampires?"

I stood inches from him. Anger percolated inside me. "It's not the job I hate. It's the crooked cops that come along with it."

He grabbed me by the neck, fingers wrapped tight. "You listen to me you piece of shit. I'm no crooked cop. I do what I have to do to keep people safe in this town and if that means keeping you out of the mix so be it. If we had brought you in on this from the beginning, he'd have gone into hiding and we'd've never found him."

I pulled his hands away. I was nearly seven inches taller and used it to my advantage. "So it also includes framing cockroaches that had nothing to do with the real murders?"

"Since when did you care if an innocent vampire bit the dust?"

I didn't know how to answer that. All I had was the word of Asa and that didn't weigh very much. Yes, he told me about the killings, but that didn't mean he wasn't involved. When it came down to it, he had the most to gain by the deaths of the Knights of the Night. "Call it a hunch, but I think you've got blood on your hands and your head up cockroach ass."

I could tell he wanted to say more, but resisted. "We have our monster. Be man enough to admit you were duped by him. If the laws are repealed, guess who gains the most power."

"And what if you're wrong?"

"I'm not. Trust me. We've been following him for sometime, just waiting for him to come out of hiding. We have the evidence that will see he never rises again." He was so nervous the blood was running out of his face. At any moment, I expected him to upchuck on all of us.

"What evidence?"

"Police business. It doesn't concern you. I shouldn't have to tell you that. We make the arrests, the lawyers convict, and you kill them. There's a reason for that. I don't get in the lawyer's business, and you don't get in mine."

"What does concern me is the fact that there's still a killer cockroach out there and the police are allowing the monsters to dictate who lives and dies for the murders. You're nothing but a pathetic pawn in their game." I watched as more officers filed into the room. Each looked at me as if at any minute I was going to freak out on them and start shooting. The way I felt at the moment, they might have gotten their wish.

"Did you ever think maybe it was you that was being the pawn here? Besides, I want a statement from you telling me everything this dead piece of shit told you."

"See, you don't even have that much right. He's a pure blood roach, which means he was born what he is." Out of the corner of my eye, I saw Asa grin. He already knew this, but poking a stick at Kansas was one of my favorite pastimes. And tonight I was going to be at full throttle.

He tilted his head and looked at me. Hands on his hips, tie flipped to one side. "It blows me away that you are siding with the vampires on this. Thank you for your concern, but if you don't mind, I have work to do." He pushed past me and grabbed Asa by the shoulder. A large silver chain hung from the cockroach's neck, zapping any power the monster might have.

"Yeah, you do have work to do. Like explaining to the public why the murders haven't made their papers. Why the Knights of the Night haven't been warned they are being targeted. Why more lives are being put into danger."

He continued to walk away from me. "I'll keep that in mind, Paul."

"One more question, Kansas." He turned, stone faced. "What do you tell the victim's family and the press when the real monster strikes again?"

He smirked. "Have a good night, Paul." With that, both monsters exited the room.

CHAPTER FOUR

Sleep the next morning was nearly impossible. I was shaken again and again from nightmares that had a foothold in the truth. Never in my life would I have believed that Kansas would allow the roaches to pull his strings. I thought he was one of the best on the force, but the fear of and the money from the cockroaches have a way of rooting out the good in anyone. Replacing it with the darkest of evils.

Worse than that, I feared for the life of a goddamn cockroach. Maybe everybody had been right all along. I did need therapy. Bring on the straightjacket and the rubber walls, I'm moving in.

Speaking of therapy, I found myself in a very familiar rut. I sat across the desk from Dr. Lydia Petty. She thought of it as therapy, I thought of it as bullshit. There are those that say I have aggressive issues and that I need to find a way to get them under control. I don't deny the problem, but I'm not exactly the kind that likes to talk about feelings. Not to mention on our first meeting I threw her out a second story window. It was to save her life, but still…it kind of hurt the trust factor.

Since then, I think we've made a lot of progress on that issue, but as far as getting inside my head? That's a tough nut to crack and I knew it.

She was in a new location since Kasey and the boys had turned her last office into a blood bath. Can't really blame her for the relocation thing. I had seen it happen and there's no way I could ever go back in there and work. Besides, I'm sure her other patients wouldn't be all giddy about a return visit.

"How did you break your wrist?" she asked. Her eyes stared at the cast as if it would answer.

"I guess you wouldn't believe me if I told you I hurt it while helping one of your patients across the street." I used my best choirboy face.

She looked at me and grinned slightly.

"My dear, Dr. Feelgood, is that a smile I see forming on your face?" I sat back in the chair and let the fun begin. Using her emotions against her was something I started to enjoy in these meetings. If I didn't find something to distract me from the real reason I was here, I'd go postal and I knew it. Sitting in a chair talking about me was just never going to be an activity I found exciting.

The smile disappeared. "It could have been had you called me by my real name." She leaned against the desk, still looking at the cast. "I'm guessing you're not going to tell me."

"I broke it killing a cockroach last night." Now those big dark brown eyes were looking at me. I had her at 'killing'. "Actually, it was a cockroach bitch that broke it for me if you really need to know."

Now anger emerged on her face. I could tell it was all she could do to stay professional. Something else I enjoyed using against the good doctor. "Mr. Isaac, how many times do I have to tell you that we don't use that term here? It is considered extremely derogatory." I could tell a wall was being built between us and all her defenses were at an all time high.

"Which one? Bitch or cockroach?"

The wide smile returned. Out of shock this time. "You know the one I'm talking about. Don't play dumb with me. That word is just so vile." For a minute, I thought she was going to spit the word right out of her mouth like a wedge of lemon.

"I meant it to be." I smiled back, trying to pull off playful dialogue, but under it all, I was serious. Did I fail to mention that she was also a cockroach activist? That's what made our little arrangement such a struggle. She got in the heads of roaches and I cut them off. Somehow I didn't think therapy was going to be the answer.

She stood and began to pace. "So what did the latest vampires do to you? Look at you wrong? Have too many unpaid parking tickets? You know that if I find reason to think that you are killing without authorization, I will have to call the police and the Vampire Council." She leaned against the desk and looked down on me. I think I was supposed to have been intimidated.

"They killed an under aged girl a few nights ago. And yes, I had the proper paperwork to kill them. You can check it out yourself if you like."

I could see her body language change. The smug wiped clean from her face, replaced with a splash of terror. The last thing a cockroach activist wanted to hear was that a fang boy had attacked and killed. Add the word underage into the mix and they clammed up good and tight. "I'm sorry to hear that. It doesn't sound like something a vampire would do without being more to the story. But I am truly sorry all the same." She returned to her seat. Eyes that had been fierce and sharp were now wide and distant.

"Sorry that the girl died or sorry that you won't be able to nail me for killing her killers?"

She jumped back to attention as if shocked. "The girl obviously. Still, I can't help but wonder what you might have done to them before you killed them."

"I'll admit they didn't like it nearly as much as I did. The advantage is that dead cockroaches tell no tales." Now it was my time to smile wide. And I did. I had the advantage now, and I was going to use it for everything it was worth. Twisting the proverbial knife in the chest of an activist was nearly spiritual to me.

"I'm sure they don't. But now tell me, how is your life going with the situation?"

"Not a situation doctor. A situation, you can work through and find a solution. I have a condition and it sucks as you might think. Having cockroach and lycan virus running through my veins makes me want to put a bullet in my brain." Just like that, she had taken my advantage away.

She took a deep breath and I could see those wheels turning. "Thoughts of suicide?"

I had to laugh. "I'm not going to let your bastard roaches cheat me out of such a wonderful life. In fact, it makes things better for me. Gives me back my edge."

"Edge?"

"Yeah. There for a while I thought this therapy might make me grow soft and I would start singing campfire songs with the daisy pushers, but now I have a whole new casket full of reasons to hunt and kill your future patients."

"Well, at least you're working through it and not keeping it all bottled up inside." She was being sarcastic but why get into something that I didn't want to talk about?

I was taking a huge chance, but I wanted to throw out a little bait and see if she took a bite. I chose to use one of the dead sun crispies as my songbird. That way I didn't have to give up my source. "When I was killing one of the roaches, it said something about the deaths of members of the Knights of the Night. To be specific, that they were murdered. You don't know of any roaches that have a beef with them do you?"

"No, I would think the opposite. Without the help of the

Knights, the vampires would still be unprotected and exposed to those like you. Are you sure you didn't misunderstand them while you had that gun of yours in their mouth?" She tried to control her shaking. Was it fear or anger? Did it matter?

"Yeah, they told me everything, *then* I put the gun in their mouths. I'm sure I got every word correct. The Knights were killed by roaches and the police are keeping it undercover for some unknown reason."

"Really?" So far if she knew something it wasn't showing. "Is it perhaps something that you read too much into? I mean, why would they say something like that just out of the blue?"

"Trying to clear their conscience, I guess."

She took a deep breath, cleared her throat and thought about what she was going to say next. "Have you gone to the police with this information?"

"I can't."

"And why not?" Her eyes were directly on me now.

"The police are the ones covering it up. Weren't you listening to anything I said?"

"Why would they cover up something like that?" Her voice almost sounded bored or at the very least distrust.

"I don't know. That's the thing I can't put my finger on. The last thing I want to do is jump to conclusions and accuse the Orlando Police Department of conspiracy."

"Like when you accused me of feeding my patients to the vampires? Don't tell me my therapy is actually starting to work?" I could see the wave of tension redirecting itself. There was a pang of humor in her voice. Every once in a while it was good to see someone smile. Even if it was at my expense.

I wanted to tell her to go to hell, but she had a point and I hated it. I had accused her of that very thing. "We will have to agree to disagree on that one."

"Please tell me you haven't harmed any innocent vampire because of this assumption of yours."

"There's no such thing." Her face turned to stone. Eyes became nothing more than laser beams of death. I had struck a sensitive nerve and I was incredibly proud of myself. She waited for me to redirect my answer.

"You still believe in the childhood myths that all things that go bump in the night are evil and out to take your soul. It's nothing more than fear from ignorance." She must have felt as though she won that battle because she was leaning back toward me again. "It's something that has been ingrained in us from the beginning. Fear the Boogie Man. It is nothing more than a prejudice against those that are different from us."

I leaned forward. "I'm never going to see your sympathy for them and you're never going to see them for what they really are. And yes, everything that goes bump in the night *is* evil. It's just that some get caught doing something evil and some don't."

"But your anger is the difference here. You think by killing them all, you can erase the pain of losing your parents and that's not going to happen. You have to channel your energies in another direction. A more positive direction."

"Until bleeding hearts like you, killing them *was* a positive direction. If I kill them all, I'm sure to get the ones responsible for my parents' murders. I think I have the right to be angry at the coffin maggots for killing my family, don't you?"

"Yes, you do have a right to be angry. I don't deny that, but you have to learn to channel that hatred and energy in a positive direction. It's the irrational lashing out that's the problem." She chewed on the ear of her glasses. A nervous tick I had discovered.

"Meaning I should take up painting by numbers or crochet?"

"Maybe it's your parents that you're angry with, not the vampires."

I wanted to reach across her desk and strangle her. She deserved it for that remark. "What the hell did you just say? If you want to cure me of any anger management issues, you better tell me I didn't hear what I think I heard." I stood, paced, ran my fingers across my head, then sat back down.

Her eyes showed the uncertain fear. To her I was nothing more than a bloodthirsty killer. She began to ease away again. "It isn't what you think. It's just that I think you have hidden animosity towards your parents for what they were."

"You actually charge people for this crap?"

"Somewhere deep inside I think you're angry at them for being supporters of the Knights of the Night. You think it's what got them killed. There's a part of you that hates them for it. You feel it's their fault for leaving you an orphan."

"Listen to me you damn quack, I don't hate my parents for what they were. Whether they supported the monsters or not is not the point."

"Will you feel the same way if you find out that your informant is right?"

"Meaning?" I was feeling as though I had fallen into her trap.

"If you find out that the members of the Knights of the Night were in fact killed by vampires rather than by natural causes, will you feel the same? That they were innocent victims of a vampire attack, or will you simply think they got what they deserved."

Yeah, she had cornered me somewhat. "Both."

"Explain."

"Yeah, they were victims, but still, they were killed by a cockroach and the cockroach has to be hunted down and killed. I can't change facts."

"Would you have sympathy for victims if you found out they were killed because of what they were?"

"Sympathy for them, no. I'd have sympathy for their families."

"So you feel the same way about your parents? No sympathy for them, but instead sympathy for you?" She shrugged her shoulders as if I had no rational comeback to her question.

"No. Yes. I don't know. You're missing the point." So, she was right.

"What is the point then, Mr. Isaac?" She sat her glasses on her desk and laced her fingers together. Again she eased across the barrier toward me.

"The point is they were brutally murdered in their home by cold blooded killers. Cockroaches to be more exact. Killers that are still walking the streets. While I have been cheated out of all the memories of having my parents around. I went from being a child in a loving family to being an orphan in a few minutes. And everyday they are making more orphans out of more children."

"Do you think your parents would still be alive if they hadn't been supporters of the vampire community and their legalization?"

I wanted to say no, but I couldn't. I wasn't sure. "Doesn't matter."

"Really? So you're going to tell me that it doesn't matter to you that you don't have any memories of them past the age of eight. You don't have any resentment toward them for not being there throughout your life?"

"I have resentment, just not toward them. They didn't desert me, they were taken from me. My resentment is toward the cockroaches and I think we both know that." I slammed my fist down on the desk. She jumped. I stood. Agitation was getting the best of me.

"I don't know that, Mr. Isaac. I think once we dig to the bottom of this we will find that you hate them for being in a position that ultimately took their lives." She stopped as she saw the reaction on my face. Her dark eyes looked up at me with a mixture of fear and stupidity. Her voice grew softer. "I'm not blaming you. A lot of children that have lost their parents to tragedy go through that phase in their life. It's something you will eventually have to address in order to move forward with your life."

"You really are full of shit aren't you?" I was confused by the double talk. I needed fresh air. There was no way of determining it, but I knew I'd lost this round of debating. Then again, I did my best thinking with my Magnum and stakes, not words. Words were for those too coward to take action. I got up and vowed to myself not to sit again. I headed for the door. I was done.

"Have you ever visited their graves like we've been talking about?"

I stopped and turned even though I told myself not to. "No. But it's not because I hate them. I just can't bring myself to going there. I remember the day of their funeral and seeing that hole in the ground. I kept hoping and praying that it was all a bad dream and they would open the caskets and make everything all right again. I never want to relive that again. Why would I?"

"Visiting the graves might give you peace and closure instead of opening old wounds." Now she was standing too. A sparing match of who could hide their uncertainty the best.

"Peace and closure? How do you think that will give me peace and closure? Doing that will do nothing more than remind me of how alone in this life I really am. That's why you'll never be able to get to me. You sit here with me and tell me how to deal with the death of my parents and that everything will be okay and in the next hour you're helping the cockroaches deal with drinking the blood of another victim. You can't do that. You can't sit on the fence and help both sides. You either have to help your own kind or serve the cockroaches."

"You've got me all wrong. I'm not going to be so bold as to say that things will be okay. I can't make the pain go away for you. But you have to face the fact that the vampires are allowed to exist and go on living. Otherwise, you'll die behind bars with nothing gained and if that happens, the killers win all over again."

"Is that what you think I'm in this for? To win?" I shook my head. "I'm trying to save the human race from being nothing more than a smorgasbord. I'm in it to survive. Extinction of the blood lickers is the only answer."

"But you treat the vampires like people treat sharks and other predators that they have little knowledge about. Truth is, only a few of them are killers. Far fewer than the humans you'll meet on your way home."

"Spoken like a true sympathizer."

"Call me what you will, Mr. Isaac."

"Some day I'll be calling you a victim."

She came around the cherry wood desk and stood in front of me. Her arms wrapped around her chest. "Can we try something?"

There was no way this was going to be good. "What?"

"Have you heard of The Crimson Madness?"

"Yeah," I said slowly, trying to figure out where this line of questions was going to go. "It's a new artsy fartsy gallery in Bat Town of the cockroach activist/artist Dubro. That's if you want to call him an artist. I've seen finger painting monkeys that do better."

"Art is in the eye of the beholder."

"His art is up his ass," I grunted. "What are you getting at?"

"Tonight is the opening of the gallery featuring his work. A lot of the members of the Knights of the Night are going to be there. I want you to go with me and tell them about the murders. If there really is a killer among them, that will be the place to be. You will have them all at your beck and call."

"Are you fucking nuts?"

"I'm serious. If what the vampire last night told you is true, it could be your chance to save the lives of some of them. Hopefully all of them. Besides, I think it will help get you out of sessions with me if you're seen mingling with the enemy. Do it and I'll give you next session off."

"You think you can get me there, I'll see just how normal they all are and begin singing Kum-ba-ya with them and that's not going to happen. Not to mention the other people and roaches there aren't exactly going to welcome me with open arms. The Knights see me as a threat not a protector."

"Trust me, there is no underlying motive. I think if you really believe there's a killer out there and that the humans are in danger, you'd be doing them a great disservice by not warning them." She inched closer.

"No, what would be doing them a great disservice would be leaving any of the roaches alive when I left. But somehow, I don't think you're going to give me that option." I remained still, wanting to see how close she'd come to me.

"I'm just asking you to try it. If you feel uncomfortable, I'll let you off the hook. But I think by warning the activists, it might be a win-win situation for everyone."

I looked at her, knowing there had to be a catch. In my line of work, there's always a catch. "And how exactly do I win?"

"You might save a life and I might put in a good word with the Vampire Council for you if you do."

"They are trying to keep it all under the radar of the media. The fang heads will do nothing but discredit my appearance and you know it. They won't see it as a gesture of good faith."

"You might be surprised. I don't think they want death in the members of the Knight of the Night any more than you do."

"And what's in it for you?"

She smiled. "I get rid of you as a patient."

I laughed. "And they say shrinks haven't got a sense of humor."

CHAPTER FIVE

s I walked back to my black 1970 hemi 'Cuda, I felt every bone in my body tense up and every muscle grow cold. A dark figure was leaning against it; waiting. His slicked back black hair shined in the parking lot lights.

"Dieter, so nice to see you and your dead face."

"This is no time for jovial sparing of words." As I grew closer to the dead man I could see the black eyes and white skin that made him all the more creepy. Dieter is the puppet of Quinn Rubio. He must be present at all victim stakings to verify that the cause of death was cockroach related. To say he's a pain in the ass is an understatement.

Beside the plasma head was another shadow. Biologically human, ethically, nothing more than dirt. It was all I could do not to reach out and punch him with everything I could. "I thought you'd be busy hiding evidence or on your knees in front of Quinn," I said to Kansas.

"Paul, I've already told you. Asa is nothing more than a lying killer. You know as well as I do that knocking out the Knights will help him with his cause. If he can kill or intimidate enough of them, he stands to gain control of the city and the laws that he sees as binding him." He gave me a disgusted look. "I don't believe you could think that thing would tell you the truth. He's in it to save his own skin and nothing else."

"Falling for the facades and lies of the killer, are you, Avenger?" Dieter's cockiness gave me goose bumps. Most of the daisy pushers used magic to make themselves appear more attractive and alive. I'm guessing he never got that memo.

"I have to admit something Dieter, you are without a doubt the ugliest asshole I've ever seen."

He looked at the cast on my arm. "Gripping things a little too tight, Avenger?"

I simply displayed my good middle finger.

Dieter never smiled. Go figure. "We have a great emotional task at hand."

I lit a Cuban cigar and blew the first lung full of smoke in his face. Cockroaches don't really breathe, so the benefit was for my own pleasure only. But I'm immature like that. "What kind of task?"

"There is a girl we must stake and behead tonight. It is of the most importance that we take care of this immediately." His red tie blew against his white shirt in the mild breeze. It was the most alive thing about him.

With Dieter you have to read between the lines. It was highly unlikely that he would come hunting for me to kill one of his own just to be a helpful little roach. "Really, who? And why are you so anxious to stake her?" His motives were always dark and deceitful.

I looked over to Kansas. "Seems a little convenient considering your recent track record."

"Think whatever you want. Reality is, you have a job to do. Do it or I can arrest you for failure to carryout a court ordered execution." He gave me a sarcastic smile.

"The neighborhood had called for us to kill her. Seems she was kept by her family and allowed to rise as a vampire. The community has threatened violence unless she is removed." Dieter moved away from my car as I reached for the door, almost fading into the blackness of the night. "Besides, when have you ever needed a reason to kill one of my kind?"

"The real question is, when have you ever voluntarily given one up?"

"It is not I, but the direct order of the Police Department. Detective Kansas has sent me here to retrieve you for the task. After all, I am a law abiding citizen above all else." His wide smile gave just a hint of the deadly fangs behind the clammy white skin.

"Detective Kansas, huh?" I looked at the detective again, trying to figure out the real reason both of them were standing before me. There was more to this and I simply had to sniff it out. If all else failed, I would beat it out of them.

"That is correct. It is of the most importance that we get to the home as soon as possible. If not, the neighborhood is threatening to kill her." He continued to pace in and out of the parking lot lights in a macabre game of peek-a-boo. His dress shoes clicked with each step. Something he was doing on purpose to give him the illusion of life. Dieter would never admit it, but I could tell he hated what he was. It wasn't unusual for him to go over the top to attempt to be as human as possible.

"Sounds like another of Kansas' shell games to me, Dieter. One that you're probably a part of."

"We have direct orders from both the judge and the Vampire Council that this task be done now and with great haste." I was uneasy with his urgency. My hand touched the butt of the Magnum as I followed his movement with my eyes.

"Where's the real dead body hiding tonight, Detective?" I asked. My eyes still following Dieter. It wouldn't surprise me that the two of them were here to permanently remove me from their little secret. Desperate monsters do desperate things.

"Keep in mind that if you do not accompany me to the victim's home and do your civil duty, any and all deaths she is accused of will be on your head. And you will be brought upon the same charges as the vampire. Not to mention your license to kill will be revoked."

Somehow, I think Dieter found the time to read and memorize every sentence in the laws on his kind and he used the technicalities to his benefit like a chef uses spices. Using just enough to get the result he wanted. I glanced back to Kansas. "And you have the proper paperwork for this killing I assume?"

He pulled out a piece of paper. One that I had seen a thousand times before. It was authentic. I wasn't sure what his true motivation was, but if I got to kill a cockroach, it couldn't be all that bad. I reached for the paper and read the name. "Annie Guzman. Winter Park." It had been issued by Judge Wyman. Unlike Kansas, I trusted Wyman. He hated and distrusted the monsters as much as I did. Call it a gut feeling, but I was willing to bet, this order of execution was just that. No wild goose chase included. Still, I'd give him a call on the way, just to be sure. And pray to baby Jesus that he wasn't in on this so-called cover up too.

"Do you know the area?" Kansas asked.

I shook my head and chewed on the butt of the cigar. "Yeah, I know it."

"Shall we go together?" Dieter asked.

"What do you mean?" I opened the door wider and got in, starting the car right away. The engine roared to life, headlights illuminated the monster's pale skin like a light bulb.

"Shall we both go in the…'Cuda?" The last word seemed a little difficult for him to say in his Slavic accent.

"Shit no. You ain't riding in my car. I'll meet you there. Can't you turn into a bat or something?" I knew that cockroaches could not turn into bats. It was nothing more than a slanderous remark for the monsters. Mythical tales of the old country, but I loved to use it every once in a while all the same. "Besides, I haven't made up my mind that I'm going yet."

Obviously, he never smiled. "Don't be late, Avenger."

I popped the clutch. The car lunged forward, knocking Dieter off balance.

I arrived at the address on the paperwork and found things a little more odd than I expected. The way Dieter talked, there were people standing on the lawn with burning torches, ready to knock the front door down. But what I found was nothing of the kind. If anyone was complaining about a newly turned cockroach, they weren't doing it from here. Other than the single light on in the home, there would be no sign of life on the property.

On the way here, I had committed to the promise I made myself, and called Judge Wyman. Everything seemed to be on the up and up, but being as paranoid as I was, I reserved some doubt.

"Glad to see you could make it," Dieter said, now standing next to my window.

I jumped at the words. "Shit, Dieter, where did you come from."

He smiled wide, allowing just a bit of his fangs show through. A throaty laugh filled my ears. "It appears as though you might be a little tense tonight."

I opened the car door shoving him away. "Let's get this over with." I moved out of the car, checked myself for the Magnum that hung in my shoulder holster obediently. I felt for my crucifix and stakes with my left hand. Having my right hand in a cast was a real pain in the ass. The last thing I wanted to do was have to fight for my life with only one good hand. Being right handed just made things worse. But to my amazement, the hand wasn't swollen or in pain anymore. I wiggled my fingers, feeling for jolts of discomfort, but nothing. Maybe Asa was right about one thing. I cursed under my breath.

Headlights from Kansas' Explorer filled my eyes as he pulled in behind me. The three amigos were ready to go roach hunting. Yippee.

As we reached the front door, a man cracked the door open just enough that I could see one eye. "What do you want?"

"We have a report of a newly turned…vampire…in your home." It was all I could do to call them that. It sounded far too formal to me. I had a bag full of derogatory slang I wanted to use. His face showed the panic before he could speak. Eyes wider than golf balls, he darted between me and Dieter through the sliver of opened door.

"There's no vampire here." He began to close the door. Dieter pushed it open again, showing no effort in the move at all.

"Who is it, honey?" a second voice asked, somewhere deeper in the dwelling, but moving closer.

A woman appeared behind the man. Her eyes mirrored his. They saw us as the monsters. We were here to kill a family member of theirs. For the second time.

I looked at the woman as the man spoke in no more than a whisper. "You must leave." Again he tried to close the door to the same result. He no longer made any effort in hiding his fear.

"You can't have her," the woman added as she reached for the door. Dieter held it firm. "We'll call the police."

"You can't keep her. It's against the law," I said as I looked at the woman now. If anyone was going to strike first, it would be her.

"Mr. Guzman," Dieter started, "Please, do not cause your family any more pain. Mr. Isaac must put her to death. It is both human and vampire law."

"You can't have her. Fuck the laws," he barked.

"I've been saying that for years. Trust me, it doesn't do any good," I answered.

He looked at me. "But you're vampires. Why does she have to die? We won't tell anyone about her."

"I'm not a…vampire…,Mr. Guzman. I'm as human as you are. He's the only fang head here," I said pointing to Dieter. "Trust me, you wouldn't want her around once she gets hungry. Chances are, you'll be her first meal."

"So why does he get to live?" the woman I assumed to be Mrs. Guzman asked.

"I've asked that very same question too, Mrs. Guzman."

"Vampires born of vampire blood or vampires that rose before the laws went into effect are protected as historical artifacts. Those that rise after the laws must be put to death," Dieter paraphrased.

"It's not fair!" she screamed again, pulling up a small handgun and shooting Dieter in the shoulder.

The dead head fell to the ground. I jumped back away from the door. Unless the shot caught Dieter in the heart, he would heal to see another night.

I pulled the Magnum from my shoulder holster. The last thing I wanted to do was shoot the woman, but if it came down to her or me, you know who I'm going to pick. My eyes tried to track her in the infinite display of shadows and darkness. To my right, Kansas was doing the same, taking cover behind a small bush that would do him absolutely no good if a bullet came his way.

Mr. Guzman slammed the door shut. The limited light coming from the doorway was swallowed whole. I could hear screaming and yelling from behind the door. Movement. Things breaking. More screaming.

I looked over to Dieter, who was already beginning to stand again. He held his shoulder, looking at the trail of blood streaming between his fingers. I caught myself in a strange dilemma. Part of me was wishing the bullet could have hit the mark a little better and another part was strangely glad to see he was still alive. We might be bitter enemies, but at the moment, we were sort of on the same side.

"You okay?" Kansas asked.

"We must get inside," Dieter ignored the question as he moved past us, showing an ever so slight hint of pain. His hand still held the wound. He looked at the trickle of blood as it painted his hand and stained his immaculate white dress shirt. For the first time the look of arrogance was wiped from his face. Replaced with a thin coat of panic and uncertainty. Oh yeah, this was going to be a good night after all.

"Plan on snacking on yourself?" I couldn't help the remark as I moved behind him, headed toward the door. Kansas tucked in behind. I kept my head low, knowing at any time Mrs. Guzman just might take another pot shot at the two of us. I planned on using Dieter as my cover until I got a visual on her again. He had less to lose if another bullet came flying by. Screw that. I just hoped he got shot again. I was here to kill a blood bat. If Dieter happened to be that blood sucker, so be it. Secretly, I was rooting for Mrs. Guzman.

"Please, God, just go away," I heard Mrs. Guzman scream from inside.

"Let us in now or we'll break the door down," I yelled back at the closed door, remaining as low as I could.

Without warning, Dieter kicked the door open. Wood splinters flew in a million directions. Violent sounds of a barrier giving way. His strength overpowered the door with ease.

"Okay, so much for negotiation," I said in a low whisper, looking at Dieter with amazement. "I hope you have a plan or we just might be in more shit than we want."

He turned to me with his fangs showing. "I thought you wanted to kill a vampire?" With that, he moved into the house, following the muffled sound of movement up the stairs. Why, I wasn't sure, but there was a sense of urgency to Dieter. For the first time, since the beginning of time, he wasn't deliberately trying to be a hindrance.

I looked to the left as we entered just to make sure one of the Guzman's wasn't waiting in the weeds. Nothing. Nothing but the bright yellow paint of the kitchen. Any other time, the home would look no different than any other home in suburbia. It's amazing what the addition of one cockroach can do. Talk about ruining the neighborhood.

"Get out of our house or I'll shoot again," I heard Mrs. Guzman threaten. "I'm calling the police!"

I couldn't see either of them. Only voices from above. We moved around the corner and began to quietly work our way up the stairs toward the hidden voices. My breath was quick and short. There was a good chance I'd end up killing more than a cockroach tonight and I didn't like that thought. Worse case scenario, they would end up killing me.

More movement. I could tell the sounds were coming from a closed door on the second floor. They had barricaded themselves in one of the rooms. Just like wild animals, cornered people were highly unpredictable in these situations.

"Mrs. Guzman, put your weapon down. We don't want to have to kill you too," I shouted. Kansas looked at me as if something was growing out of my forehead. "So I'm not all that good at negotiations." I had my Magnum in my left hand. If I lived through this, I was going to break the cast off. With the combo of cockroach poison and lycan virus in my veins, I was healing at an incredible rate. I was more concerned than happy. I didn't want their strengths or weaknesses. Some say it gave me an advantage, but anytime I asked them to put themselves in my place, they changed the subject.

We moved up the stairs, inching our way forward, stopping to listen from time to time for any sounds. At the same time, we grew at risk with each sound we made. For all we knew, they were waiting to open fire when we got to the top stair.

The cockroach in front of me stopped and held up his hand for me to do the same. I did. He pointed to another door just to the right of the one the Guzman's were believed to be in.

I shook my head in disagreement. I pointed to the door I thought I heard Mrs. Guzman behind. "The sounds were coming from that door."

Dieter turned to me, his dead black eyes showing no emotion whatsoever. "You do want to kill the female vampire do you not?" He gave a nervous smile.

I shook my head.

"Then we will proceed to enter the room to the right. That is where we shall find our vampire. Mr. and Mrs. Guzman are only attempting to give us a diversion."

He could feel the cockroach's power better than I could. Something inside me wanted to fight it, but for now, I had to trust Dieter. Just another reason to hate him.

As we moved to the top stair, another shot rang out. It hit harmlessly into the wall across from them, but I found myself on the floor just the same.

"I'll kill you all! Don't come in here," Mrs. Guzman screamed.

"Mrs. Guzman is only trying to throw us off the scent of the vampire in question. Trust me. I can feel our vampire's power behind this door. We must proceed. If we are lucky, we can kill her before they realize we have found her."

I stood again. Looking at the door. I slowly felt the handle. "It's locked."

"You thought it would not be?" Dieter answered.

"Go to hell." It sounded childish as it came out of my mouth, but then again, maturity was not among my greater strengths. I moved back away from the door and kicked it open with everything I had. It gave way a lot easier than I had guessed and that oversight threw me forward into the room. I lost my balance, fell to the floor, and landed on the arm with the cast. The Magnum poised upward ready to kill.

"I fear our advantage of silence has been severely breached." Dieter held out his hand. "Do you wish for me to help you back to your feet?" His voice was filled with humor.

Kansas snickered in the background. "Graceful to the end aren't you, Isaac."

I could feel the anger grow from the embarrassment and waved off the assistance. "I'm fine. Find the roach before the Guzman's kill us." I came back to my feet and turned in circles. There was no other monster in the room. "Where is she?" Dieter's dead eyes moved to the closet. "In there." His voice was low and matter-of-fact.

I stood in front of the closet and braced myself. "Open the door and I'll blow it away."

Dieter did as I asked and quickly open the door. My eyes tried to pick it out among the multitude of stuffed animals and toys inside. It was then that I noticed we were in a child's room. Tingles of disbelief ran down my spine.

"Shit," I said as I saw her.

"Please no, don't kill her. We won't let her out, I swear," Mrs. Guzman screamed. Dieter held her as she kicked and moved in his arms. He pitched her pistol on a small dresser to his left.

Mr. Guzman stood behind her, still as a statue. "Please, she's just a baby."

I looked at Dieter. I couldn't believe my eyes.

He smiled. Knowing all along what I would find behind the door.

"You knew this didn't you, you son-of-a-bitch." I wanted to hear it come from his dead mouth.

The cockroach looking at me was no more than eight. "Who did this?" I looked back to Kansas, only to see a blank stare. Now I wished this had been nothing more than another wild goose chase. I wished it had been anything but this.

"We've got money," Mr. Guzman said. Tears streamed from his face.

I kept my eyes on the small cockroach. Just because she was small didn't make her any less dangerous. Maybe more because she would be underestimated. I wished I could say something to the father that would ease his mind, but there was nothing. I was going to have to kill his daughter. And the last thing I wanted to do was kill her in front of him.

"I'm begging you, please don't do this," he pleaded again. He held out his wallet and keys. "Here take these."

"Dieter, I'll take the Guzman's out of here. You do what you have to do," I said, finally turning my eyes to the dead man.

"I am afraid I cannot do as you ask. I do not have the authority to bring about her death. The deed is yours." His voice showed the pleasure in his statement. Mrs. Guzman continued to fight in his arms.

"You knew this all along didn't you?" I grabbed him by his tie with my left hand.

He stood like a statue, never attempting to break free. "Is it such a good idea to turn your back on such a cold blooded killer?"

"She's just a baby." My words nothing more than a whisper. I could feel the cold sweat run down my back.

"She is a vampire. I thought you had no pity for our kind. Do not tell me you have lost your lust for death?"

I turned to the parents again. "Who the hell did this?"

Mr. Guzman shook his head. "We don't know. A vampire broke in and attacked her. It was in the middle of the night. We didn't even know something was wrong until we went in to check on her the next morning."

I looked back at the small child in the closet. I couldn't bring myself to seeing her as a cockroach. She was cowered in the back, snuggled against the stuffed animals, shaking. Eyes still of a child. Innocent and full of fear. Perhaps it was just me that saw the child in those eyes. Most likely, it was simple wishful thinking.

"Please Sir, we'll pay you anything you want. Don't kill her," Mr. Guzman said again.

I pointed the Magnum at Dieter. "I should blow your brains out right here and now. You set me up."

Dieter shrugged and grinned. "But Avenger, I am doing nothing more than upholding the human laws. Surely you will not think ill of me for doing such an honorable thing?" Mrs. Guzman screamed again. "Kill us all if that will help the pain go away, Avenger, but the truth remains. The young Miss Guzman must die. It is human law not ours."

I looked back to the family. There was nothing I could do to ease their pain or fears. If I let her live, it left me outside the law. I could live with that part, but she would feed and probably kill. That part I couldn't live with.

Dieter had beaten me this time. I knew it. He knew it. I wished the small child would hiss, attack, do anything except act like a timid child. This was not something that would be easy. In the long run, I'd be saving the lives of her parents and the children of others. That's the way I had to look at it. Either I killed one small child now, or she would kill others later. "Put them under," I said to Dieter.

He shook his head without saying a word. He knew what I meant. When humans lock eyes with a cockroach, the monster can put them in a dreamlike trance. They remember nothing. Feel no pain. Best of all for the monster, the victim doesn't scream or fight. Alerting no one.

In a moment's time, Dieter had the Guzman's under his charm and led them down the stairs and out of the house.

I turned to Kansas. "Did you know about this?"

He was as white as a sheet. "No. Nothing like this. I'm sorry, Paul. I didn't know."

By his color, I could tell there was at least truth in what he said. To what degree remained to be seen. "I want to know everything they know about this." I turned to the small child. Still hoping she showed signs of something undead. I needed something more than me to finish her off. Her scared soft eyes looked back at me. For the first time in all the years I had been hunting and killing cockroaches, I had remorse for what I had to do. All the roaches I had killed in the past had been the adult, blood sucking, mean as hell monsters we've all come to know and hate. But now I was face to face with something different. I had met her parents. Seen them cry. Heard them beg. Emotionally, I had been hit with a dilemma that left me with no easy way out. Inside, I hated Dieter more than I had ever hated him before. This was his circus. He knew what this would do to me and he was enjoying every minute of it.

I wanted the bastard that did this.

CHAPTER SIX

I came out the front door with little fanfare. Tonight I wouldn't celebrate my kill. There was only tragedy and revenge working in the air tonight. Revenge would be taken on as many of the monsters as I could get my hands on. What these creatures did to humanity was disgusting in every way, but when they start preying on children, I see no reason to offer mercy.

Unlike when we arrived, the area was flashing with blue strobe lights of at least six police cruisers. In the distance, I could see the white and orange of an ambulance. I felt the shivers run down my spine. Neighbors of the Guzman's were gathered at the end of the driveway, craning their necks, hoping to see part of the show. In situations like this, my fellow humans can be so insensitive. Kansas was busy gathering information from as many witness as he could, working the crowd like a circus ringleader. After all, this was his show and he wasn't shy about telling anyone.

Ahead of me I saw the first cockroach that would experience my wrath. Dieter stood next to the 'Cuda, a thin smirk on his pale white face. I didn't think he was responsible for the child's murder, but he was guilty be association.

Dieter still had the Guzman's in a deep magical trance. Lifeless as zombies. And for that I was grateful. At least the cockroach had the decency to do that much. It was one thing to find your child murdered, but to know that it would rise as coffin bait and eventually be killed again was something that I wished no parent would have to witness. It was gruesome and bloody. I had to cut off the head and remove the heart. The law on the act was clear no matter the age. I couldn't do it in front of any civilians. Only authorized witnesses. "You have done what was necessary I presume?" he asked.

Kansas turned and stared at me as if I now walked around with two heads. Suddenly, what he had done with Asa didn't seem so bad. Given my druthers, I'd kill Asa along with the other fang heads of this town and still sleep like a baby, regardless of innocence or guilt.

I continued to walk toward Dieter, never slowing my pace. With everything I had in me, I slammed my cast in the side of his pasty head. He rocked back, hitting the 'Cuda. Knees buckled, but not falling. The dead were much stronger than the living for some reason, but tonight I didn't care or even think about that. I had a lot of built up anger that needed to get out.

A second jab hit Dieter across the left shoulder. This time I didn't stop my momentum. I continued to pound as many punches into his face and body as I could. He fell to the ground. I stayed on the attack. Grabbing his hair with my left hand, I slammed his head against the ground. Repeatedly.

The cockroach stopped my hand as I attempted another swing, pushed me over top of him. I hit the ground with a violent crash. I continued to roll until I was standing again. Moving back toward my punching bag.

"What has you so angry, Avenger?" he asked as he moved out of the way of the swing. He was pathetically calm about everything. Being a roach as long as he had been seemed to drain him of any human emotions.

"You know damn well why I'm mad. You bring me here to kill an eight-year-old girl? Are you really that fucked in the head?" I looked down at the arm with the cast. The white shell was shattered like a broken egg. Instead of throbbing with pain, it felt good. I had healed at an alarming rate, slower than a shifter, but faster than a human.

I caught Kansas staring at the cast with his mouth open. I wasn't sure if he was connecting the dots yet or not, but his reaction was priceless. At least he was smart enough to give me room to vent. He knew he was already on my shit list, why poke it with a stick.

"According to the human law, all vampires that rise must be killed. Please forgive me if I have misinterpreted the law when it comes to age. Besides, I thought you killed without a conscience. Do not tell me you have grown a soft spot for those that share the same sickness as you."

"Meaning the poison you put in my veins to turn me into a blood sucker. Don't think that I won't kill all of you for that. You, Quinn, Veronica, all of you."

"Nay, it was not I that did such a deed. Maximillian acted alone in that effort. As for the other vampires, I assure you they were nothing more than pawns in the game as well."

"You've lied to so many people over the years, you're starting to believe your own bullshit aren't you?" I pulled the Magnum out of my shoulder holster. "Give me a good reason why I shouldn't spill your lousy guts all over this lawn right now."

Dieter stared at the weapon and took a hesitant step back. "If I know you as well as I think I do, I know you do not want this act of violence to happen again. We must stop it before he strikes again."

"We? You got someone in your pocket? I ain't helping you do shit. You're as much a part of this as anyone." I looked over to the

Guzmans. "What are you going to tell them that's going to make it all right? It was your kind that did that to their daughter." I pointed to the house. "For this, I work alone. I'll bring the head of this creep back with me and on my own terms."

"So what do you plan to do?" Dieter looked at the Magnum, then to me.

"Why do you care? You were only here to see me squirm. You don't give a damn about her. You don't give a damn about her parents. It's all a game to you. You brought me here just to watch and see what I would do. It only goes to prove just how soulless you really are."

Officers began to fill in the empty space around us. Occasional stares came our way, but so far they knew me well enough to leave me alone. Dieter's voice slithered into my brain. Whatever he was going to say next was for my "ears" only. *"I brought you here to help not only the Vampire Council, but me personally. I know of your current distrust of Kansas and the police department. And of the Council. Unless you saw this first hand, you would not understand the urgency behind this. Now unless you start to think with a clear head, you may compromise not only the lives of the child's parents, but all those that may still be on the cusp of this monster's grasp."*

I pushed him again, hoping he'd grow aggressive. "You're wrong. I'm going after the piece of shit that did this. You can count on that. Better than that, I'm going to find him, torture him and kill him. Don't think for one minute I can't kill both of you. Multitasking is my middle-freaking name."

"If I told you the small child in the home is not the first of this kind, would you spare me my life?" It sounded condescending and it was meant to be. *"It seems so unnecessary to kill me and become the hunted."*

He was right and I hated it. I couldn't just kill him. Yet. Kansas would have to go take a piss sooner or later. I'd kill Dieter then.

And as I've said before, if you're not going to kill the monster you have the weapon pointed at, you just start to look silly. I pulled it down and put it back in the shoulder holster. Besides, he had something that changed everything, but I needed to hear it again just to soak it in. "What did you say?"

"I said the small child inside is not the first of this type of killing."

I simply stood there, unable to think or speak. Paralyzed by that one simple sentence.

His face lost the smirk that I was used to. Replaced with an unknown fear. Something I had never seen in him before. *"Over the past three hundred years I have seen this type of activity before. A vampire that feeds on the small and weak. The small child is possibly the next victim of the vampire that not only the humans fear and hunt, but also the Vampire Council. Forgive me, but I wished you to see and feel as you do now. I came calling on you to help both human and vampire in killing this creature."*

"Who is it?"

"No one knows. In all the centuries that he has fed, he has been able to elude the authorities." He gave a nervous smirk. *"Now we have you."*

"What's that supposed to mean?"

"In all the murders and years that have accompanied them, there has never been a hunter fearless enough to hunt him down. All have been found with every internal organ removed. That seemed to deter the humans' revenge."

"You think I will hunt him down and kill him for the sake of the Council?"

"For the Council no, but you will do it for the Guzmans and the other families that have suffered." His fangs showed through an evil smile. *"It is in your nature. Whether it is above...or below the human laws."* For the first time in all the years I had known Dieter, I could see sorrow and hurt on his face. Something about this death

scared even him. *"I fear this is the work of the same vampire as the ones I knew of in Europe, centuries ago. If so, this will not be the last."*

"I want to know everything you and the Council know about him." I looked around as the officers seemed to be pre-occupied with other activities. "And get the hell out of my head. Talk to me…normally."

He gave a light smile and bowed. "As you wish. I know what the Guzman's must feel." His voice grew cold and distant. He looked away for a second. In his silence I could hear the multiple conversations around us. The blue flashing lights reflected off his pale skin like a bleached sheet on a clothesline.

"How would you know how the Guzman's feel? You've had no feelings for anything alive in centuries, you soulless bastard."

"I am not here to debate rights and wrongs with you, Avenger. Please keep in mind that I too was once a man. I had a family. A loving wife and a young boy."

"And then they saw what a work of art you were and hated you like the rest of us," I finished.

He grabbed me by the throat in a swift movement that shocked me. One minute he was an arm's length away, the next he was on me. My hands grabbed around his instinctively. "You have asked me to tell you all I know of him. Listen to me, Avenger. This is difficult enough to tell you without your commentary."

For the first time, he actually seemed to have emotion. Good for him. I fought for air, felt my air passage collapse under his grip. "My son was killed by a vampire on our farm. Taken from me in the middle of the night. His body rose, much like the one we saw tonight. And like the Guzman's, I felt compelled to keep my son close to me, fear of anyone else finding him and killing him. In the nights that followed, my son grew aggressive and was no longer the loving child I once knew. He killed my wife and left into the thick darkness of the night. I, like you, grew vengeful toward the monsters and swore to find them and kill them. Two years later I found an old crypt where vampires were known to dwell. I entered only to find an unspeakable world of vampire children. All had been killed and turned at an early age. An unspeakable world of dried corpses and smells that will never leave my memories. In my moment of discovery, I found my son among them. He was nothing more than a shell of the child I raised and knew. He no longer knew me. A monster parasite that had taken his form. I along with the others of the village drew flame to the crypt, killing all the vampires inside." His hands released my throat. He looked away from me. "I killed my son. Out of pity, not vengeance."

I wasn't sure how to respond. I was having a bitter taste fill my mouth. I wasn't about to feel sorry for the monster in front of me. For all I knew, everything he said was nothing more than a lie. He was manipulative, evil and nasty. I wanted to believe he deserved everything he got. I had to. I thought about my own loss. If I had been older, I might have had to witness, or God forbid, kill my parents myself. As much as I wanted to deny it and push it from my thoughts, if Dieter was telling the truth, we had more in common than I wanted to admit. "What does that wonderful story have to do with this?"

"We never caught the vampire responsible for the murders. From time to time, we have found signs that he still exists. Now I have reason to fear he might have been here picking the scabs off the wounds of my heart. I fear the vampire responsible for my son's death is the same monster that fed here."

I continued to fight the ability to feel sorry for him. I refused to allow that to happen. "Now you know how every family feels when they lose a loved one to your kind. It doesn't matter if the victim is eight or eighty, the result is the same. If that crock of a story you just told me is true, then you should know why we hate your kind so much." I walked up to his pale white face. "Make this very clear, Dieter, I will find the killer of that little girl, and your story will not spare my feelings for you. I still hate you and every other vein whore in this city. I always have and always will. Do us all a favor and go to your little coffin, fill it with holy water and take a sponge bath. I still see you as the problem. Compassion for you will never enter the equation."

"We can agree on our hatred of each other, but there is a larger darkness among us." He looked at the Guzman's again. "Their magic will wear off shortly, so time is of the essence. I wish to find the killer of the child with you."

I laughed. "With me? You mean like Starsky and Hutch?"

He turned his head like a dog that had heard a strange noise.

"The answer is, 'Hell no.' I work alone. Got all the help I need." I tapped the Magnum in the shoulder holster and began to walk toward the 'Cuda. Distractions and scenarios filled my head so much I couldn't think of anything and thinking of everything, all at the same time.

"Then there may be more that perish at his bite."

"Don't worry about that, Dieter. I have my ways of flushing out the filth." I reached for a cigar. Time for a nicotine fix. I stopped, lit it and finished my thought. "If things go well tonight, I'll be bringing you the head of your blood maggot by sun up."

I thought about the opening night celebration I had been invited to with Dr. Feelgood. It seemed like as good of a place to start as any. Asa had me thinking about a killer stalking and taking the lives of the Knights of the Night, Dieter wanted me to track down a child killing cockroach, and I was about to go into the heart of their kindred dressed to the nines in a tux. Could life get any more twisted? I looked back at Dieter. I had one more question that seemed to be screaming at me. "How did you become a cockroach anyway, Dieter?"

"We shall save that tale for another day, Avenger."

CHAPTER SEVEN

Red neon glowed in the night. It cut the darkness with artificial light, signaling the far end of Bat Town like a freshly cut wound. The night was still young for those that ventured looking to party with the undead in the countless clubs and restaurants along Church Street. For me, it was sad to see what had happened to the historic street, once alive with tourist simply looking for nightlife outside of the theme parks. It had somehow turned into the macabre world of the undead, filled with a buffet of tourist that actually thought they were safe. Pathetic fools. It was a false sense of security that the city tried to promote. Trying to run a campaign that made the cockroaches appear as harmless and caring. Those that bought it, usually bought into more than they wanted.

I sat in the 'Cuda in a parking garage close to The Crimson Madness and took a deep breath. After what I had seen and done, I wasn't ready for this. My initial plan was to be Mr. Nice Guy. Now, pulling that off would be a miracle. Still, to find my killers, I had to earn a percentage of their trust. I swallowed and leaned my head against the headrest. I watched as others moved past me through the rear view mirror. The gentlemen dressed like penguins, the women like princesses in long flowing gowns. I could hear bits of conversation and laughter, but couldn't catch any of the words. I was pretty sure they were all humans. I didn't feel power anywhere.

I had called Dr. Feelgood and told her I'd meet her here at two in the morning. I checked my watch. 1:40. My stomach had a familiar sick feeling. Butterflies to the max. I kept telling myself I didn't have time for the party. That I was a fool to think that anyone here, human or otherwise, was going to give me the time of day, much less information on a possible killer cockroach.

I looked at my watch again. A nervous tick for the night. Just enough time to smoke a cigar before the good doctor arrived. It would help calm my nerves. With a quick push, I opened the door to the 'Cuda and stepped out. My hands patted along my chest for the hidden arsenal underneath. Nervous hands straightened out my shirt and lit the cigar. I turned in slow circles making sure I wasn't being stalked by some unseen vein weasel. I took a long drag on the cigar and blew the smoke out as slow as possible. To say I was nervous was an understatement. I was about to go face to face with powerful cockroaches and the humans that supported them. And to make matters worse, I was here to save them. Go figure. Note to self: I was overdressed for the job.

"To say you look handsome would be the understatement of a lifetime." A familiar voice. Soft. Seductive. Sensual.

I jumped at the break of silence but calmed at the sight. "Angie."

Her long flowing blue hair fell teasingly across her ample breasts. "Still mad at me?" She gave the same smile that I had grown to know and love. If she was serious, it didn't come through.

"Mad at you? About what?"

She walked up to me, hips swaying like a hammock. She had my attention and she knew it. She was dressed in a white leather halter-top with fringe, tight shorts, and white knee high fringe boots.

I had never met anyone else in my life that could pull it off and not look trashy. On her, it fit. So to speak.

I smiled. She was the werewolf that bit me a few months ago, leaving me with traces of lycan virus. It saved my life, but the last time we had talked, I hadn't been exactly pleasant about it. "No, I'm not mad at you."

"What're you doing here?" Her fingers ran along the outline of the 'Cuda. Fingers craved to touch more.

I sat the cigar on the top of the car as I put on my black jacket. "You wouldn't believe me if I told you."

"Whatever it is, you're nervous." I felt her power as she stepped within inches of me. Her sweet smell filled my senses. My body ached with urges that were about to make me very embarrassed.

"What makes you think that?" I adjusted the jacket across my shoulders. For some reason it didn't seem to fit as well as it did at the rental store. Then again, I hadn't been dressed up in so long, I wasn't really sure how it was supposed to fit anyway.

"You just have that vibe about you. I know you better than you think. First, you turn in circles looking for the Boogie Man. Then you smoke on that stink stick up there until you can't breathe." She moved closer to me. She had a way of making me forget about the bad stuff in my head. Replacing it with raw urges that begged to be met.

I looked deep into her hazel eyes. I wanted to deny everything she just said but she was right. "Lucky guess."

She leaned up and gave me a light kiss. Enough that it lingered. "I've missed you."

I swallowed hard and readjusted myself. "I've meant to call you."

"Why?" She wiped the wisps of blue hair out of her face. A smile in her eyes drew me closer. I could look roaches in the eyes, but not Angie. I had no power over her.

"To tell you thank you for what you did."

"Is that all?" Her hands were tracing along the buttons of my dress shirt.

"And to say I'm sorry for everything I said at the hospital. I was just a little scared at the time." I paused. "And acting like a man."

"You mean, ass."

I smiled and took my verbal beating.

She straitened my bow tie. "I want to hear you tell me the truth."

I could feel the blood rushing to my face. "What do you mean? I am telling you the truth."

"You're not a very good liar. Tell me that you missed me. Tell me how you can't think of anything else at night." Her breath danced on my skin. Warm lips traced my neck. She gave out a purr so soft I almost didn't hear it.

I stepped back away from her. I needed air. She followed me step for step. As she passed the car, she grabbed the cigar. "It amazes me. You can stalk and kill the most vicious and powerful vampires in the city, but I scare the hell out of you."

A laugh escaped before I could stop it. "I'm sure you scare the hell out of a lot of people dressed like that."

"So why are you here of all places. To kick ass I hope." Her eyes grew wide with excitement.

That was Angie in a nutshell. Sex and violence were her vices. "Believe it or not, I was invited here."

Now it was Angie's turn to have a laugh escape. "You? Why? Were there too many vampires invited?"

I stopped backing up and allowed her to softly run into me. "What have you heard on the streets about the Knights of the Night being killed?"

"Nothing. Should I?" Certain parts of her hit me before others. I breathed in, just to feel more of her.

"No, not necessarily. It's just that I've had a lead that three members of the organization have been killed by roaches."

"The papers say they died of other things. A car accident, a suicide and a heart attack or something like that. Why? Do you think that's not the case?"

"I don't know yet. Asa seems to think there's a big cover-up going on. I hope to find out tonight. If I live that long." Before I knew it, she had my hand in hers. I looked down, as I tried to re-gather my thoughts. "They have Asa under arrest. I don't think he had anything to do with it."

"Since when have you and Asa become such big buddies?" Arms now wrapped around me like a constrictor.

"I'm just living up to that old phrase of keeping my enemies close."

She looked toward the entrance of the gallery. "You honestly think anyone in there is going to cooperate with you? They'd die first." She took a draw from the cigar and let the smoke out in circles. "Literally."

"Probably. But if there's a killer out there taking them out one by one, maybe they'll at least take extra precautions. At least until I can find out what's truth and what's not."

Another laugh. "And again, they'd die before they'd listen to anything you had to say. I say let them meet their demise. You know Kincaid is in there right now looking for new talent. Without gaining the trust of the vampires, his porno business wouldn't be what it is today. It's all about money, not equality. Of all people, I shouldn't have to tell you that."

I shrugged. "I do know that. He's nothing more than a sleazy skin dealer for men who like to see undead sex, but still..." I gathered my thoughts again. "I always thought my purpose was to protect the humans over the roaches. No matter what."

She handed me the cigar. "I've missed seeing you." That's my Angie. Better to distract than to disagree.

"Will you tell me if you hear anything on the streets? Like you said, I'm not exactly trusted by the monsters down here. Tonight will probably be nothing but a waste of my time." I wished that was all I had to ask her about, but there was the other little cockroach I met tonight. There was no doubt I'd have nightmares about her for the rest of my life. "There's something else."

Her lips glistened, moist and wanting. "I never thought you'd ask."

Even with the grim question I was about to ask, I smiled. Truth be known, I was already second-guessing my decision to tell her. I wanted this to be my personal project. No witness. No mercy. No compromise. "I need you to be serious for a minute."

"Okay." Her face showed the sincerity. Again, she grabbed my hands in hers as though we were about to play a seductive game of 'Hot Hands'.

"I found a child that had been attacked and fed on by a cockroach tonight. She had been attacked in her sleep. Her parents were keeping her, thinking she would rise as the same child that went to bed that night. Dieter says this isn't the first time something like this has happened. You know as well as I do how little emotion you get out of his dead ass and he was shaking in his boots."

"My God, what did you do?"

I took another drag on the cigar. Something had to mask my fears. I didn't answer, just shook my head.

"You didn't kill it?" The way she said it, I wasn't sure if she was appalled that I *did* kill it or that I *didn't* kill it.

"It was a small child, not an it!" I yelled. The last thing I wanted to do was take my anger out on her. I pinched my nose and ran my hands across my bald head. "Sorry, I didn't mean that."

She smiled. "I understand. My mistake. I didn't mean it that way, you know that."

"If you hear anything, anything at all…" My words trailed off to nothing.

"I will. You have my word."

"Angie, I want this son of a bitch. I want to kill him so slow it's not funny." I tried to wipe the horrid images from my mind. It wasn't working. "And I am sorry for everything. If you forgive me, I'll make it up to you somehow."

"It's gonna cost you, lover." She kissed along my neck, sending shivers up my spine. Her caramel skin glowed in the soft moonlight.

I pushed her away enough to see her face. "I need your help on this. If you hear anything, please let me know." I looked at her far-from-innocent beauty. "But don't tell anyone what I told you. I'm going after this one my way. No strings attached."

"Let me tie and blindfold you to my bed and I'll do anything you want." Her breath slid along the wet skin from her kisses.

"As good as that sounds, I think I have a better chance coming out alive with the cockroaches in there," I said pointing to the gallery.

"At least we agree on that," she smiled and licked her lips, "but I can guarantee you won't have as much fun."

"Just let me know if you hear anything."

"Are you here alone?" Typical woman. They all have radar about things like that. I called it bitch radar but I think that might be politically incorrect. Then again, who's counting?

"No, you're here." I hoped to get away with a thin joke.

"You know what I mean. It's not in you to get this dressed up."

"I'm dressing to impress. Is there something wrong with that?" Try number two.

"Impress who? The vampires? Albert Kincaid?" She glanced down at my crotch. "I don't think so. Who is she? It's not like we're dating. I'm not going to care." She gave a sinister smile. "Yet."

If there was one word in the English dictionary that I hated it was that one. "I was invited here on the behalf of Dr. Petty."

Her face changed. The jealousy filled every inch. Bitch radar was about to be in full bloom. Lucky me. "Dr. Petty? Is she out of her mind? You pushed her out of a two-story window and she gets a date with you? I should be ahead of her." I couldn't tell if we were still having friendly bantering or not.

"Does everyone know I did that? Besides, you bit me and nearly turned me into a werewolf. I'm not sure that exactly puts you in the lead for my affection." I was still joking. For now.

"One of these days Paul, you've got to trust your heart. Besides, you might as well give in to me. I'm relentless." She smiled with the last word. It was said in jest, but I knew she meant every syllable of it.

"No need for a cat fight tonight. We're not on a date. She's just my cover for getting in. If I live through tonight, you can have my heart and my body." This time I was wishing I was joking. I wanted nothing more than to have gorilla sex with her, but I couldn't get past the fact that she was one of the monsters. No matter how much I tried to see the human in her, I couldn't.

"Who said I wanted anything to do with your heart?"

"Am I interrupting something?" a voice from behind said.

"Dr. Petty," I started. I had no reason to feel it, but I felt like a man that had just been caught with his two lovers. "Glad to see you could make it."

She looked over to Angie. They knew each other. "Well at least if you turn furry tonight, you won't have much to take off."

"If I turn furry tonight, it's your head I'm taking off," Angie responded.

"Ladies, please." I was trying to keep the catfight from happening. I looked to Angie. "I'll be in touch. Keep your eyes and ears open."

"For you, that's not the only thing I'll keep open." Too bad she was so shy.

"You can take the girl out of the trash, but you can't take the trash out of the girl," Dr. Feelgood huffed.

Angie began to walk toward Feelgood. This wasn't going to be pleasant. I stepped between them and grabbed Angie by the shoulders. "Don't pay her any attention. She's just trying to get a reaction out of you. Tell you what, be the bigger person and walk away, and I'll let you help me kill the big bad monsters when I find them."

She smiled and looked at Feelgood. "You're lucky I have the hots for him honey or you'd be nothing more the skin under my fingernails." She looked back at me. "You could do better." With a quick bounce she moved to the balls of her feet and kissed me on the lips. I wasn't sure if it was for my pleasure or Dr. Feelgood's pain, but it was nice all the same.

With that, the sexy werewolf faded away in the darkness. I walked beside Dr. Feelgood toward the Crimson Madness, checking under my black jacket for the hidden Magnum and crucifixes. I hoped the night went smoothly or I'd never get my deposit back on the tux.

CHAPTER EIGHT

The long walk across the parking lot seemed to take forever. There was that nagging voice inside me, telling me that no matter how good my intentions were tonight, things were going to go bad. I looked over to Feelgood, who was looking forward and an arm's length away. I could tell she was as awkward about us being together as I was. Even though we weren't even close to being on a date, there was an indescribable tension in the air. We wanted to say things to each other, wanted to appear cool, but the emotions just weren't allowing it to take place.

Feelgood was dressed in a deep red dress that stopped just short of her knees. Silver sparkles lit it up like a summer's night. Her hair was pulled on top of her head with curls of loose hair falling to both sides of her face. She looked so different than the woman I had met at the office. She looked almost sexy. I shivered at that thought. There was no way I was going to date and fall in lust with my therapist. Yuck.

"You look nice." I meant it to sound much better than the mellow-toned effort I gave it.

"Wow, you must be unstoppable with the ladies."

I wanted to come back with something smart, but she was right. Complimenting a woman wasn't something I had practiced lately. "Look on the bright side, it's the best compliment I've given all evening."

"Compared to your other date tonight, I'm dressed more appropriately as well." She looked over to me and smiled.

I felt the blood rush to my face. "Depends on what you call appropriate if you ask me."

"What is it with men that all a woman has to do is show a little cleavage and you all turn into putty in our hands?"

I gave her a little evil smile. "That wasn't a *little* cleavage."

"Men," she huffed as she gave in to the smile just under the surface.

The entrance to the gallery was glass from top to bottom, red glowing neon working its way around the over-sized windows. It was two stories high, open and chic. Art Deco design with a modern pop culture feel. The whole building seemed to glow like a huge light bulb. Two giant glass doors allowed all that passed by to see the inside of the gallery, enticing all to stop, look and hopefully buy. Giant spotlights cut through the darkness like a knife.

There was a line forming outside the gallery. Five couples ahead of us. A doorman was checking credentials as well as religious items, as they filed into the main gallery. There was the same sign at the entrance that you see at all cockroach places of business. **No Religious Articles of Any Kind.** From time to time one of the couples would look back at us, or better put, me, and whisper. I was an anti-celebrity to them. For me to be here was something to raise questions from even the most jaded in the city. Then again maybe I was just paranoid.

Even from the door, I could feel the power. It hit my skin like a bee sting, raising the little hair I had. Intoxicating and alive. Never

before had I felt so much power in a single spot. It was like grabbing a live power line.

"Dr. Petty, so good to see you," the doorman said to Feelgood,
but he was staring at me. "What do you think you're doing here?"

"He's with me." Dr. Petty lightly put her arm on my shoulder.
Nothing playful or endearing. Simply pushing me forward.

The man stopped us again. "With all due respect doctor, he isn't
welcome here, credentials or not." It was said about as polite as I
could have expected, but I could already tell tonight was going to be
a repetitious account of that same old tired line. I wasn't welcome
here and I knew it. It made me both nervous and excited. To know I
was the party crasher on this little shindig brought about a small
grin on my face. To think I might have to fight my way out of here
tonight gave me a smile nothing could wipe off.

"He's here on diplomatic terms tonight. I promise, he'll be no
trouble at all," Feelgood answered back with a smile of her own.

"What type of diplomatic terms?" He continued to block our
way inside the gallery. Others were starting to form behind us. I
caught myself starting to make the nervous circles Angie had picked
up on earlier. I smiled thinking of her.

"To find the killer of a …." I was cut off.

"He's one of my patients and he is here on vampire sensitivity
therapy. Orders of the Council."

"My darling Lydia, so nice to see you here tonight." I jumped at
the new voice. From inside the gallery, stood a short roach, no more
than five foot six, red hair and large sunglasses, covering nearly all
of his face. A flamboyant roach to say the least. He took Feelgood's
hand and kissed it.

"Ahh, Dubro, such a charmer," Feelgood cooed. Her eyes
sparkled as she looked at him. Like with me, nothing romantic,
simply admiration.

"What was that about the Council?" He fanned the air with his
hand. "You can tell me inside." Dubro pulled her in by her hand.

His hot pink tux made me smile. Complete with top hat and cane. It took a lot of balls to dress like that. "There are just so many fabulous people I want you to shmooze with."

"I want to, but we are having trouble getting my friend in."

Dubro looked to me. I honestly don't think he knew who I was until he looked me in the eyes. I saw the elegant charm evaporate. "Oh dear, Mr. Isaac?" He looked back to Feelgood. "Oh, honey you cannot be serious. I agree he is quite charming to look at, but this kitten has claws."

"Mr. Isaac is here on…diplomatic issues."

He looked as though someone had licked the icing off his cake. "With all due respect, dear Lydia, I can understand why he would have trouble getting in." He looked back to her. "Have you lost your mind in bringing him here? I heard you say something about therapy, but this is insane. I have investors from all over the world here tonight, not to mention the press. I believe in therapy for everyone, but there is a time and a place for everything."

"He's not here to be a problem. In fact, he wishes to warn some of your supporters of possible harm and ask questions about a serial killer." She made sure her voice was just for him. No need to draw attention just yet.

"Oh, dear. I don't think asking about such a rumor will go over well. A possible serial killer will not get anyone in the mood to buy art. Tonight, everyone is required to think happy thoughts and write big checks." He gave a nervous laugh and bent closer to us. "Save the blood and guts for another night."

Time for me to speak. "If another supporter dies because I can't ask a few questions, I'll let the press in on our little talk. I don't think your investors will think protecting a killer is a good career move. And if they find out that you could have helped stop the deaths and did nothing, what do you think they'll do?"

"But I have nothing to do with the death of anyone. You are simply threatening slander."

"The public won't know the difference. And their doubt could be bad for business. Truth won't matter."

"He's just trying to keep others out of harms way. He's here to warn not accuse." Dr. Feelgood held the fang breath's hand, patting it lightly. "Please. As a favor for me."

"I'm sorry, but I just don't think it is a very good idea to allow him in. As you know, tonight features the who's who of vampires and vampire supporters in Orlando. He would be, well, a distraction at the very least. The press will be all about him. That's not what I'm paying all of this for."

"I'm very much aware of the reason for tonight's occasion. I don't mean to cause you any problems. I know how important this night is to you. I wouldn't ask you such a favor it I didn't think it was very important to you and your guests that he be here." My best effort at political correctness.

Dubro looked back and forth between Dr. Feelgood and me several times. His mouth opened and closed just as often, the words just not making it out. With obvious angst, he tried again, "Do you realize what a huge chance it would be for me to even consider such a mad idea? How could you even put me in such an awkward position?"

"I do," started Feelgood, "but I think for the good of the vampire community, it would be something that you might consider. It could be very good press if spun right." She gave a light smile. Feelgood was a real snake charmer.

"Consider? You bring one of your patients here as your guest for one, which I find very unethical, and two, you bring the one man that has killed more of our kind than anyone." He looked back in the room at the mingling guests, who were starting to stare as well. "To say everyone would be too nervous to have a good time is an understatement. At the very least, they will be on pins and needles over this. No one will spend money on art if they are looking over their shoulder. My credibility would be shot for even allowing it. I will not have any blood spilt here tonight." He shifted his attention from Feelgood to me. "Regardless to what you might think, Mr. Isaac, we are a peaceful group. Unlike you and your kind, we are here to love, not hate."

"Look, I'm not here to kill anyone. As hard as it is for me to say, I'm actually here to keep more of your supporters safe," I chimed in.

He quickly moved my jacket open, exposing the Magnum in the shoulder holster as well as a 9mm in a hip holster. "For someone that does not plan to bring death, you sure have enough weapons."

Believe it or not, but for a moment, I'd forgotten I had them. They had been a part of me for so long that it was just natural to have them with me. "It's just for my protection. And possibly the protection of some of your supporters," I lied.

"Protection from what may I ask? We are here for a celebration of art. If you are here to help and protect us, you should be willing to leave your weapons at the door."

I shook my head and smiled a fake smile. "I have too many enemies for that."

"Then we have nothing more to talk about." He turned to walk away.

"Play his game," Feelgood whispered angrily. It was followed by an elbow to the ribs.

"If you allow me to enter without any problems, I'll leave the weapon at the door." I placed the Magnum on the small table near me. I still had a couple of vials of holy water in my jacket pocket. It wasn't a good trade for me, but you have to lose some of the little battles to win the war.

Dubro turned to speak but was cut off.

"We are not here to negotiate with killers," another cockroach said as he moved behind Dubro. He was the palest cockroach I had ever seen. No doubt an albino. Movements more fluid than any other I had ever seen. Eyes red with blood. "I will not ask you to leave again."

I could feel his power. Close to four hundred years old would be my guess. Not the strongest I had ever felt, but enough that I was reconsidering the Magnum for entrance trade I just put on the table. "And you are?"

"I do not answer to you. You will not take away anything from my lover's grand gala tonight. He has worked far too long and much too hard for you to take his moment in the spot light." His long white hair flowed like ice water down his shoulders and to the small of his back. The ends of the hair were dyed black, getting lost in the black suit he was wearing. Even the dress shirt and tie were black. He looked like a walking salt and pepper set.

"Sylvester, it is fine. I can handle this," Dubro said, patting the albino on the hand, lovingly. "According to Dr. Petty, he is here to warn our friends of imminent danger." He looked back to me. "Is that not true, Mr. Isaac?"

Playing Mr. Nice Guy with these roaches was not the easiest thing I had ever done in my life. But I knew cockroach politics and the mind games they liked to play. I looked back to Sylvester. "Yes, of imminent danger." I gave my best choirboy smile.

"How ironic. I had always thought of you as the imminent danger. And how has it come to be that you are here to protect rather than slaughter?"

"I have word that members of the Knights of the Night are being murdered by a rouge ..." Shit I was going to have to be political correct for the second time tonight. "Vampire."

Sylvester laughed. "So am I to understand that you, the vampire executioner, are now saving us from one of our own?" He moved away from Dubro and came face to face with Feelgood. "Are you really that good at therapy? That you can turn the hunter into the lover? Should I be honored to have such a warrior watching over me?"

"No that's not it at all. I don't give a fuck about your kind. It's the humans I'm here to save." Okay, I was losing my battle with being nice, but come on, he started it. I walked slowly toward him.

"What Mr. Isaac means is," Feelgood slid between me and the monsters, "he wants to make sure the events tonight go off without a hitch. There are a great deal of potential buyers and investors here tonight. All have money. It would be a shame if they were put into danger tonight over something so trivial as Mr. Isaac's profession."

"And how is it that we have not heard of this imminent danger? Could it be that you are simply using it as a Trojan horse to enter and kill at will?"

I stepped forward, forcing him to take a step back. Feelgood was now trapped between the two of us. "But there is only one of me and so many of you. How could I possibly put you in danger?"

He looked at the 9mm still tucked in its holster. "If you wish to put all of us at ease, I am sure the weapon you still have is nothing more than a slight oversight."

I handed over the 9mm to the human at the door. "Satisfied?"

Sylvester never reacted to the gesture, simply continued with his inquisition. "Why would you think that any of us are in danger of losing our lives tonight?"

"I was given information about them from a secret source."

His large fangs glistened in the artificial light. "Really. And who might that have been?"

"Telling you wouldn't make it a secret anymore, now would it?" I gave him a big smile. "Let's just say it was one of your kind." I felt my heart rate rising. The coffin crunchy was trying to paint me into a corner, and I was being stripped of everything I had to defend myself.

"A vampire?"

"And they said you were slow." I grinned.

"Sylvester, sweetheart, I said I'd handle this. Go mingle and fill the glasses with drink. The humans are more free with their currency when a little tipsy." Dubro looked at me and gave a nervous smile.

Sylvester smiled and looked behind him at the growing crowd. "He leaves all his weapons at the door." Back to me, "All of them. Crucifixes, holy water. Everything." He moved within inches of my face. "If you so happen to look at one of our guests wrong, I'll personally rip your throat out."

Oh, there were so many things I wanted to say at this point, but I bit my tongue. "You have our word," Feelgood answered.

A large man approached, looking to Sylvester for orders. A human servant. The typical big and dumb kind. I guessed he was some sort of security. "Check him for all weapons," the albino roach said, then floated away. "I keep my promises," the pale roach threatened.

"I am counting on you to keep your guest out of sight and trouble tonight," Dubro said looking at Feelgood. I'd be as good as I could be, but if one of them tried anything, all bets would be off.

Feelgood looked at me. I could read her eyes. "You won't even know he's here."

Dubro looked back at me and glared. "Somehow I seriously doubt that."

CHAPTER NINE

"I owe you one," I said to Feelgood. I hadn't realized it but I had been holding my breath for a very long time. I could feel my pulse thump against my temple. Blood pressure so high, I was slightly dizzy.

Feelgood patted me on the back. "No problem. Now just keep your end of the bargain. Don't pick a fight." She looked up at me. For a moment, she had become my therapist again.

The gallery was open and large. Hundreds of small bulbs filled the room with soft light. Oversized paintings decorated the walls. Colors deep and bright all at the same time. I had taken art lessons, so I could appreciate talented art when I saw it. This wasn't it. I know art is in the eye of the beholder, but this was nothing more than paint thrown on a canvass. More like pornographic macabre. Naked statues that I swore were living humans, twisted in eternal sexual positions.

There were small crowds around each of the pieces, nodding and talking to one another while holding glasses of red wine. I hoped it was red wine. Soft classical music filled the open space, giving everyone a false sense of sophistication. They looked back to me from time to time, watching and waiting for me to do something. I hoped I'd leave them all disappointed.

I looked up the stairs along the far wall and saw more art and more over dressed rich patrons, talking to the cockroaches and laughing on cue. Nude waitress carried trays of drinks. The hum of conversation filled my ears. I had to look for members of the Knights of the Night. After all, that was why I was here. My main goal was getting out of this tux and finding a killer roach that likes to take the lives of the very small. The hair on my arms rose as I thought about it.

At the top of the stairs I saw the leader of the cockroach activists. Albert Kincaid. He had led the charge in making the monsters legal. Not everyone knew it, but he ran the largest distribution of roach porn in the country, known as Necro-Pussy. Now the profits he made were being laundered into the filth like tonight's gala.

"Excuse me," I whispered to Feelgood and patted her on the shoulder.

She followed my eyes to the top of the stairs. "Be good."

"You know me." I smiled as I began to walk.

"That's why I said it."

Kincaid was flanked by two very attractive women. Their eyes were dilated from roach magic. I was willing to bet they were fang whores, but from where I stood I couldn't be sure. It didn't matter. I wasn't here to judge who he slept with or who he filmed.

I made it to the bottom stair when a woman stopped me. "So we meet, Mr. Isaac."

Her sweet perfume made me breathe deeper than I had wanted, almost hurting myself. "Do I know you?" I waited for the typical response of how I had killed her fanged lover or how I wasn't wanted here. Instead I looked into a docile face that matched the perfume.

"Not face to face. I'm Isabella Dunlawton." She held out her hand. I ignored it.

"So?" I tried to keep an eye on Kincaid. In this thick crowd, it would be easy to lose him.

"I work for Dubro. I'm his assistant."

She was short and petite. Pretty smile, almond eyes. A purple dress draped over her form falling just above the knees. I tried to think of something clever to say. Something to let her know not only was I good looking but eloquent as well. "Oh," was all I said back.

"He and Sylvester have asked me to be your personal guide tonight. Can I get you something to drink?"

"No, I'm fine." I wasn't here to indulge her.

"You have everyone here a little nervous as you might have guessed." She gave a small giggle and touched my hand playfully.

I pulled back, more from the surprise than anything. "I've already told them, I'm not here to cause any trouble. I'm here to talk with Kincaid. After that, I'm out of their hair. If there's drama tonight, it'll come from some other source than me."

She followed my eyes to Kincaid. "Looking to invest in his little business?"

I'm sure she saw the repulsion in my eyes. "Hardly." I looked up the stairs again, trying to keep my eyes on Kincaid. "I don't mean to be rude, but I'm not here to mingle and talk. In fact, I suck at conversation."

She grabbed my hand and pulled me to an art piece on the wall. "Some say death is an art all its own. Do you like art, Mr. Isaac?"

I followed her like a small child, all the time keeping my eyes on Kincaid as if he would vanish into thin air. "I like good art. Not really this. But I guess when you're a cockroach you can wait until it's appreciated."

She looked up. "Because they're timeless?" A grin formed on her small face.

"No, it's just that this is crap. Whether it was done by a human or monster doesn't make a difference."

"They hope to make quite a profit tonight. If this gallery makes as much money as we think it will, our investors will be rolling in money. Millionaires. Crap or not, they all win."

"Vampire artists are just like any other artists as far as that goes. The paintings are more valuable after the artist is dead. What these poor idiots don't understand is that vampires can live forever. They'll never make their investment back." I scoffed at the painting and shook my head. "I guess there's a sucker born every minute." I started to walk away, only to have her grab my wrist once more. I thought about jerking free, but I was trying to play nice. Instead, I gave a stare that gave me the same result.

She turned to face the painting, hesitated, and then faced me again. "I need to tell you something very important." The woman looked around the room as if about to reveal the secret to life. "Something that can't wait."

I was only half way paying attention. She hadn't said anything so far that made a difference to me. "If it doesn't have to do with a name of a killer cockroach, it *can* wait." I watched as Kincaid faced into the crowd again. His bimbos laughed and continued to be the perfect pieces of arm candy.

"What would you say if I told you I wanted to see these things become a pile of ash more than you do?"

I was confused. "Then I'd say you have no idea how bad I hate them." I stared at her as she looked into my eyes, never blinking. "Why are you telling me this?"

"I'm not a vampire activist. I hate the damn things. Simply a woman with a useless degree in need of a good job. I took it to get close enough to them to kill them. When I heard we would be opening the gallery here, you have to know I was excited beyond words."

"Good for you." I wanted to get away from her as soon as I could. "Activist or not, you're not the one I'm here to see or help."

"I want to hire you to kill Dubro."

"What did you just say?" Was my hearing really going that bad?

"Help me kill Dubro."

"Are you crazy?"

She hesitated. "If you help me, I'll make it very much worth your while."

Before I could answer, power moved across my spine. We were no longer alone.

"I have waited so long in meeting you, Mr. Paul Isaac." She was six-foot tall, hair no more than an inch long on her head. Crippling power radiated off of her. "My name is Sanguine."

Chances were, she was a vein weasel porn star. I looked her from head to toe and simply answered. "Well now you have." I was blunt and meant it to be. With what just came out of Isabella's pie hole, I really wasn't in the mood for small talk.

"You have a lot of nerve coming here tonight. There are a lot of vampires here that would love nothing more than to kill you where you stand." She moved around me like a deadly cat. "I happen to be one of them."

I moved with her, never allowing her to get to my back. "Many have tried, but they all end up dust when it's over."

"He's not here to cause trouble, Sanguine," Isabella said. "Only to talk with Mr. Kincaid."

"And why would you say such a thing, Ms. Dunlawton? Is he not the great vampire executioner of the city? He is at best a distraction. His reputation cannot be ignored. Dubro has put everyone here in grave danger." She continued to circle me. "I say we kill him and have a buffet to remember."

"Don't let your fear cause your ass to be ash." I gave her my patented fake smile.

She licked her lips. "Oh, it is not fear, Mr. Isaac. Do not

presume to think I fear you at all. You are nothing more than a minor distraction that must be squashed at the first opportunity."

"And I think you've been on your back so long that it's starting to affect your thought process."

Her black leather outfit fit her. She looked like a dominatrix from hell. Large tattoos covered most of her body up to the neck. "Is that a challenge?" The stilettos on the thigh high black leather boots clicked against the marble floor as she moved. "I for one would love nothing more than to go down in history as the one that killed you."

I had to be careful. I was talking to a very powerful roach and all my weapons were sitting in a box somewhere far away.

Eyes were starting to look our way. "In another time and place, if your mouth is empty and the cameras aren't rolling, I will accept the challenge. Right now, I'm here to talk to a few of the guests and leave. Seems there are a few of you out there that aren't as excited about the Knights of the Night as I would think."

"From what I have heard, the local police have the vampire in custody."

"No. They have *a* cockroach in custody, not *the* cockroach."

She closed the distance again. Cobra-like actions. "I did not think it would matter to you whether it was the right one or not. Perhaps since your altercation with Maximilian, you have grown a soft spot for the vampire in you."

"Please excuse us, Sanguine. Mr. Isaac wishes to speak to Mr. Kincaid," Isabella added. I could tell by her voice she was as nervous as hell. She had every right to be. I was used to meeting and killing things like Sanguine, and I was just as nervous.

Sanguine dropped Isabella with magic. As if she had been hit with an invisible fist. Quick, powerful and deadly. "Do not ever interrupt me again, Isabella."

I pushed Sanguine back, allowing Isabella to stand again. It had been a test to see if I would jump and lose my innocent façade. She had tricked me, but the game wasn't over. Not by a freaking long shot. Now, a lot of eyes were watching us. And I didn't have to guess who would get blamed for the altercation.

"How sweet, the executioner being led around by the balls by a vampire human servant. What's next howling at the moon with the wolves?" Sanguine laughed. "That's right, Avenger, we all know about your little dog bite." Evil that crawled into my ears like a deadly virus. *"Count you blessings, Avenger that I did not end your pathetic life just now. Next time I assure you, you will not be as lucky."*

"Careful Sanguine, or someday I just might cut off *your* balls."

She looked to Isabella with eyes of ice, and then moved them back on me. "I anticipate the challenge, human. Killing you will be sweet and erotic for me. I will expose you for the monster you are."

"We must go now, Paul before Mr. Kincaid gets away." Isabella grabbed my hand and led me away from Sanguine. "Don't ever tell her that she's not powerful or beautiful. I've seen her kill on the spot for that." I glanced at Isabella to see if she was joking. She wasn't.

Kincaid saw me and I could tell he wasn't happy. He began to move down the stairs and I was sure more slanderous remarks would be coming my way. They were getting old, but I was getting used to them.

I had asked the question, but was already growing impatient as Isabella spoke. There was another question I wanted to ask even more. "Do you mind explaining your comments earlier about killing Dubro?"

She looked back to see how far away Sanguine was. From the side, Dubro was slithering toward us. Her words were hurried and vague as she started to vanish into the thicket of people. "We may not have time to get into detail now, Mr. Isaac, but I will be in touch soon." She slid a card into my jacket pocket.

"I see you have met my lovely assistant, Ms. Dunlawton."

Dubro looked me over like a piece of meat. "Have you been able to talk with Mr. Kincaid as of yet? No offense, Mr. Isaac, but I'd like to have you out of here. We want the auction to take place as soon as possible." He looked over to Sanguine. "People are already starting to talk. I do not want you to be the focus of their conversations."

Before I could answer, Kincaid was in front of me. Large round man with more money that God. His balding head reflected the swirls of light coming from the room. "May I ask what the hell you're doing here?"

"Possibly saving your life," I answered.

CHAPTER TEN

"This is Mr. Paul…" Dubro started.

"I know who he is, Dubro. I just want to know who the idiot was that let him in here," Kincaid said, trying to stare me down. I think I was supposed to be intimidated. With a shoo of his hands he broke free of the two bimbos.

"He's leaving soon, sweetheart. It's okay," Dubro chimed back, patting Kincaid's hand. "Answer his questions and we can get back to the business at hand."

"What is it this time, Isaac, afraid the vampires will take over the world? Maybe you want to kill an innocent vampire in front of his mother?" Behind me I could hear the patter of light laughter of the arm candy. I balled my fists, but remained in control.

"I'm trying to warn you that your pathetic life might be in danger. If you're not into listening, it's fine with me. Go ahead and stick your head up your ass if you want. It won't keep the danger from coming all the same. If you wake up dead from a roach attack, I'll be there waiting to send you to the afterlife personally." I was now an inch from his face. I made a point not to blink. He may not listen, but I'd have his attention all the same. "Maybe you can make a movie about it."

"He thinks there is a vampire trying to kill you. I told him that the likelihood of that was quite preposterous," Dubro added with a nervous laugh. "Now that all the bad news is taken care of, can we get back to the party?" Dubro hooked his arm in Albert Kincaid's in a light effort to end the conversation.

Kincaid pulled his arm free. "You mean Asa," he said, still staring holes in me.

"No. He's not the vampire that has been killing all the members of the Knights of the Night."

"I'm sorry to inform you of this, Mr. Isaac, but Asa is in jail for killing the members of the Knights. And if he's behind bars, I don't think my life is in all that great of danger." Like prize fighters, we continued the stare down. "Don't tell me you're here to join the Knights and help set poor Asa free?"

"Truthfully, I don't care if he lives or dies, but I thought you might. Did the police tell you the reason they arrested Asa?"

"Asa is not one to follow human law all that well. He is a thousand year old vampire pretty set in his ways. According to Detective Kansas he's being held in association with certain murders. He has asked us to keep the arrest quiet until the investigation is complete."

"And you agreed?"

Kincaid laughed. "I will never understand you, Isaac. First you come busting in here unannounced and unwelcomed, and now you're telling me there are vampires killing us, the police are involved and they have the wrong vampire behind bars for execution. I'm not sure if you're truly insane or just pathetically stupid."

"Time and opportunity are wasting," this from Dubro as he looked back at the crowd of people that were now staring at us.

Kincaid waved him off. "What's in it for you, Isaac?"

"What do you mean?"

"You aren't here to save us from the vampires and we both

know that. So I ask you again, what's in it for you? Publicity? You'd have thought you had enough of that when you and that quack priest gunned down that vampire in cold blood."

"I simply want the right blood sucker killed. Neither the police or the Council seems to want to do anything about it. And you're right, I'm not here to save you from the fang heads. I'm in search of a killer and his trail led me to you. What you or the authorities do with the rest of them is up to you. I do have suggestions, but I doubt you'd like to hear them."

"Asa has not been a supporter of our cause and we both know that. He and his are nothing more than rouges that should be weeded out. He's uncivilized and insane. I think he's finally getting what he deserves. If you ask me, the police have their vampire. He's been nothing but a pain in vampire rights since the laws came down. Killing him will gain in our cause, not deter from it. Good riddance I say."

"Maybe so, but the threat on your life as well as those around you still exists. Being pompous or ignoring it won't change anything. You've been warned, so the blood is on your hands from here."

"According to you, Mr. Isaac and only according to you. I have seen no proof that there's any threat at all. Why would the police not report the deaths as murders if that is in fact what happened? I tell you why. People panic and stories grow into bigger stories. I applaud them for their discretion."

"The police and the Council want it that way. There are murders happening under your nose and you don't even know it. The killer responsible could be here tonight for all we know." I looked around the room for effect.

"Asa told you this didn't he?"

"That's right. But I have checked it out myself as well. Not to mention when I went to the morgue, the doctor went to a lot of trouble to keep me from nosing around. Quinn and the Council threatened his life if he let the truth out."

"And where are the bodies of these so-called victims of vampirism?" By his tone, I was guessing he already knew that answer.

"Cremated."

"How convenient." He gave a demeaning smile.

"There are those close to you that are at your throat waiting to go for the jugular. You should be demanding, not only the truth, but protection for your people as well."

"Investors are getting lonely," Dubro sang.

Kincaid ignored Dubro. "Mr. Isaac, the way I see it, you are the only thing we have to worry about tonight. Now if you will excuse us, we are trying to have a wonderful evening with friends." He placed an arm back around each of his women, then shot daggers at Dubro. "How could you let him in here? If every investor leaves here tonight and doesn't buy a goddamn thing, it'll be our best case scenario, mark my words. Start acting like this is a business and get him the hell out of here." Kincaid began to walk away.

"What about Susannah ? You know that she's dead too don't you?"

"Died of a heart attack. What of it?" Kincaid said as he continued to walk away.

"Don't you find it just a little odd that three members of your organization are dead within a couple of weeks? Seems like it would at least raise a red flag or two."

He turned with a half grin. "I agree that it's a streak of bad luck, but to think we are being targeted is absurd. Besides, as we have already discussed, there is a vampire nice and warm in a jail cell. I think our time of worry has passed. Just like your welcome."

"Have you seen the body?"

The grin turned into a weak chuckle. "Like you said, it was

cremated. Now if you don't mind, Mr. Isaac, my patience have worn thin."

"Or perhaps you've known all along that they were being killed. Nothing more than a shepherd leading his sheep to slaughter."

I could see the anger growing quickly on his face. He moved close to me and spoke in deep hushed tones. "Be careful with your threats, vampire man. I have lawyers that will eat you alive."

"Literally, I'm sure." I stood my ground. He wasn't going to intimidate me.

"I don't have time for this game. Leave or I'll make this very embarrassing for you." He began to move again. "Have a nice evening, Mr. Isaac."

I put my hand against his shoulder to stop him. "What's happening here isn't a game, Kincaid. It's murder. Personally, I should let you find out the hard way I'm telling you the truth. You'd deserve it, but I have a bad feeling the blood bum responsible won't stop with you or your clan."

Kincaid looked down at my hand, then slowly rose his glare to my face. "You have about three seconds to take your hands off of me or I'll call the police."

"And it doesn't bother you that the police are covering it up?" I asked. "If you truly are in the dark on this one, I'd think it would scare you to death."

"Kind of hard to be a cover up when there's no killer out there, Mr. Isaac. You know, this isn't the first time we've had these conversations and in all that time, we have agreed to disagree. Now you can either leave peacefully, or I'll have you escorted out of here and it won't be nice. You are nothing more than a flea that is in need of being squashed." Kincaid moved close to me again, yelling in a loud whisper. "If there's a cover up, then it was for the benefit of the families of the victims. I see nothing wrong with that as long as the vampire is dealt with properly. And we will deal with the threats in our own way. Chances are, Asa is probably guilty of the murders if they happened the way you say, but it is still a moot point. If there was a vampire killing the Knights, they have their monster. If they didn't think so, they'd have called you by now."

"Besides, to bring up a story like that would just ruin the vampire district. If it is true, I commend the police department for their discreetness on the matter," this from Dubro. "Enough about death and gore. Let us get back to the celebration at hand. There is no reason to talk about things that none of us can change anyway."

"I knew you were all sick pathetic bastards, but I didn't know you'd go this far. You're nothing more than death dealers yourselves. Make sure you stop by the coroner's office on your way home so they can fit you for a body bag. You're gonna need one. "

"Your time is up here." Sylvester pushed me back against a wall. Scary part was, I never heard him come up from behind.

I started to leave when Kincaid added, "You know something Paul, you remind me of another loser that I used to know that thought the vampires were out to take over the world. Oh, what was his name, Stephen Isaac I think it was."

I came back to him with my hands shaking. "What did you say you filthy bastard?"

"I'm sorry, that's right. He was your father wasn't he? Now I know why your name rings a bell."

I hit him before I knew I had done it. My body was numb with anger as I looked down at him as he held his bleeding lip. Screams filled the open room. People started to scatter. "Don't you ever say anything about my parents again. They died trying to help these fang shits and you know it. You're lucky I don't stake you here and now, myself."

"I think it's time to leave." I felt a pull of my hand. Dr. Feelgood was on the scene. "This isn't a good thing anymore. I should have known you couldn't get through the night without starting something like this." Nails suddenly dug into my skin.

Sylvester grabbed me and pulled my arm behind my back.

"With any luck there won't be anyone on the street and I can kill you tonight."

"You can try it pale boy, but the truth is, I don't think you have the balls to do it. If you did, you would've done it already, so let me go before I embarrass you in front of your boyfriend," I finished.

"When I kill you, you will beg for it to end," he said in my mind.

I looked to Albert Kincaid, who was now standing, wiping away the dots of blood from his lip. Cockroach eyes were on him. If I've said it once, I've said it a million times, bleeding in Bat Town is not a good idea. "Keep in mind what I said. There's still a killer out there and you're the highest target on his list. If you end up in a body bag, you have no one to blame but yourself." I pulled away from Sylvester's grasp. "You can all be coffin bait for all I care."

I had only taken a few steps toward the door when the shots exploded in the room.

CHAPTER ELEVEN

Chaos spread quickly throughout the gallery as more shots rang out. The screams filled the room, humans and cockroaches alike moved in various directions; hiding in corners, falling to the floor. Above the screams and gunshots, I could still hear the classical music playing, giving the gallery a surreal feel to it. Ignoring the pending death as the two worlds collided into one another.

I reached into my shoulder harness to get the Magnum, only to remember it was far away in a safe somewhere. Feelgood pulled me to the ground, nails dug in my arms, eyes wide as cannonballs.

"Still feel the same about your monsters, Dr. Feelgood," I said as I lay flat on the floor.

Her eyes were fixed on a man no more than twenty feet from us. "We can debate this some other time, but the shooter looks to be human."

She was right. God, I hated therapy.

"I'll kill you all!" I heard from the entrance of the gallery. It was

Mr. Guzman. "Damn you all. You know what you did. You set me up. I'm innocent."

I moved from the spot where I was pulled down, keeping low, crawling along the floor through the sea of bodies. As I pushed forward it became very clear to me that I could just as easily be attacked and killed by one of the roaches as the attacker.

"Another of your tricks I see," Sylvester said as I moved past him. He grabbed my arm, pale white skin, cold and dead.

"I didn't do this. Either help me save everyone or get out of the way." I broke his grip and dared him to make the same move twice. To his benefit, he didn't.

"You all did it!" Guzman screamed again. He waved the pistol across the crowd. More screams followed. Like schools of fish, many of the trapped pushed from one side of the gallery to the other. I used them as cover as I grew closer. My eyes locked on Guzman.

"How could you? You killed my daughter." Another shot rang out. "This is not over. I'll tell the police all I know. Every dirty little detail."

Guzman moved through the sea of bodies still scrambling to stay out of his way. I looked around the room and into the eyes of those wanting me to do something. Others blamed me with their glare.

"Which one of you killed her?" He pointed the gun at random. "I want the one that killed my baby. The one that made my little angel a monster."

I pointed to Sylvester just to watch him get shot. It was guilty pleasures like that that sometimes got me into trouble. Still, watching an angry man shoot these bloodsuckers could be called entertainment to me.

As the bullet found its mark I looked at him and smiled. He gave an angry growl while holding his new wound. Thank God looks can't kill. I shrugged and blew him a kiss.

I wanted to tease him more but now was not the time. Not everyone was immune to the bullets and I had to get the situation under control. "Mr. Guzman, please put the gun down!" I yelled instead. One of two things would happen if I didn't. One of the roaches would kill him or he would shoot and kill me. The second was not that appealing to me. Empty handed, I wasn't much of a threat to them. "Give me the gun!" I tried again.

The gun instinctively moved on me. "Make one more move and I'll kill you where you stand. I want the ones that ruined my life. Tell me or I'll start shooting them all." Tears streamed down his cheeks. I couldn't blame him for the actions. I had nothing but apathy. Thanks to Dieter's little magic trick, I didn't think he remembered who I was. Things were looking up.

"I'm here trying to find out, Mr. Guzman. Please put the gun down. You're not helping the situation by doing this. I'm a vampire executioner. Let me handle this." I made sure not to make any sudden moves and kept my voice as soothing as I could make it.

I saw one of the humans get up from the floor and run for the door. Guzman turned and shot as the woman moved past, catching her with a bullet to the ribs. Blood shot from the wound as she fell to the floor just short of freedom.

I cursed under my breath. The situation was getting more and more out of hand. If he continued to shoot, what little order there was would be lost. I looked at Dubro, shivering and screaming. "Get one of your roaches to run him. He doesn't have anything but regular bullets."

"Why should we sacrifice ourselves? I didn't kill his daughter. Besides you allowed him to shoot my Sylvester."

"Kincaid! We need to talk!" Guzman shouted, looking to the second floor. Gun still fanning.

"You useless coward," I whispered to Dubro. Guzman was calling out names. Kincaid? He wasn't even a fang head. But if he got shot just the same, so be it.

Guzman pushed the barrel of the gun into the head of Isabella. He pulled the young woman to her feet by the hair on her head. Isabella screamed and looked to me. I tried to tell her I would help her with my eyes, but even I doubted I could do anything at this point. "You told them didn't you?"

"She's not a vampire," I said. "She had nothing to do with your daughter's death."

"You're all responsible for killing my baby. Now you'll all pay." The gun pushed into Isabella's head harder. She screamed and began to cry.

"A little help here would be nice," I yelled in general. I was appalled at the fact the monsters were willing to allow this man to assassinate everyone. Acts of heroism were something unfamiliar to them. I tried to use my wits and do, other than killing, the thing I did best. Lie. "Mr. Guzman, the monster that killed your daughter is in police custody."

He looked at me, eyebrows pulled low on his eyes. "What do you mean?"

"I caught him tonight. We're planning to execute him for the act." I kept my hands in front of me to show him I was unarmed. I tried not to breathe any more than I had to.

Guzman moved toward me slowly, still dragging Isabella like a rag doll. "You're lying. Besides, even if what you're saying is true, my life is over. Over because of all of this…this greed. Lust. You're no different than all the rest of them. Monster or not, you're all liars."

"No I'm not. Now let her go. Your daughter needs you more than ever. If you kill that woman, you'll never get to see your daughter's killer die. I'll take you to the police station right now." I looked at the woman Guzman shot. Blood was running everywhere. Time was running out for her. "No one else has to die."

In the glass doors behind Guzman, I saw a quick shadow. More of a reflection really. Movement so fast it was blurred. Just what I needed, more things to kill. I tried not to let my eyes give the distraction away. I might be able to use it to my advantage if it made its way inside.

"They're all responsible for this. They all deserve to die." He shook Isabella. "She dies. Kincaid dies. All the vampires die. No compromises."

I couldn't disagree with that logic. "At least let the humans go. They've done no harm to you. The woman you're holding is not a vampire. Just hired help."

His eyes were like spinning balls. Menacing and unforgiving. "Then you know nothing about why I'm here."

I moved toward him one-foot step after another. Methodical and deliberate. I looked to the woman that had been shot again. A small group was gathered around her, all looking up to me, then to the shooter. "We need to get her help as soon as possible. The last thing you want is murder on your hands."

I was only inches from Guzman now. My eyes still locked in on his. I had to give him a façade of trust. If not we'd all be corpses and dust. And I wasn't ready to die just yet. "I'll tell you why she and Kincaid dies just like all the rest. Lies and blackmail. All of them. Up to their bloody necks..."

Power moved past me. Nails grabbed like vice grips around the throat of Guzman. The smell of warm copper filled my nose. Blood streamed from Guzman's neck. Blank eyes stared back at me as he buckled and fell to the floor in a lifeless slump.

Sanguine stood next to the body. Her hands were thick with dark blood. Gooey. Shimmering in the light. Hands that instinctively went to her mouth. Licking fingers with a long pink tongue like a large jungle cat. She laughed deep and demonic, as my face must have showed the horror. "Umm, AB Positive, my favorite." She held her hand out to me. "Care to taste him?"

"You twisted fucking bitch. You didn't have to kill him."

"You are right, I did not. But it was quite clear that you were not going to do it. Besides, you kill for far less." She looked down at me. "I could tell you lost your nerve. I on the other hand have no hesitation." She looked back down at what was left of Guzman. "If it was not for my actions your whore would be wearing a bullet. A little gratitude would have been nice." With that, the dominatrix porn star strutted next to Sylvester and Dubro.

From underneath I heard a whimper. "Please help me."

I looked down to see Guzman; his throat ripped open, blood still gushing from the wound the size of my hand. Emotionless eyes looked up at me. Not in peace, but in infinite horror. I rolled him over to find Isabella, covered in thick syrup-like fluid. She was shaking. Hands covered her face like a frightened child.

Dead hands caked with blood had me by the throat and slammed me to the ground. Above I could see Sanguine. Fangs pink with fresh kill. Power so thick I couldn't move. "I told you I would kill you. I always keep my promises. The difference between you and me is I have the nerve to do it. Now it is my turn to bring death to this place." Blood breath hit me like a Mac truck.

My hands reached for her throat. It was a move that would do me no good. It was hard to choke something that didn't breathe. Advantage: Cockroach. I balled my fist and jammed it into her stomach, feeling her give but the grasp on my throat remained. If she had been a man, I'd kicked her in the balls, but that wasn't an option either. Well, at least I didn't think so. Finding them on the roach at my throat wouldn't be all that big a surprise.

Above me I could see the hundred or more other faces, looking, watching. But in no way helping. For the second time I reached for the Magnum. And for the second time it wasn't there. As if it would magically appear out of thin air. *God, were they all just going to stand there and watch?*

"How does it feel knowing you are seconds from dying, Avenger? Knowing my face is the last thing you will ever see."

I looked up at her with all the strength I had left, seeing large ancient fangs exposed through a gapping mouth. Inching closer. Saliva dripped from her mouth in syrup-like strands. Just the thought of that shit hitting me gave me the creeps.

Above me, I saw Albert Kincaid and Sylvester, smiling and waiting for Sanguine to do the deed. My fault. What was I thinking? I came here to help my fellow humans, but now they wanted nothing more than to watch me be sucked dry. So much for gratitude. "Help me," I instinctively screamed.

"Looks like you were right, Mr. Isaac. There was a killer vampire among us. Forgive us of the oversight." Kincaid smiled then walked away.

"Let him go!" I heard Dr. Feelgood shout to no avail. "Dubro, stop her."

The monster was now at my throat and I closed my eyes. The last thing I wanted to see was her mouth wrap around my jugular. *"Look in my eyes if the pain becomes too much for you."*

"Sylvester! Albert!" Feelgood continued to scream.

My hands reached along the floor, landing on Guzman's pistol. Hungry hands wrapped around it. I thanked God for being the only thing in the room with a conscience.

I moved the gun into her mouth. "Kiss my ass if the pain becomes too much for you." I pulled the trigger on Guzman's gun only to find the gun had jammed. My finger again pulled hard on the trigger only to find the same result. Sanguine began to laugh her little evil laugh. Her fingers began to squeeze a little harder. I didn't know it was possible. For one last time, I pulled the trigger and felt the bullet leave the chamber and move through her throat. A shower of blood fell on me.

With the last ounce of strength I had, I head butted Sanguine. Skulls cracked from the impact. I saw stars, but at least there were no fang holes in me. My situation was the better of the two evils. Sanguine gasped in surprised pain, but her fingers never faltered, still gripping me tight.

"Kill him, Sanguine," Sylvester said with boredom. The remark was followed by twisted cheers from the others. Death turned them on. Erotic and demented. Sylvester moved close to my ear as I struggled against the cockroach bitch on top of me. "I owe you one for that stupid act a few moments ago." An evil laugh vibrated through my bones. His hands were on me once again.

I felt more blood munchers moving in on me like lions on a gazelle. Things weren't going well for the good guys.

Glass shattered in violent motion. The front door spun from its hinges and hit just to the left of me. I heard screaming. Glass danced close by. Motion. Quick. Chaos. Something was shifting the power away from me.

With any luck it was the police, but then again, I wasn't even sure they would come to my rescue. We didn't have a good working relationship as of late.

I tried to turn my head as much as I could to see what had caused the distraction. It was hard to see through the drops of blood from Sanguine's throat. I closed my eyes and thought happy thoughts.

A violent hand collided with the side of Sanguine's head, reeling it backwards. More blood sprayed from the hole in her throat. I felt her weight shift above me. Again, I tried to see what was now attacking, but I no longer needed my eyes. My sense of smell gave me all the clues I needed.

Angie again slammed a claw-like fist into the side of the cockroach's head. A trickle of blood streamed from Sanguine's nose. Sylvester and a few other cockroaches moved to stop the lycan's assault.

For the second time, I head butted the monster on top of me, sending her to the floor beside me. Angie pounced on top of her before the roach had time to react. Sylvester moved on top of the lycan, pulling her chin upward, trying to break the neck. Other cockroaches began to move in on her, bringing her to the ground.

More screams filled the gallery. I wasn't for certain, but I didn't think Dubro's little gathering was going to go quite as well as he had hoped.

I came to my feet just as Isabella met me face to face. "Here," she said handing me my Magnum as I cleared my eyes of blood and guts. "Do it now and it will be justified."

My eyes asked the question. Words couldn't form.

"Kill them. It's perfect."

I aimed the Magnum down on the back of one of the nameless roaches and put it to his head. "May you burn in hell." I pulled the trigger and let the bullet drive deep into his skull. He rose up from Angie and looked at me just as he turned a beautiful orange color and crumbled into ash.

All the other vein lickers seemed to stop in mid motion and look at me for a second, then backed off of the caramel skinned woman under them.

"About time," Angie said with a wild smile. Eyes filled with excitement.

Before basking in my pleasure, I moved the Magnum on Sylvester and started to pull the trigger again as a hand reached and pushed the gun upward. The bullet went into the ceiling, causing a flurry of sheetrock to shower downward. More screams. Running. Power crippled me. Death just got a little deadlier. Gotta love it.

CHAPTER TWELVE

I turned to see the source of electric power. Quinn Rubio looked back at me. Long flowing black curls framed his timeless pale face. Until now, I was unaware that he was even present tonight. As though he had magically appeared out of thin air. And he was pissed.

As I tried to catch me breath, I looked for Feelgood. She stood in the corner like a statue. Getting in the heads of the monsters was one thing, dealing with them when they misbehaved wasn't turning out to be all that exciting for her, I guess.

"I think that will be all," Quinn said as he looked down at the pile of monsters. It was amazing how his power seemed to bring order in a matter of seconds. That was the power of a Master Roach.

It was as if the room froze. No motion. No sound. Nothing but obeying eyes. Sylvester and the others on the floor rose slow and with caution. Angie looked at me and smiled. I had to hand it to her, she liked this more than I did. Her chest heaved as she caught her breath. Hypnotic and erotic all at the same time.

"Please tell me, Mr. Isaac that you have an explanation for not only being here, but for the chaos as well," Quinn growled. He looked along the floor at my handy work. He grimaced as he surveyed the damage.

"I was here warning against you and the police if you must know. Now that you're here, it saves me the time to hunt your dead ass down."

He turned and waited for me to explain. His eyebrows lifting, asking the question for him.

"Oh, don't play stupid with me. You know exactly what I'm talking about. The deaths of the members of the Knights of the Night. They weren't accidents, or deaths by natural causes. They were murders. Murdered by your very own. You had the police cover them up as a car accident, a suicide, a heart attack. The only thing I haven't figured out so far is the why behind it all."

"You mean the deaths Asa has brought upon us all."

"No, I mean the deaths that you and the police are trying to put on him. You know as well as I do that he's not the killer. You on the other hand..." I kept the Magnum primed and ready to shoot. It would come to that. It was only a matter of time.

He shrugged. "I trust in the police's ability to determine the truth. Perhaps you should do the same."

"Truth? You must be kidding me? You wouldn't know the truth if you sucked on it all night long. With the number of people and roaches in on the cover up, don't begin to use that word with me."

"We owe you no explanations," Sanguine said, her voice far more raspy than before. Her hands were deep red with Guzman's blood as well as her own. A pink tongue licked fingers as she continued to hold the wound in her throat. I was surprised the she could still talk. "You come in here with your bitch and accuse us of murder and then you attempt to kill us."

Angie again moved between me and the roach. "We didn't attempt to kill anything." She looked down at the pile of ash where the one monster had fallen. With the same stripper stalk she used with me, she moved close to Sanguine. "We *did* kill. You just happened to be luckier than they were." Her wide smile was now up in Sanguine's face. "If you don't want that nice wound to grow a little larger, I'd suggest you back off. In fact, you better thank Quinn for saving your dead ass. And more than that," she began as she looked to Quinn, "if you don't like it, we can kill you too."

"Life is all about knowing your place." Quinn stood his ground. "Do not allow your lust for your human cost you your life, wolf."

"In my opinion, she already has," Sanguine moved in on Angie. "I will bring you her sacrificial heart."

Like a never-ending catfight, the two women were once again at each other. Instant scratch marks formed, trickles of blood followed the trail of fingernails. Angie and Sanguine wrestled to the floor, each trying to gain an advantage. I felt guilty for being a little turned on. One woman wanted to jump my bones, the other wanted to break them.

"Enough." Quinn's power rushed over us like a tidal wave, again. Life came to a standstill as though he was death itself. And in many instances, he was. He turned to me again. I lowered my eyes, not wanting to get caught in them. I could look into the eyes of some of the less powerful roaches, but not Quinn. Or at least I didn't think so. It was a mistake I couldn't afford to make. "How is it that you were able to darkened our door tonight, Mr. Isaac?"

"Therapy."

It was not the smartest answer and I knew it as I said it, but it wouldn't be the first time my mouth had gotten me into tighter spots than I should have been. Quinn never smiled as he spoke. "Do you find this game of yours entertaining?"

Angie came to stand by me, Sanguine by Quinn. I guess we had both picked teams. Goodie.

"I did before you stopped it. I killed one of you blood suckers and if you don't mind there are a few more here I'd like to work on as well."

Quinn looked over to Dr. Feelgood, her eyes red from crying. Visibly shaking. "You bring the vampire executioner here among us? Tell me you had a reason for such calamity of thought." He began to walk in her direction, visibly holding back a lot of anger.

"I made her bring me," I started. "I came here to save lives not take them." I now found myself between Feelgood and Quinn. Not the smartest thing I've ever done.

He looked down at the pile of ash. "You come here under the pretension of saving a life, but instead you take one. Ironic is it not?"

"Your bitch attacked me. I was only here to warn against a killer. Something you and the police should have done a long time ago."

Quinn smiled, but I knew better than to think he was amused. "Sanguine is a little high strung I know, but to warn against a killer that had been arrested hour before you arrived." He paused, almost as if searching for the right words. "I find it a little confusing."

"The police have a cockroach in custody, but you know as well as I do that it's not the killer. It's nothing more than a power move by you to end the rivalry between you and the pure blood roaches. It's really not that shocking to me that you'd pull shit like this, but to involve the police? And now you are allowing the very people that helped give you your freedom to be slaughtered for it."

"I can feel you trembling inside, executioner." Quinn's voice reverberated through my bones.

He moved closer to me, almost floating. Closer than what I should have allowed. He was as powerful as he thought he was, but he was also one of the roaches that had poisoned me months back.

"I think we should all just call it a night. You have made your presence known here. You have disrupted the party and you have killed. I do believe that you have accomplished all you set out to do tonight." At least he was speaking out loud now.

"I don't know, Quinn, you're still alive. I think there is a lot more to be accomplished if you think about it." In as fluid a move as I could make, I brought the Magnum up to his head. I wanted to pull the trigger.

I felt Quinn's magic hit me hard. I fell to the floor as the invisible razor blades tore through my very soul. My fingers pulled at imaginary claws but still the pain dug in.

"Do watch your tongue, executioner. I will not allow you to disrespect me in front of my own. Is that very clear to you now?" Quinn calmly said in my head. With methodical care he reached down and pulled the Magnum from my hands. At first, I thought he was going to kill me with it, but instead he simply emptied the bullets and handed them to Sylvester.

Defeated, but not dead. It was the better of the two. I slowly moved back to my feet trying not to show the pain that still ran down my spine. Everything in me was telling me to run. But like a true idiot, I stood there.

Isabella moved with visible hesitation behind me. Angie pounced with animal-like speed to her throat. Before I could say anything, Isabella was on the ground, with Angie on top.

"It okay Angie, let her up," I shouted. Angie came back up with anger still in her face. Intensity was her calling card. "She's not going to do anything. She's on our team. Sort of."

"Looks as though you are having trouble controlling your women," Quinn said, voice laced with humor.

Angie began to say something to him as I held up my hand to her. Isabella, still confused by being thrown to the floor, stood, keeping her eyes on Angie. She was a quick study on what the monsters can do, even the ones that are on your side.

"Look at what you have done to my gallery. I am ruined," Dubro began to cry. "I should not have listened to Lydia and allowed you to come in." He slapped me lightly on the chest. "Now I have nothing to show for this night other than blood and ash." A handkerchief wiped his eyes. "I need to call my lawyer."

"Do not cry, My Sweetness. I will promise you revenge for tonight." Sylvester kissed Dubro's cheek lightly.

"I must go lie down." Dubro pushed through the crowd and disappeared. I couldn't contain the smile as I watched the over-the-top dramatics. Sylvester followed behind, but turned to look at me. Something told me I was supposed to be scared. I threw him a kiss.

I turned back to Quinn. "Tell me about the child I found tonight." Even if I was about to die, I wanted to know about the child killer. I knew he had secrets locked away about the monster responsible. Running away only gave the vein weasels in front on me more power.

The crowd inside the gallery had all but disappeared. Albert Kincaid stopped short of me. "You will pay for all of this, Mr. Isaac. If it's the last thing I do, I'll make sure you pay for every death you bring to these innocent beings. I hope they drain you dry."

"If we don't find the killer of your little group, you might not live to see that day."

He smirked. "Always the conspiracy expert aren't you, Mr. Isaac. Three people lay here dead tonight, and all you can do is point fingers."

"And if you noticed, I didn't do the killing."

He looked at the pile of ash. "I think he might disagree."

"Not anymore." I grinned for Kincaid's pleasure.

"Go to hell." Kincaid's face turned red, but he made the right decision and walked away. Then again, I spoke too soon. He turned and looked at Quinn. "If you don't do something to stop him, I will." A slight glare back to me, "Trust me, the police will hear about this."

I watched as he left then turn back to Quinn. "Now about the child."

Quinn watched as the exodus continued toward the door. "What child?"

"You know what child. I was sent to kill a child tonight by

Dieter so you can stop playing stupid with me." I said, pointing at what was left of Guzman. "If there's one thing I know about you blood monkeys it's that none of them act without your consent."

"I assure you, Mr. Isaac I know nothing of the sort."

"Are you going to tell me Dieter knew about it and you didn't?"

"If he has knowledge of a child being killed by a vampire, then yes, he has acted on his own." Quinn's demeanor changed. I couldn't put my finger on it, but something made me think maybe he didn't know about the killing. There was concern in his dead face as though a dark secret had been uncovered. He followed my stare down to Guzman. "Do tell me about his child."

The way he phrased it made the deaths seem personal again. For a moment I had been the one that had forgotten that. I had been focused on the killer rather than the wake it had left behind. "Dieter and I went to kill a cockroach, which turned out to be an eight year old girl. He tells me that it isn't the first time something like this has happened."

Sylvester moved back into the circle. Like most of the older roaches, they could be gone one second and in front of you the next. "No civilized vampire would do such a thing."

"Show me a civilized cockroach and I'll kiss your ass, Sylvester." He moved toward me.

Sylvester stopped as Sanguine's pie hole opened. My mark on her was starting to heal. In another day or so, there would be no trace of my handy work. "He is not worth it, Sylvester. He is nothing but a walking paper tiger. Besides, we will kill him in time." She looked back at Angie. "If we play our cards right, we might get a wolf as well."

Angie smiled. "Whenever you feel froggy, bitch."

Sanguine started to speak, but stopped before the words escaped her mouth.

Quinn shook his head. His stare was on Sanguine, but he was still talking to me. "Please tell me about the child that you killed."

"I didn't kill a child. She was a victim of your species. One of *you* killed a child. I simply kept it from being a cockroach anymore."

Quinn nodded. "I apologize if I have used the wrong terminology. Tell me about the child you had to decapitate tonight."

Leave it to Quinn to make it sound uglier than I wanted it to.

"You do not really think he has found such a child do you?" This from Sanguine.

"It is nothing but more lies. He brings lies here to disrupt and kill and now he tells us that there is a child that has been killed. Do not get caught in such a web of deceit. He has no proof of such child." Sylvester moved close to Quinn.

"Is this true, Avenger? Is this nothing more than more fabrication?" Quinn asked. "Do you indeed have no proof of such a death?"

I should have known better. Trying to communicate with cockroaches leaves me nothing short of frustrated. The little riddles and patronizing remarks were getting old. "Time will tell, Quinn. When I bring you the head of the cockroach that did it, we'll see who is fabricating the story. And as for the killer of the Knights of the Night, I'm warning you and all the blood suckers here, if you're responsible, I'll not leave enough ash for the dirty cops to find." I began to walk for the door, along with Feelgood and Angie.

"Where do you think you are going, Mr. Isaac?" Quinn asked.

"I've already told you blood boy, I'm going to bring you the head of your killer…and stick it up your dead ass."

"I do not think you are free to go. I was told there would be food and drink." Quinn and the other cockroaches began to circle around Angie, Feelgood and me. I wasn't getting a good feeling about it. "I do not believe any of us will fear such empty threats."

Sylvester, Sanguine and other roaches caved in on us. I swung wildly at the monsters trying to free myself from certain death. I began to panic. Gapping mouths moved closer. Claws scratched skin. Angie began to turn into the wolf that only knew how to kick ass, but tonight, I wasn't sure how much ass we were going to be able to kick. We were outnumbered and there seemed to be fangs everywhere I looked.

In the distance I heard the screams. Torturous and frantic.

I saw Quinn move past us in a blur of speed. Like typical lemmings, the others stood at attention, watching their leader move toward the female cockroach at the door. She was covered in blood and crying hysterically. Her long golden hair covering her face.

I got to my feet as fast as I could. I wanted to stake them in the back. And would if I had any at my disposal.

"It is Dieter," the bitch roach started.

Now they had my attention.

"I think Dieter is dead!" Quinn caught her as she collapsed to the floor.

CHAPTER THIRTEEN

Outside the Crimson Madness Gallery, I saw the chaotic confusion of shadows move in the neon lights of Bat Town. Humans and non-humans alike were running away and spilling into the street. Screams filled the air. My eyes began to focus on a nightmare I never thought I would ever see. My knees buckled and for the first time in my life I hesitated, not believing the gothic horror before me. "Impossible," I said to no one in particular. It had to be cockroach magic. For years there had been the rumors of a roach war, but that was all it was. Rumors. Now the pure bloods were drawing blood of a different kind. Bodies lay in the street. Heads severed and still rocked back and forth. A river of death flowed into the drains along the sidewalk. Carcasses still twitched as life left them.

The hand with the Magnum refused to rise. Without bullets, it wouldn't do me much good anyway. Angie looked to me, then back to the crowd of on-lookers behind us. She was waiting for me to do something, but I wasn't sure what I could do.

"Get everyone back inside." I tried to shout it, but my own

growing fear choked the sound down to a whisper. Making a stand would be a noble idea, but without firepower, I was no more a match for what my eyes saw than any of the dead that now lined the street.

"If you don't want to die get back inside," Angie barked. No pun intended.

I looked at her in disbelief. "I was hoping to do it without causing a panic."

"There are dead headless bodies in the street being killed by vampires. And you don't think that might cause a panic?" She began to move into the street where four large cockroaches now stood. Deadly shadows that were not going to back down. A hunch, I know, but I trusted my gut on this one.

I saw the crumpled mass that was Dieter. If he wasn't dead, he was dying. Maybe things weren't going so bad after all. Then again, we were all probably going to die tonight, just from different cockroaches. Pure blood cockroaches.

Sanguine stood guard over Dieter, protecting him from the cockroaches that threatened to take his head. Her clothes stained with blood. All the other commercial coffin munchers looked out in the street with mouths open and as lifeless as mannequins. I would never say it out loud, but Sanguine had just earned a little respect from me.

I spun around to face Sylvester and Quinn. Power gave them away. Instead of trying to save Dieter or help Sanguine, they simply stood at attention like wax figures. "Give me my bullets," I demanded through gritted teeth.

"And what is my guarantee that you will not try and place the first bullet in my head? Would you have not already killed me if your weapon was not empty?" he answered. "It looks as though you have brought death to our doorstep for the second time tonight. I will not aid in your killing." Like me, Quinn stood looking at the carnage in front of him. Even the sights before us didn't seem to rattle much of a true emotion from him.

"Just like an arrogant cockroach to think only of yourself." I shoved him as hard as I could. "Give me the bullets before they kill all of us." I began to panic. It wasn't a matter of *if* the pure bloods would attack, but when.

More screams filled the street. Angie and Sanguine were doing their best to keep the roaches out of reach, but they wouldn't be able to hold them at bay for much longer. Moving like a pack of demons, they had left their wrath in the street and now stared back at us. The pavement flooded with spilt blood. It ran like newly fallen rain. Reflecting neon in its flow. I watched it. Saliva built in my mouth. I wanted to dip my finger in it and taste it. Run my tongue through the bitter sweetness. I shook my head hard. Before I allowed the cockroach in me to take over or even attempt to take over, I'd put a bullet in my brain. Sweat turned me cold. I forced myself to vomit just to rid the imaginary taste in my mouth.

"Do something!" Feelgood shouted from behind me.

I turned to see her along with a small gathering of Knights of the Night members, all with eyes of disbelief and panic. Faces no longer sure if the cockroaches around them were friend or foe. One thing was certain, they were seeing what true cockroaches were capable of. It served her and the rest of the Knights right. They came here hating me for what I was, and now they hoped all they had heard about me was true. Oh, the poetic justice in it all.

A part of me wanted them to see what these monsters could do. I grabbed Feelgood by the chin and turned her toward the carnage. "I want you to see first hand what all your efforts and money's helping. Tonight, I want you to experience the cockroaches as something more than historical artifacts that deserve to live. Get a front row seat into the world of a cockroach killing party. A first hand look at being seen as a meal rather than a cockroach activist."

"These are not the vampires we've helped. They are uncivilized and you know it."

"Civilized? Do you think Quinn or any of the other cockroaches here are civilized just because they invite us to an art gallery? Own a nightclub? Live in your neighborhood? Wake up and smell the reality, woman. Death and power is all they know."

"Preach to me some other time, Paul." Feelgood screamed again. "Just kill them!"

"Shit, Feelgood! I need something to fucking kill them with!" I caught myself screaming at her.

Eyes looked back at me as if I would be the one that ate them. Feelgood looked to the master fang head. "Please Quinn, he's the only chance we have."

In his body language I saw something I had never noticed before. Fear. It was as if he were frozen in time. Haunted by what he saw. Quinn looked to Sylvester and nodded in slow motion, almost in an act of defeat. Sylvester handed me the box that contained all my arsenal I had left at the door. I grabbed the articles and loaded the Magnum with hands that were not at their best yet. I still hadn't made up my mind if I was going to kill Quinn and Sylvester or the cockroaches eating in the street. With a strike of luck, maybe I could make it a daily double.

"Even if you kill them, Avenger, all is not forgiven between us. All debts must be settled," Sylvester added. He licked his lips as if tasting my blood.

"I was hoping you'd say that, pale boy." I moved my attention to the Amazon neck biter moving in my direction. "Spilling your blood is going to be a lot of fun."

Sanguine pushed through the crowd of both blood junkies and humans to get to me. Her hands grabbed me by my shirt. "I shall have my retribution by spilling *your* blood."

The 9mm was on her head before she could make her next

threat. "How would you like me to reopen that nice little bullet hole of yours again?"

She sniffed. "You threaten me with silver? How pathetic."

I pulled the silver nitrate cartridge out of the 9mm and replaced it with ultra violet, keeping my eyes on Sanguine.

"The least you could do is help me save the innocent," I said to her and the other cockroaches around me as I watched the humans move back inside the gallery. I pointed to them. "After all, they're the ones that keep the wooden stake out of your heart." I broke her grip and pushed her away from me. "We'll settle our differences another time."

"Count on it," Sanguine snapped. In another grasp I gathered up the holy water and crucifixes and stuck them in my pocket.

"I say we kill him now," Sylvester said as he swung at me.

I caught his arm and stopped the blow to both of our amazements. Without hesitation, I brought one of the crucifixes up to his face. Sylvester stepped back, trying to avoid the certain burn it would cause. I followed with every intention of leaving a small scar on his perfect pale skin. "Just give me a reason to waste you here and now, you albino piece of shit." In an act of random violence, I drove the crucifix into his chest. If I was lucky, Sylvester and Sanguine would retaliate. If I was real lucky I might be able to save a human life or two. "Now grow some balls and help me kill these sons of bitches."

Quinn appeared between us. "Put aside our differences for now. If we do not work together, it will be all our blood that is spilt here tonight." He looked back out to the pure bloods that were closing in on us. I doubted he would do any of the dirty work, but at least he was able to keep Sanguine off my back until we either killed or were killed.

When I turned, I saw two of the roaches on Angie, biting and tearing at her animal form. Rivers of crimson rolled from her back and legs as she fought to stay on her feet.

I grew hollow as I took it all in. Angie had no obligation to help me or the humans under attack. The first shot hit the roach on Angie's back, sending it rolling across the street in a blaze of fire. Another shot rang out, taking down another as it rushed toward me.

The other two stopped and stood perfectly still. Keeping to the shadows, but it did them no good. I knew one of them. Sasha hovered above me like a demonic cloud. "This has nothing to do with you, Avenger. Step aside and I assure you, you will live. This is their problem, not yours." His Russian accent still thick, even after hundreds of years of living here. Hands red with death. "Take your humans and leave at once."

"When you started killing, it became my problem." I kept the 9mm on him.

He laughed. "So we find ourselves in a Catch 22."

I looked at Angie. She was bleeding and balled up like a baby. It was the first time I had ever seen her as anything other than confident and self-reliant. "I don't think so." I pulled the trigger on the 9mm but missed him as he dove out of the way. He was way quicker than any roach I had ever seen before.

"Our anger is not with you, but with Quinn and the human police. An innocent vampire sits in a cell tonight facing execution because of their lies and violence," Sasha said, reappearing to my left. "My master vampire."

"But you are innocent, peaceful?" I asked, looking at the carnage at his feet.

"Precisely. Was it not your kind that developed the phrase, "An eye for an eye?" Quinn and his vampires must pay with their lives for the life of Asa. Now allow us to finish what we have started."

"I don't think so." I moved toward Angie. I had to get to her as soon as possible. I didn't want the dead head in front of me to know it, but if it came down to killing him or saving her. I was going to save Angie.

"So you have aligned yourself with the commercial vampires?"

"No. I hate you all equally. My gift to diversity."

"I assure you, you do not want to be caught in the middle of this. You and your humans do not need to die tonight." Sasha floated to the ground and took a step toward Angie. He waited for me to make the first move, like an old west gunslinger. "Your wolf is bleeding in the street. Maybe I should put her out of her misery."

"Funny, I was about to say the same thing to you." I began to flank Sasha's moves, trying to stay between him and Angie. The other plasma pirate with Sasha began to shift toward me in an act of defiance. Wrong move.

I pulled the trigger, catching him in the throat. Blood splattered high into the air. He hit the pavement on his knees. Screams of demonic pain bellowed from his mouth. Hands tight against the wound. Orange light illuminated the street as he turned to black ash.

Out of the corner of my eye, I saw Sasha move past Angie with the speed of lightning. I turned to him and shot again. I looked all around me. He was gone. As if he had melted into the darkness of the night. Vanishing without any other trace than the dead and dying he had left behind. My eyes scanned all directions, knowing the daisy pusher could simply be using the darkness to wait me out. But his power was gone. And so was the monster.

As fast as I could run, I went to Angie. She had collapsed in the middle of the street. Violence stuck to her without remorse. Across her back were four rivers of blood. She had returned to human form. Soft caramel skin wadded up like paper. He had cut her deep, but it was evident to me that he didn't want to kill her. Simply his way of letting me know I couldn't protect her.

I held her head up and placed it on my knees, moving the strands of hair from her face. She looked up at me and wrapped her hand around my arm. A forced smile formed. "What took you so long?"

"I had to thank Quinn for a wonderful evening."

With a soft laugh she tried to pick herself off the pavement.

"Just rest for a minute. You're gonna be okay." It was the best bedside manner I had in me. Probably sounding a bit forced, but I was trying to determine my next move. She bled so much, my jeans were soaked heavy.

"You have to stop them." Her eyes almost pulled me down to her. Lips quivered, fighting back the uncertain fear that hovered over all of us.

"I will as soon as I get you some help. I'm not going to leave you here alone." I screamed for a doctor, only to see silent empty eyes of the undead on the streets. Many feared treating the lycans, afraid of catching the virus themselves. Even though it was a proven fact that it couldn't happen while the wolf was in human form.

That playful grin formed. "Why Mr. Isaac, I do believe you care." She would live, but that didn't make the situation any easier for me. A decision had to be made. Either I could stay with Angie, or chase after the cockroach. And I had already proven I couldn't protect her.

To my right, I noticed the slaughter. Five dead in the street, dressed in evening wear, as if death were a grand event. Three more dead were along the sidewalk. I prayed Sasha was telling the truth and that there were no human deaths.

"You have to kill them all." Angie's voice was soft but dominating at the same time.

Reaching down, I put her hand in mine. "I can't leave you here with these things."

"Why not, to you I'm nothing but another type of monster." Her eyes glowed with pain, but I could tell it wasn't from her wounds. Not the physical ones anyway.

"Don't say that."

"Because it hurts you or because it hurts me?" Tears welled in her eyes, but she fought against them escaping.

"I don't think this is the time to bring all this up." I acted as though I was scanning the area for a doctor. Truth was, I couldn't look her in the eyes. We both knew the truth. Even if I said nothing, she'd see it in my eyes.

A tear rolled down her cheek. I caught it with my finger. "If I wasn't a monster, do you think you could ever love me?"

I took in a deep breath and tried not to roll my eyes. "You're a very beautiful woman, but…"

"But I'm a monster."

"No, I don't think of you as a monster." I lied.

"At the hospital…"

"At the hospital, I was being a jerk. One of the only things I'm really good at." I ran my fingers through her blue hair. "I'm about as huggable as a cactus." I desperately needed her to smile back at me.

"Then what are you so afraid of?" She rolled off of me and looked me in the eyes.

It was a good question. One I had asked myself many times. "Losing."

Her eyes thinned as she tried to understand.

"Afraid of losing someone else in my life, or them losing me. You saw what happened here tonight. It could have been you or me. The blood suckers use the ones we love to get us to do their bidding. Without love there is no compromise."

"You would rather die alone than take a chance on finding happiness. Not much of a life if you ask me."

"Angie, we don't have time for this right now. There are some really naughty cockroaches I need to find."

She shook her head and tried to smile again. I smiled back. Her superficial wounds were already beginning to heal. "Take your guns and your stakes and kill them all. Then what? Do you think the pain will just go away? If you're not going to kiss me then go kick ass."

"Maybe." I leaned over and kissed her on the cheek.

"Wrong. You'll just be bitter and alone." She wiped a tear and looked away.

"It's my choice not yours. No one asked you to come down here tonight and rescue me. And it's not going to make me instantly fall in love with you."

She laughed. "Who said anything about love?" A light shrug, "I'm just looking for a chance."

A groan broke our conversation. One of the bodies tried to rise on its elbows, and then collapsed to the pavement again. I moved the Magnum on it without hesitation. Slick black hair, thin build, bad odor. Our good friend Dieter. In all the commotion, I had actually forgotten about him. It was a nice feeling.

He turned his head to face me. Like Angie, the roaches had taken a few bites out of him. His pale ugly face was covered in blood. "They will be back, Avenger. They are many."

I looked in the direction leading into Bat Town, seeing the red and blue flashes of rescue and police vehicles moving toward us. But no danger of another attack.

My eyes looked back to Dieter as I stood, lighting a cigar. Feelings grew inside of me. Fantastic feelings of being able to watch him die. One more cockroach I wouldn't have to kill one day or possibly even tonight. A cockroach I had wanted to see separated from his head since the moment I had met him.

"Are you going to die or simply lay there and smell up the city?"

Dieter remained flat on the pavement. His wounds were severe, but unless I finished what the other roaches started, he would make a full recovery. "We must put our differences aside for now. For the good of the entire city. There is much more at stake than my death. Of this I am sure you will agree. If we do not stop Sasha, more lives will be lost. Human and vampire."

"Make no mistake about it, Dieter. I will find Sasha and kill him. But let's get one thing very clear. There is no *we*. I hunt alone. Just tell me what you know before you bleed and die in the street." I moved the Magnum on his head. "I'll make it quick and painless if you spill your guts on what you know. You know as well as I do, I'll find him and I *will* kill him. Do us all a favor and go out a hero."

"Looks to me like you've already done enough killing tonight." I turned to see Kansas. He looked over to the bodies in the street. "Paul, tell me you had nothing to do with this."

"I had nothing to do with this."

"Quite the contrary." Power hit me full on. Quinn stood at attention, his black hair flowing in his face as it danced in the light breeze.

"Mr. Rubio, I didn't notice you there. You look quite dapper tonight," Kansas said.

"Want him to bend over so you can kiss all his ass, Kansas?"

CHAPTER FOURTEEN

"Why am I not surprised to find you in the middle of this?" Kansas asked as he looked around at what seemed to be endless carnage.

"Mr. Isaac has found a way to sabotage tonight's festivities, detective. He has brought a great deal of death to both our people." Quinn looked along the street at the littered bodies. "Now it appears as though he is instigating total genocide."

I glared at Quinn. "Go to hell, both of you. If it wasn't for me, there would be ten times as many dead."

"Really? I guess you just showed up at the right time and the right place. It's amazing how lucky you are sometimes, Isaac," Kansas snapped, his comb over blowing in the light breeze.

I was so close to Kansas our noses were touching. "When it all comes down to it, Kansas, this is all *your* fault. There's nothing truly dead here that doesn't tie to you."

He looked at me, but never spoke.

"All this is a direct result of your cover up of the Knights of the Night murders and the inevitable conviction of the wrong cockroach. The blood junkies attacked here because of the injustice your department has done. All the pure bloods needed was an excuse to declare war and you gave it to them. Sasha has taken that excuse and run with it."

"How many times do I have to tell you, Isaac? There is no cover up." He turned and looked at the growing scene, sprouting with medics, onlookers and more. "Since you got vampire virus in your veins, you seem to care about them a little too much if you ask me."

"I care when it involves a dirty cop." I had him by his shirt before I knew what I had done. Punching him right now would be most therapeutic. "If it wasn't for Angie, they'd all be dead right now. Human and blood suckers."

Kansas looked at me with an inquisitive look.

"You know what I mean. Really dead. Pushing up freaking daisies dead." I walked by the cockroaches around me and puffed on the cigar.

"You think I had something to do with the vampires showing up here tonight?" Kansas huffed. His hands firmly on his hips. "Such a big imagination for such a little brain."

I turned and walked back to Kansas. I was so ticked, I couldn't stand still. "You had everything to do with the blood heads showing up here tonight. You see, Kansas, you aren't fooling anyone in this game of charades, but yourself. I don't buy the deaths, the cock-roaches don't buy it, nobody does. You've opened a wound that's been bleeding since the beginning of time and you don't even know it."

"We have reason to believe that Mr. Isaac might have had a hand in bringing the vampires in question to our location," Quinn chimed in. "He would love nothing more than to see death be placed on those loyal to me or bankruptcy for the Crimson Madness for that matter. If he had not shown up here tonight, I assure you everything would have gone off without incident. We were here to celebrate art, nothing more. It was peaceful until he arrived. Now we have death inside the gallery and out."

"If I hadn't been here, Quinn, you'd all be little spots on the street." I looked at Kansas. "My question to you is, do you know who the real killer is? Because if you don't, God help us all. Sasha will slice this city apart until justice is served. And I mean fang style."

"His name is Asa. You were there when we arrested him."

"What are you going to tell everyone when the next murder takes place? You already have your scapegoat behind bars. So you've either painted yourself into a very small corner, or you already know who the real killer is."

"Look around us. This was the work of Asa's vampires. How can you think he had nothing to do with the deaths? Besides, I am not going to let a vampire go free simply because his followers retaliate with violence. This is nothing short of vampire terrorism."

"Where's the bodies of the victims? They will have fang marks on them that will prove me right."

"Cremated. Just like the families requested." Kansas looked back to Quinn. "Can you tell me what happened here? I doubt I'll get any real answers from him."

"Mr. Isaac harassed and threatened Albert Kincaid. I was a witness to him striking him as well. I'm quite sure he would like to press charges." Quinn turned to face the gallery and spoke again. "He has killed one vampire inside the Crimson Madness and allowed others to help him kill and maim. If it were not for Sanguine, I fear more lives would have been at stake. She had to kill Mr. Guzman in order to detain him."

Kansas snapped around to me again. Blood vessels popped through the pink skin on his balding head. "You involved the Guzmans?"

Sanguine continued, "Apparently an accomplice to Mr. Isaac. Says that he was here to avenge the death of his daughter. He started shooting madly inside the gallery. Mr. Isaac appeared to be pointing out the vampires in the room to him."

"She killed Guzman," I added, pointing at Sanguine. "A little quick if you ask me."

"I had no choice in the matter. Mr. Isaac's hesitation was leaving too many in danger. If he had have acted quicker, chances are, none would have perished inside the gallery tonight."

"Not to mention Mr. Isaac told the man to shoot me," Sylvester finished.

"What is this? Valley of the undead tattle tails?" I asked.

"Tell me you aren't recruiting others into your mad sick world?" Kansas' eyes were as glazed as fresh doughnuts. "Feeding off of the loss of parents? I knew you were a sicko, just didn't know how bad of one."

I took another draw on the cigar. "His daughter was killed by a cockroach. He was a father hell bent on revenge. Nothing more, nothing less. I had nothing to do with him being here and they know it."

Angie moved into the circle of the conversation. The young wolf placed her arms around me from behind. I felt my body tense. Not out of lack of trust, but from animal magnetism. Even in pain she moved with unstoppable sexuality. "You have plenty of witnesses inside the Crimson Madness that will tell you what happened if you really want to know the truth. If it hadn't been for Paul, Sasha would have killed everyone out here. He saved both human and vampire life."

I shook my head and looked at Angie. "They're not looking for answers. They're looking for a rug to sweep all this under. And forget about witnesses. You know as well as I do that people's point of view will be skewed. Now that they're safe, they'll see me as the monster again."

"I know the feeling," Angie grimly smiled.

Other cops and paramedics moved in on the scene. There was

no way the police or the cockroaches were going to be able to keep this quiet. There were far too many bodies and far too many witnesses to even think about it. For that, I was very happy. At least some good came from this very bloody evening.

"Should have left the blood suckers to kill each other," I said to myself as I stepped over one of the dead fang heads.

"Maybe so." I jumped as I turned to see Detective Frank Price. His shirt already wet with sweat. His chest heaving from a short run. His body, plump like a balloon. Glasses at the point of his nose, eyes looking above them. It was the first time I had seen him since he spent a couple of nights in the hospital with chest pains.

Panic flooded into me as I spoke. "What do you think you're doing here?"

"My job, what do you think?"

"I mean running. Isn't one heart attack enough for you?"

"Save it for someone who cares. Doctor says this old heart will last me another ten years easy." He smiled, but we both knew the heart attack he had about two months earlier was more serious than he wanted to say. I caught myself handling the old man with kid gloves since the attack, but knew in my heart all it did was make him resent me more. I followed his eyes to Quinn, who was now about twenty yards from us, talking with Kansas and Sylvester. "Should have shot him out of principal."

"The thought did cross my mind." It was good to see the bear of a cop. He always made me smile. Even in the valley of death.

"Tell me, off the record. What the hell really happened here?"

"I told Kansas everything. I came here to warn the members of the Knights of the Night that a vein leech was killing their members. You know as well as I do that Asa isn't the killer. All you're doing is fanning the flames of war by keeping him under arrest. I think Kansas has lost his mind on this. At least give me enough rope to hang myself."

Price took in a deep breath and looked me directly in the eyes. "It's not what you think, Paul."

"Then what is it?"

"Fear." He said it as low as he could.

"What do you mean, fear?"

"Kansas is scared of them. Quinn has him in his pocket. He ain't no dirty cop like you think. It's just that he has a lot more to lose by going head to head with them than you do."

"So that gives him a free pass?"

"No, it doesn't. But that's the way it is. You deal with the vampires with anger, he deals with them through his own fear. It doesn't make either of you right." He pushed his glasses back up his nose.

"So why don't you do something to stop it?"

"This isn't my case. The department is letting him head this one up. Seems I'm too old school to lead the investigation. Since the heart attack, I ain't allowed to do nothing but push papers and help little old ladies across the street."

"Bullshit."

"Call it what you will, but it doesn't change anything. I retire in six months and I've been told in a round about way that if I don't play the game, I'll lose all my benefits. I can't afford to do that. All I can do is try and help you when I can. Find the killer and maybe we all win."

"So who's the real killer?"

"Don't know yet. All I know is that it's a true vampire doing it. Bodies sucked dry, heads cut off. We don't know for sure Asa didn't do this, and we don't have proof that he did. If you want him to stay alive, you need to find this maniac soon. I don't know how long I'll be able to keep him safe. Quinn wants his mouth shut. For good. One, it keeps the cat and mouse game alive and well and two, with Asa out of the way, he gains a lot of power in this town, not to mention the possible loyalty of Asa's vamps." He took a breath and pushed his glasses back up his nose again. "I hear talk that Sasha started this, what can you tell me."

"Off the record?"

"Off the record."

"Yeah, he was here. He and the rest of the pure bloods are angry with the arrest and framing of Asa. According to Asa, they want the city to know they did this. Sasha's trying to scare us into releasing him."

Price watched as Kansas moved through the sea of dead bodies. "Do me a favor, Paul and get lost. I want you away from here as soon as you can. The vampires will make Kansas take you down for questioning and that could give the killer a window of opportunity."

"Do you know something I don't?"

"With the vampires, there's no telling. I believe in your side of the story, but I doubt I'll find many here that will back it up. Find Sasha and see what you can find out. And I give you full permission to do it your way. Off the record of course." I saw a different look come into the old man's eyes. Cross between fear and mischief. "How are you pretty lady?"

"Never been better," Angie smiled back as she kissed his cheek. The shifter was still walking gingerly, nursing her wounds. She had been given a large blanket to wrap up in. One of the problems with being a shifter is that clothing usually got ripped or lost in the transformation.

"Get him out of here before the vampires turn on the both of you."

"You say that like it's a bad thing," Angie said with thick charm.

He chuckled, and then grew serious again. "It just might be. I don't trust any of these things any farther than I can throw them. I'll have Paul fill out the paperwork some other time. I'd rather have him secretly helping us find the killer."

"You heard the smart man, let's get you home and out of those clothes." Her devilish smile was returning, wounded or not. She wrapped her arm around me and started to lead me away.

I pulled her off of me but smiled back all the same. "That's not what he said. Besides, I have to work up the courage to do something I've been meaning to do for a long time."

CHAPTER FIFTEEN

I had killed some of the meanest cockroaches in the world but I had never lost my nerve or been as scared as I was on this very evening. It had been three days since the big shootout at the Crimson Madness and I had been on a constant search for not one, but very likely two killer roaches that were munching on my fellow humans. So far I hadn't come any closer to either of them, even though I had turned the city over and shook every coffin.

There was no doubt I was losing it, but at least I was trying, which was more than I could say for Detective Kansas and the Orlando Police Department. Inside, I knew the truth. I was drowning myself in my work so I had an excuse to put off what I was about to do.

I pulled into the cemetery that I hadn't been to in nearly twenty years. Large magnolia trees draped over the thread of a road leading through the endless tombstones. I could still see that fateful day all those years ago running through my mind as if it were yesterday. My hands were sweaty against the steering wheel as I tried to keep from talking myself out of doing the inevitable.

I parked the 'Cuda, closed my eyes and took in a deep breath. Somehow making the next step of getting out of the car was not happening. I felt as if my legs were paralyzed and refused to move. But my mind was made up, I had come this far and I wasn't going to back out now.

With all the willpower I had in me, I opened the door and shoved my six foot four frame out. I walked around the other side and picked up the pot of daisies I had bought. From what I had heard, they were my mother's favorite. Thanks to selfish bastard cockroaches I would never know first hand. Like with most information about my parents, it was told to me by those that knew them. That's what made this all so difficult for me. I was bitter and angry in that I didn't have that many memories of either of them for myself. My mother and father were only steps above being total strangers to me.

I saw him from the car. "Do you come here often?"

"I thought I'd never see this day," Father Garcia said, as he remained knelt down by the tombstone. He was dressed in old blue jeans, a flannel shirt and a wide straw hat. I couldn't see his face so I wasn't sure if he was smiling or not. He was pulling renegade weeds away from the base of my parent's tombstone.

"I wasn't sure I would see it either." I sat the daisies down next to the marker.

He looked at the flowers, and then turned back toward the stone. "They were always your mother's favorites you know."

"Yeah, you told me that once. Do you come here often?"

"Every day."

"Guess I have a lot of catching up to do."

"So, are you here because of therapy or because you want to?"

"Does it really matter?"

He faced me and gave a sheepish smile. "That point is up to you. Just be true to yourself on the reasons."

I knelt next to him. "It's just that they're strangers to me. I mean, I have some memories of them of course, but not enough that I knew them as people. Not like most people anyway." Now I looked at him. "Father Garcia, what were they really like?"

With a slow turn of his head, he looked me in the eyes and gave me a painful smile. "They were good people. They loved you very much."

"That's the easy answer to the questions I want to know and you know it. I mean, tell me something about them. Something tangible."

"Why? It's not going to bring them back from the dead. The last time we talked didn't go so well."

"That's because you told me they were supporters of the Knights of the Night and the cockroaches. That's a lot for anyone like me to swallow."

"And so am I to assume that you have swallowed it?" He continued to grab the weeds by the handfuls.

"Hell no. But that doesn't change anything for me."

"So just remember them as loving parents. Nothing else should matter."

"That's just it, Father. I don't remember enough about them to know if they were loving or not. Almost everything I know about them has been told to me by you or others that knew them. It's as though I love strangers. Sometimes I wonder if all the good memories I have of them might not be made up by a kid that missed the most important people in his life."

Father Garcia smiled, but I could tell there was pain behind the façade. "They aren't made up and you know that. We might disagree with their beliefs, but that has nothing to do with how they felt about you. You were their world. Your father was the proudest father I had ever seen. Never missed an opportunity to show you off. Never ever doubt that."

"But I can tell there's a dark side to all this. Tell me the truth.

Even if it hurts me. I'd rather it hurt than go on not knowing or making up things that only I believe."

"What will it help? Just know they loved you and that you love them."

"You're wrong."

"About loving them? You don't really mean that and you know that."

"No, I'm saying I love them because everyone says I love them. They were gone before I had a chance to know them as more than parents of an eight-year-old boy. No matter what you tell me, I'll still love them, but I want to love them because I choose to, not because someone else says I should. I want to know them more than people in a picture frame."

"Maybe you should pray to God about it."

"Don't bring God into this. He's a lousy communicator on the subject, so you tell me."

"He works on his schedule, not yours." He placed the handful of weeds in a metal bucket next to him.

"Save the faith lesson for someone else, Father. I want to know about my parents and I want to know it now." I stood and started to pace.

"There are so many lies and rumors that might change how you feel about them. I don't want to be responsible for that."

"Let me know everything and decide for myself what's truth and what's a lie."

He stood and walked away from me a few steps. Turning, I could tell I was about to learn about my parents and it wouldn't be sugar coated in any way. It was about time. "Your mother was someone your father really admired when he first met her. Love at first sight I think they call it. He was crazy about her. Never stopped talking about her. At first, I thought she was the best thing that ever happened to him."

"What do you mean at first? Somehow I feel a 'but' coming on."

"Look, Paul, I don't want to go into all of this. I don't feel comfortable talking about the dead."

"Father, I deserve to know."

He shook his head. "You're right. Your father was a great man of God, and a fierce vampire killer. He hated them so much. You remind me a lot of him when I watch you. You have his same manncrisms." He wiped his hands on a towel and threw it in the bucket.

"Here comes the *but*."

He smiled and looked down, gathering his thoughts. "Your mother began to influence his thoughts about them. I dismissed his changes at first, blaming it on puppy love, but as time went on, I began to see it influence him in many ways."

"What do you mean?"

"After they were married and had you, your mother began to persuade him from killing the vampires, saying it was too dangerous for a man with a small child to raise. And in the beginning, I agreed with her. But soon it became much more. She began to become most outspoken about vampire rights and how they were not the satanic beings that we all thought they were. Saying that our opinions of them were based on myth from times long ago. She, along with long time friend Albert Kincaid started the movement that would become known as the Knights of the Night."

"My mother was mixed up with Kincaid?"

Father Garcia shook his head. "Albert Kincaid was a big influence on her and she began to put more and more pressure on your father. His love for her was stronger than his hatred for the vampires. I had talked to him weeks before his death about it, but I knew I wouldn't win. He had too much to lose at that point. His heart was with his family, even though I could tell he hated what he was becoming. Our talk had some power I guess. He confronted Albert Kincaid and told him to leave your mother alone and stop filling her head with lies. There was a confrontation that night and from what I have heard, harsh words spoken. I don't wish to fill your head with thoughts, but there have been rumors."

"What kind of rumors?"

"Do not take this as the gospel because I have no proof of it. But there has been accusations that Albert Kincaid might have had something to do with their deaths."

"And to think I was trying to save his life the other night."

"You saved Albert Kincaid's life?"

"Not yet anyway. There's a killer cockroach that seems to be targeting members of the Knights of the Night. I went to warn him of the attacks and was practically blown off."

"Don't let what I have told you, affect your judgment. I have no proof that he had anything to do with the murders of your parents. Large trees grow from very tiny seeds."

"What makes you think I'd let it affect my judgment?"

He gave me a genuine smile this time. "Because you are just like your father, of course."

"I still have one more question."

"What would that be, my son?"

"Let's say you are right about Kincaid and that he had something to do with the murders. Hypothetically speaking. I can see why he might want my father killed and out of the way, but why my mother. Seems to me, according to you anyway, that she was a big part of what he wanted to accomplish."

If any of the smile remained, it was gone now. Somehow I think I had asked the wrong question. "Perhaps she wasn't supposed to be with him that night. Maybe it was mistaken identity."

"How long have we known each other, Father?"

"For your entire life."

"Then you should know that I can tell when you are lying to me. And as a man of God, you should be ashamed."

Father Garcia looked to the sky. "It is time to go. The sun will be setting soon. I don't wish to be walking back to the church in the darkness." He grabbed his bucket and started to walk.

"I'll give you a ride, now tell me the part of the story you are leaving out."

"All of it is lies and you will only jump to conclusions that are unfounded."

"And how is that different from anything else I've ever done in my life?"

"We should be taking baby steps in this. Let us stay with the facts and things we know to be true."

"Why would Kincaid want to kill my mother?"

Father Garcia took in a deep breath. "The root of the rumor is that Kincaid and your mother had a love interest. Your mother had broken the affair off after your father found out. That's what the confrontation was over, not vampire issues."

I felt my jaw drop. Father Garcia was right. I didn't want to know the rest of the story, but now it was too late. There was no way to take it back. God I hoped I had heard it wrong. Minutes ago, I thought I was part of a loving all American family. I assumed my parents were deeply in love, but now all that had been shattered and it was my fault. I asked for it. "Did you say love interest, as in an affair?"

"I tell you because I would rather you hear all the bad from me instead of someone else. I only do it to protect you. Your father had told me about the suspicions at confession that night."

I was pissed at my own mother and like Father Garcia said, it was nothing more than hurtful things that others had said. "So my mother fell out of love with my father? For that piece of garbage?"

"I'm not sure she truly ever loved him, but that is not for me to say. Looking back on it all, I think she used your father to take down one of the biggest vampire executioners in the city and not draw a drop of blood."

"How long?"

"How long what?"

"How long had Kincaid and my mother been having the affair before her and my father were killed?"

He hesitated. "Some say the entire marriage."

"God, no." I needed to keep my mouth shut and stop asking questions. Each ended up being another punch in the gut.

"There is more if you want to know."

I didn't, but my curiosity wouldn't allow it to sit out there untouched. "Go ahead."

"It might be the most hurtful to you of all things."

Reluctantly, I said it. "Tell me."

"There are a hurtful few that say Albert Kincaid might in fact be your true father."

"Go to hell." I wanted to take it back as soon as I had said it.

"I don't say it to hurt you. Only giving you all the information that might come up one day. Information that you deserve to know. Even against my better judgment. I find no truth in any of it, but want you to decide for yourself." |

I stepped away from the grave as if it were now something evil and vile. "It's not true. Cockroach lies. That's what it is." I looked back to the daisies at the foot of the tombstone. "They took my parents away from me once, I'll never let them take them away a second time."

"What are you planning to do, my son?"

"What makes you think I'm going to do anything?"

"I know you better than you do."

"I'm gonna have a real heart to heart with the city's slimiest scumbag."

With that, I moved toward the 'Cuda never looking back, still convincing myself that everything I had heard was nothing more than cockroach bullshit.

CHAPTER SIXTEEN

The large moon and darkness were my only allies and with the events that had happened in the last few days. I needed to regroup and think about my next move. I wasn't sure if I was any closer to finding the cockroach responsible for the deaths of the humans or not, but all that seemed like a distant memory compared to the life twisting testimony Father Garcia had just thrown on me.

There was only one thing to do. Have a stiff drink with a very beautiful woman. Ironically for me, it was the safest thing I could do.

I pulled the "Cuda into a spot near the Lunatic Moon. Despite it being three in the morning, the place was still alive and kicking. From inside, I could hear the repetitious beat of the bass. Looking at the front door, I felt my blood turn cold. The last time I was here, things didn't go so well. It was not long ago that I had been a hostage to one of the most ruthless shape shifters in the world. Piel.

During one of his so-called shows, he had killed a woman and eaten her right on the stage. Or so I believe. You see, I sort of passed out and missed the actual eating part.

I was here to meet the only female that seemed to stick in my mind and make me want to do something other than kill. I wanted to make sure that she was okay. She was just as responsible for keeping everyone alive at the Crimson Madness as I was. No, I take that back. She was far more responsible. And I'm sure not a single person had thanked her. And that included me.

"Where do you think you're going?" the doorman asked as he stepped in front of me. He was a cockroach. I couldn't feel any power flowing from him, meaning he wasn't all that powerful.

"In there," I said as I pointed forward.

"Not on my watch."

"Let me give you a little advice. Tonight's been a long night and I'm all out of fuzzy feelings. Do us both a favor and step to the side and you won't die. 'Kay, Sparkie?" I moved the coat away to allow him to see the Magnum.

"You can't go in with that unless you got a court order."

"Is there a problem?" a deep voice from behind said.

"Kasey."

"What are you doing here, Paul?" His long flowing hair was down to his waist. His face left me with no idea whether he was here as a friend or a foe. He was every bit as tall as I was and nearly as friendly.

"I'm only here to see Angie, nothing more."

"Why?"

"To thank her for helping me the other night."

"You nearly got her killed."

"I apologize."

"I'll give her the message." He started to move forward.

I stopped him with a hand to the shoulder. "I'd kind of like to do it myself."

"So?"

"I'm asking as a favor." I had always heard you attract more bees with honey than vinegar. Might as well give it the old college try.

Kasey looked to the cockroach, "I'll make sure Mr. Isaac behaves." He nodded with his head and I obediently followed.

We snaked our way through the sea of blue that was found on everything. My eyes continued to search for the woman I had come to see. My chest was tighter than if I was here to kill a cockroach. Lust was a monster all its own, but far more irresistible.

"She's over there," Kasey said, pointing. "Do something stupid, Paul, and I'm not kidding, I'll eat your throat out."

I had no reason to believe he was lying and did the only thing I knew to do. I nodded and watched him disappear again into the thick crowd. Kasey and I had a short but eventful history. I still wasn't sure if he liked me or hated me. No matter. I wasn't about to lose sleep over it.

Ahead of me I saw the woman I had come to see. She was dressed in glitter and nothing else. Heavy amounts covering the necessary items, but leaving very little to the imagination. I froze as I saw her in a heavy petting session with a man, his back to me. My feet were already turning to run for the door. I was trying to save what little dignity I had left when her lips left his mouth and she saw me.

I found myself paralyzed as I tried to move. Her eyes pulled me closer. As deadly as a cockroach's. But far more intoxicating. I was angry, but I wasn't sure why. Or at least I wasn't willing to admit it.

"Paul?" She began to move close to me as the lights went low.

Screams filled the club. The show was about to begin. It would be the last of the night. Or would that be morning? If you've never seen a strip show at a monster club, you were missing something that even your imagination wouldn't be able to think up. Monster magic had a way of making everything, alive or dead, appear beyond beautiful and sexy.

The music grew to deafening levels and I could see Angie's lips move between more smiles, but I couldn't tell what she was saying. Didn't matter. I had already seen this was a bad idea. I felt stupid for even thinking that something could come from being here. The thought of getting laid was not an option any more.

She grabbed my hand. I pulled it away and began walking toward the door. She grabbed my hand again and slowed me to a stop. "Paul, what are you doing here?" she yelled above the deafening music.

"Nothing," I refused to look at her. There was something about seeing the woman you were thinking of having raw intercourse with tongue locked with another man.

"Stop and look at me."

Still, I tried to move forward, feeling everyone in the club knew why I had come here and were laughing at me. "I've got to go." She smelled like sweet vanilla with a hint of sex. Delicious and vulgar at the same time.

The stripper began to move down the T-shaped runway above us to the music that was now beginning to break down every cell in my body. She was blonde, long hair flowing across a tux top and black thong. Her beauty made it impossible to keep from looking. Her large breasts bounced inside a see through shirt that was stretched so tight if the buttons popped, they would surely kill someone.

Angie pulled me to a service door on the side of the club, leading to the receiving area. I immediately heard the music go from unbearable to muffled. I was thankful for that alone. The cheers and screams continued to battle the bass for superiority. I was well aware that the beautiful woman on the stage was giving all the men in the audience all the sexuality they wanted. After all, why else would they come here?

Angie moved between me and the distractions on the other side of the door. It was all I could do to keep from looking at her. She was incredible to stare at. Practically naked. A glittering caramel dream. Her hair was in pigtails to each side of her head, silver glitter sparkling like newly fallen snow. "What's wrong?"

"Nothing." I tried to cover my anger, but with Angie, there was no such thing as hiding emotions.

"For nothing, it seems like it has you all worked up."

"Well I'm glad that you can make something out of nothing, but really, nothing's the matter. Sorry to burst your bubble."

"You're doing that thing again."

"What thing?"

"The thing where when you're nervous you turn in circles."

I hadn't noticed doing it. I ignored the comment.

"What are you doing here?" Vanilla filled my nose. I took deeper breaths, afraid to miss any of it.

"I said nothing. Does everything with you have to have a reason?"

"So you came here for nothing?" I could tell she wanted to smile, but resisted.

"Do you have a problem with that? I guess I wasn't aware that I needed your permission to come in here."

"Why are you so angry with me? Did I do something wrong?" I traced the silver glitter on her body and tried to keep her from catching me. It was like an erotic game of connect the dots. She grabbed my chin. "Hey, my eyes are up here. I asked you if I did something wrong?" Deep eyes looked up at me, lashes drawing me in like a spider's web. An evil smile formed. "I can tell you're happy to see me, yet you're trying hard not to admit it."

"No, not at all. In fact I'm surprised that you even noticed I was here with your tongue that far down that guy's throat. Then again, that's what you sell here isn't it?"

"If you think you can make me cry, it's not going to work.

There's a line of guys before you that have tried it and failed."
Suddenly, she was on the defensive.

"I'm sure they have."

I saw the hurt enter her eyes and already wished I hadn't said it.
"You're upset that I was talking to someone? What was that thing
about permission you said a minute ago?"

"From what I could see, you were doing a lot more than just
talking. Besides, I have better things to do that justify myself to
you." I began to move back out the door. Angie stopped me.

"Wait. You were here to see me weren't you?"

"That's crazy. What makes you think that?"

"Because you're angry."

"You know, you give yourself far too much credit. In fact, I'll
have you know I was in here to find a cockroach that needed to die.
You being here had nothing to do with it."

"Then why are you leaving? Shouldn't you kill the vampire
before running away?"

"I don't owe you any explanations to anything. Go tongue
wrestle with your client and leave me alone. I was crazy to think
that you could be anything more than an animal in heat. Kiss every
guy in here if you want. I'm sure the respect you're getting is
incredible. Dressing in nothing more than glitter has nothing to do
with it."

"I respect myself. I don't ask for it from anybody. Who I kiss
and don't kiss is my business and what people think of me, and that
includes you, doesn't concern me. If that makes you angry then you
have yourself to blame, not me."

"Really? And why is that?"

"Because if you're angry about me kissing another man, it can
mean only one of two things. Either you're jealous of him or in love
with me."

"Get out of my way before I push you through the door. Me
being here has nothing to do with wanting to see you. I don't date

women I can't trust and I don't date monsters. You happen to fall in both categories."

"So you lied to me the other night when you told me you didn't see me as a monster, didn't you?"

"Maybe I did. You're no different than anyone else that's passed through my life and far less significant. I've learned to survive on my wits and anger, but at least I won't be betrayed by some under dressed exhibitionist working in a cockroach strip club."

"That's not it and you know it. In fact in your pathetic little life, I'm about the only one that hasn't betrayed you and you know it. That's why you're so mad at me isn't it? It's not that you saw me kissing someone else. It's that I haven't betrayed you. It makes you scared doesn't it?"

"I'm not scared of monsters. You're a monster. Therefore I'm not scared of you."

"Logic. Bet you wish you could practice what you preach." I could see the animal growing in her eyes. It was like watching a thunderstorm form.

"Whatever twirls your tassels, sweetheart."

"You're mad at me because you want to see the monster in me, but you can't. You want to give in to your heart, but in doing so, you lose your control. You think by being vulnerable to me, you're being vulnerable to the monsters. What really pisses you off is that you see more monster in you than in me." I felt her long finger stab me in the chest. I jumped at the sharp pain.

"Trust me, I see the monster in you. In fact it's all I see in you."

"When I first met you I thought you were the angriest man I had ever met. But that's not it is it? It's not anger, it's fear. Fear of the monsters, fear of love, fear of life, fear of dying. That's why you don't let anyone near your heart and get to know you. You're afraid they'll see it too."

I moved back toward her, simply to keep the music and cheering from drowning out my words. If I was going to sting her verbally, I wanted to make sure she heard it. Comebacks lose their zing when you have to repeat them. "You listen and you listen good. If making a choice between falling in lust with you and keeping hold of my hatred are the only two choices I have to make in life, you'll lose every time. You're nothing more than a naked piece of meat in a strip joint. You're a dime a dozen. So go find some other chump to fondle around with because I see through your game. Just a twisted illusion, a fetish for desperate husbands with a monster fantasy. You make them feel good, they make you feel important, but after you both get dressed, you realize you still are *and* have nothing."

With that she slapped me hard. I deserved it and took it like a man. Inside I knew she was right about everything she had said. I had simply taken my anger of little secrets out on her. Not a smooth move at all.

"Don't you ever come in here and judge me again. You know nothing about me or what I do. I'm happy with who I am and if that involves having fun so be it. Unlike you, I don't hide behind my pain and fears and allow them to dictate my life and who I spend it with. I'm not a gold digger or con artist. I make my own choices and that intimidates you. I don't bow down to you simply because you're a man and you're not used to that. I'm not here to feed your ego. When you start thinking with the right head, talk to me."

"Stay out of my life." I started for the door yet again.

"You came here looking for me remember? Not the other way around. And you can play tough guy with me all you want but you know you'll be back so save yourself some time and stop fighting with me over something this silly."

"What do you mean by something this silly?"

She moved toward me with her patented stripper stroll. Hips swaying like a palm tree in a light breeze. Her body touched mine, hands going around my neck. She looked me in the eyes. Her voice lost its intensity. It grew soft and hypnotic. "I'm sorry that you saw me kiss him. It was nothing and I mean that. If you want me all to yourself, all you had to do was ask. Now you've stained everything with words you can't take back."

She was right. I had blown my chance at sex, might as well feed the other vice. It was time to send a message to Kincaid and his skin flick business. I turned and never said goodbye.

CHAPTER SEVENTEEN

I stood over the body of a cockroach I had just killed. "Where are they?" I asked the trembling naked freak only feet away. Like her punctured neck, my stake was dripping with fresh blood as I threw it to the side.

The other vein weasels in the house had scattered before I had a chance to give them the same welcome. The house was being used as a filming sight for one of Kincaid's necro-sex films. Simply put, young girls that had been filmed doing the nasty with neck biters while being fed on. Kincaid's meal ticket.

Cameras and sound equipment now littered the floor, leaving only the human girl on a satin-sheeted bed in what had once been a living room. I was here tonight, not to stop the freak porn industry per say, but to damage Kincaid. He had a vested interest in the films and profited off of them. Not to mention I needed to work off a bit of the aggression from my conversation with Angie.

I saw Kincaid as more than just another activist up a coffin sleeper's ass, or as some slim ball that ran a sex film business just outside the city limits. He was possibly linked to the death of my parents. Tonight, I'd send a message to all the bat heads and those that stood with them. If the police wanted lawlessness in this town, I'd gladly do my part.

"I won't ask again, who brought you here?" I grabbed the freak by the hair. She was naked, bloody and in need of a hot bath.

"I don't know, God I swear, I don't know," the freak screamed. She was high, but not on a street drug. She was high on cockroach magic. Her pupils still dilated with the effects, reflecting in the dancing orange glow of the candles. In a few minutes that would melt away. The source of her high was now a true corpse at our feet.

I jerked her hair a little harder, twisted the long blonde ponytail in my hand and pushed her face down on top of the dead cockroach. Partly to scare her and partly to shake the magic out of her. "If you don't want me to do this to you, you better start spilling your guts. Tonight is not the night to look for compassion from me. I'm here for a reason and it's not to protect or rescue a tripped out piece of white trash roach freak." I looked at her in the dim light. "How old are you?" I pulled the Magnum from my holster and made sure she saw it. With any luck it might scare an answer or two out of her.

"Sixteen."

Good. Now the killing of the sun crispy was justified. I looked around the room at the camera and other filth and got sick to my stomach. I had killed her co-star, but there was still a lot of killing to do.

"Where did the rest of them go? I want the one that's running all this."

"Do I look like some kind of freaking psychic to you?" Another good sign the magic was wearing off. She was getting mouthier.

I twisted the hair a little tighter. Shoved her face down a little harder. "Just in case you don't know it, there is a very messy gun against your temple. I'll waste no time in planting a bullet in your skull. This is your last chance. Where's the monster in charge?"

Tears rolled down her cheeks, smearing her mascara in

grotesque lines of melting sickness. I didn't want to feel sorry for her. Unlike a lot of humans I find myself trying to keep alive, this one was here of her own free will, but then again, she was simply a young naive babe in the woods.

"Or what? Will the great Paul Isaac kill me like a common vampire?"

So she knew my name. "Just here feeding the monsters is that it? What did they promise you? Fame? Money? Love? Eternal Life? Tell me you're not here out of your own free will."

"So what if I am? Are you going to kill me just for that?"

"I probably won't have to. These things will do it for me. *Then* I'll kill you." She tried to pull away, but I held tight. I looked at the bite on her neck. "Tell me something. How bad does your life have to be to allow something that's been dead two hundred years do this to you? I'm not even going to get into the porno part."

"I'd rather be one of them than a pathetic piece of shit like you." She looked at me with eyes of steel. Scared, yes, but there was something more dangerous there now.

"You won't think that when things get ugly. To them, you're nothing but an endless link in a food chain. And don't think you have anything between your legs that will save you when they're done with you."

I looked in the corner of the small room and saw a second girl curled up with her hands hugging her knees, rocking. Her eyes were wide with terror. "Who's she?"

"None of your fucking business."

The dark girl on the floor looked up at me and tried to move. It just wasn't happening. Her legs wouldn't lift her up. A trail of fresh blood oozed from her shoulder, staining her light coffee-like skin. I could hear the small whimpers.

"Please don't kill me. Please don't kill me," she cried.

Dragging the first girl by the ponytail, I went to coffee girl. My Magnum was still in my right hand, the free hand. I was sure it wasn't helping me bond with the crying girl, but there was no way I was going to put it away in a house filled with cockroaches.

I grabbed ponytail girl by the chin and made her look in the eyes of the girl on the floor. "Look at her. She's scared shitless. How much did they pay you to bring her here?"

I threw ponytail girl to the ground and walked to coffee girl.

"What's your name?"

She shook uncontrollably. I was afraid she was going to hyperventilate, or worse, puke before she could speak.

"Don't tell him nothin'," Ponytail girl shouted.

I kept my attention on coffee girl. "Now, if you want to live through the night, I'd strongly suggest you work with me. What's your name?"

"Amber," she said, nearly in a whisper.

"I told you not to say nothing. Jesus," Ponytail snapped.

"Amber, listen to me. Tell me where they are. They'll kill you if I don't kill them first."

"We feed them of our own free will and if you kill us, there'll be others that'll do it. You can't stop it. It's too big for you, you pathetic pig," Ponytail girl continued.

I turned to her. "If you don't tell me where they are, one of two things is going to happen. One, you will be killed by the very same monsters you're trying to protect, or two, you'll go to jail for helping them to escape." I looked back to Coffee girl. "This girl can't be more than fifteen. How sick can you get?"

"The only thing that'll be found here is your dead body." Her face seemed a little more animated than it really was. Pale skin caught the light, then threw it back into the room.

I saw the flash of light before I felt it. Cold at first, then turned to burning pain. She had stabbed me with a knife in the upper leg. "Fucking little whore."

I slammed the butt of the Magnum against her head as I tried to decide whether to kill her or not. Leaning toward killing her. She fell to the floor holding her new wound. A small whimper of pain followed it.

I picked her up and threw her out the door into the black night. I had wrapped a crucifix around the doorknob. If any of the roaches had any bright ideas about escaping or entering the house, the cruci-fixes would burn their hands and hopefully trap them inside. I had done the same to the back door before coming into the house. Coffee girl looked at me with eyes even wider than they had been before.

"Go!" I shouted. Lucky for her, she didn't argue. She lifted up and ran out the door. I turned and looked at the room before me. They were still here. Watching and waiting. Now the fun would begin.

The camera stared at me. A sign of the vulgar abuse that had taken place here, not only tonight but an infinite number of nights before. With everything I had, I kicked it from its tripod and smashed it with my boots. My efforts might not even make a dent into the fang and freak porn business, but it sure made me feel better.

It hit me on the top of the head like a demonic raindrop. With my head being clean-shaven, it wasn't hard to feel it or hear it for that matter. I raised my hand to my head to touch it.

Looking at my fingers, I could tell it was blood. Still warm. Dripping from the ceiling. Not something you find everyday.

With blurring speed, I grabbed my 9mm and lifted it from its holster with my left hand and brought the Magnum up with my right. Raising them to the ceiling in deadly synchronized fashion, I pulled the triggers. I dropped to the floor and rolled for cover. Ultra violet bullets met the cockroach on the ceiling with deadly force. It screamed for a split second before turning into an undead tiki torch.

A second and third cockroach jumped out of the doorway to my right. And like their dead friend, completely naked. Faces dripped with fresh blood. Mixed with saliva. From the opposite direction a fourth cockroach appeared. It was as if I had lifted a rotting log. They were scattering in directions all around me.

I pulled the triggers on both guns. The Magnum pointed to my right and the 9mm pointed to the left. The move sent two cockroaches into ashes at almost the same time. Flashes of violent fire. Turning into a bright orange ash storm. Above me more movement. Fast. Rush of air as it moved overhead.

I tracked the cockroach clawing above me. It moved down on me quicker than I expected, hitting me across the head and rolled me toward the wall. A candle fell to the floor. Drapes caught fire. Orange flame grew in hungry movements. Heat hit me in the face. Sounds of material being devoured.

My hands held the guns as tight as I could. Losing them was not going to be an option. I had learned early on, that being in a fight with the undead is a lot more difficult without them. I rolled away from the flames, avoiding the heat more than anything.

The cockroach moved toward the door. My hand with the Magnum swatted at its foot as it moved. Knocking it to the ground. My fingers stung with pain from the contact.

The roach bounced along the floor. It came back to its feet as if it had been snapped up by an invisible hand. My fingers pulled back on the trigger of the 9mm. Exploding music filled my ears. The bullet caught the monster in the back of the leg. Lodging in the upper thigh. The cockroach spun wildly to the ground. It howled in pain. Rocking back and forth on the floor. Blood gave way to smoke and fire as the ultra violet bullet poisoned and burned its way through undead skin. Howls gave way to screams. Screams gave way to silence. God, I loved my job.

I moved back to my feet, keeping my eyes and ears open for anything that might still be in the house. These cockroaches were not powerful enough to give off a lot of power, so it was harder to sense them.

Thanks to the Bitch of the Year, my leg throbbed with undue

pain. I was still kicking myself for not just shooting her along with these filthy parasites. I had been lucky. The wound wasn't deep. It stung and was bleeding, but nothing I couldn't handle. It would be healed by breakfast.

Smoke and flame was flooding the room. My eyes burned. My breath shallow and labored. Heat forced me to move. I squinted to see, looking for shadows, feeling for power.

I moved through the house, trying to stay low enough that I could breathe. I wiped my eyes every few seconds, trying to keep what little vision I had. In the kitchen, I found another cockroach. He was holding his hand as if he had been burned. "I see you found the crucifix on the doorknob. Funny how things work out that way."

The monster jumped toward me with non-human speed, ripped fingernails across my face as he moved back toward the living room, stopping just short of the flames. He turned to face me.

"See you in hell, asshole." I pulled the trigger on the 9mm three times, hitting him in the head once and in the chest twice. He screamed briefly, before turning into a Roman candle. Undead flames intertwined with those already devouring the house. A sulphuric smell filled my nose.

For now, my work was done here, but there were more demons to fight. Some out here in the night waiting to get to me and some inside me waiting to get out.

My cell phone rang. I could tell by the ring tone it was Detective Price. Everyone on my cell had their own ring, just for situations like this.

From my pocket, I pulled the phone up and pressed the green button to take the call. Smoke began to choke me. Water filled my eyes. Breathing became labored. I could feel my own pulse in the wound on my leg. As the adrenalin wore off, the pain set in.

I opened the back door and raced outside, filling my lungs with much needed fresh air.

"Yeah," I answered.

"Isaac, get down here to Isleworth. We have another body for you. It's Albert Kincaid." I could tell by his voice he was walking.

"Kincaid?"

"Yeah. Get over here as fast as you can. This is going to blow the lid off their little game of hide and seek. I need you to tell me what I don't know before it disappears."

I never answered, simply folding the phone shut and putting it back in my pocket.

CHAPTER EIGHTEEN

I sleworth is one of the wealthiest areas of greater Orlando, made up of multi-million dollar homes, sprawling along streets like little hotels. Sport and luxury cars in every garage and trophy wives in every bedroom. It is a neighborhood that said you had made something of yourself. To live here, you are an executive of a Fortune 500 company, sports star, entertainment mogul or in our victim's case, a man that preyed off the exploitations of both the undead and young human girls. I was out of place as I drove up to the large mansion in a 1970 black Plymouth 'Cuda, thumping with American muscle.

In fact, everything I noticed seemed a little out of place. Usually when I go to one of these shows, there is a line of cars a mile long, complete with far too many officers than are really needed, but not tonight. Tonight there was a lack of both. There wasn't a police cruiser in sight. No ambulance. Nothing. To the unknowing eye, nothing was a miss in O-town.

There was a silence in the air that almost hinted to the fact that the night itself had lost its life somehow. I didn't hear a single police radio. Not a conversation to be heard. A quiet so solid it was deafening.

I stepped out of the car and looked around at the odd normality of the scene. According to Price there was a dead man in the house, murdered by the same psychopath that had killed the other Knights, yet there wasn't a single thing here to solidify it other than Kansas' Ford Explorer and Price's truck.

You might think I would be giddy about the death of Albert Kincaid, but actually, I was pissed. I now had a million unanswered questions that I'd never have the chance to torture out of him.

"What brings you here on such a warm night?"

I jumped as I turned to see Victor. A vein weasel I knew well. I had forced information out of him with a mixture of holy water and silver. A combo just short of deadly for the undead. It burnt the skin, caused unbelievable pain, and the wound never would heal. I smiled as I looked at my handy work. Even with roach magic, he looked hideous.

He remained hidden in the crape myrtles, only an outline of his body and deformed face visible. My hand moved toward the Magnum as I watched him slither from the darkness and walk toward me. It went without saying he had retribution coming to him.

"There will be no need for that," he calmly said.

"I'll determine that."

The evil confident smile grew on his face as the streetlights illuminated his features. "Why are you here?"

I returned the smile. "Maybe I should be asking you the same question."

"Looking for take out." He slithered out of the shadows.

"At Albert Kincaid's? Sucking on a widow of a blood sucker attack so early in the game, Victor?" I shrugged. "Then again to be married to a man like Kincaid, maybe she's nothing but a freak herself."

"There has been no vampire attack here. Simply an unfortunate accident. A slip and fall. Cranium meets porcelain. So you see, you have the evening free to frolic in the swamps with you newfound vampire friends."

"I beg to differ." I began to walk toward the house.

Victor stopped me. "I do not think that will be necessary. I think the best thing for you would be to fade away for the night." His voice hung in the air as if taking flight.

"I couldn't possibly be rude after coming all the way out here like this. Besides, if there wasn't a murder committed here, neither you nor I have anything to worry about." I took a step back. "Then again, they say a killer always comes back to the scene of the crime."

I could see the harnessed anger in his body language. He wanted me gone before I saw too much and I knew it. Inside, I enjoyed watching him squirm. A deep laugh bubbled from his throat as he continued to scan the area. "I have a more refined taste than the likes of Albert Kincaid, Avenger."

My eyes focused on the wound that ran along his cheek and throat. Infection oozed in creamy icebergs of puss. "How's that wound healing?"

His face grew into stone. "You know, I could kill you and no one would know or care. If I were you, I'd respect what fragmented form of life you still have." I began to walk toward the house as Victor grabbed my shoulder. "Besides, I know the secret you and the Father hold close to your chests." I felt his power grow stronger behind me. It would only be a matter of time before he had to stop me and I knew it. When he tried, I'd justify the stake in his heart. "It would be such a shame to know that both father and son had been killed on the same night do you not think?"

Every ounce of air in my lungs left me. Cold chills raced down my arms. He had stopped me without laying a hand on me. "What's that supposed to mean?"

"Seems as though he and your mother had quite a love interest under your poor father's nose. I hear there are even inappropriate films of her and nameless vampires as well. Freak films I think they are called."

I pulled a bottle of holy water from my trench coat. "Looks like I should go ahead and finish what I started with you."

"What the hell are you doing here?" Kansas asked from behind. Without breaking momentum, he began pushing me back toward the 'Cuda.

I pulled free of Kansas and reached for the dead man in front of me. I still wanted my hands on Victor. "I'll kill you Victor! If it's the last thing I do, I'll see you burn in hell."

He dodged my swings with little effort at all. *There is no shame in what your mother was, Avenger. If your father had been more of a man than he was, she would not have had to seek lust in other men.*

I started to open the holy water vial, when I felt Victor's power shock me. I fell to the ground as the pain ran through me. My fingers started to paralyze. I could hear Victor and Kansas above me, but they seemed far away, almost dreamlike. Then, like waking from the nightmare, the power was gone. I looked up at Kansas while still on my hands and knees. "I want to see the body. I want to know everything about what happened here."

"This is police business, Paul. I don't owe you any explanations or access."

"You do if there's a dead body in there that's the result of a cockroach." I stood again. "How long, Kansas? Don't you think sooner or later people are gonna start talking? When are you going to stop being a puppet on Quinn's string? You're covering up murder for God's sake. And why?"

"Honestly Paul, no one has been killed by a vampire. You've been misinformed. Either leave now, or I'll have someone remove you."

"Then why are you here? Where's Kincaid?"

"Dead."

"Really? And how did he die?"

"Heart attack."

I looked at the two in front of me and wondered which was the more dangerous lying monster. "Kincaid died of a heart attack?"

"That's right, so see, there's no need for you to be here. Now if you don't mind, I have work to do."

"Let me see if I have this right. Kincaid died of a heart attack, yet you're here with police officers instead of paramedics. I never knew having a heart attack was against the law. But then again, according to the blood sucker here, Kincaid died from a slip and fall. You two can't even get your lies right."

"There's nothing here but a dead man. A man with a bad heart. Quite possibly caused by your little tirade the other night. And as far as the bathroom fall Victor has told you about, it was caused by the heart attack. Seems as though he hit his head on the sink."

I couldn't believe what I was hearing. "Do I really look that gullible to you, Kansas? The man was killed and it had nothing to do with a heart attack or a slip in the bathroom or anything else except fangs." I looked at Victor, but was still talking to Kansas. "Perhaps you already know who killed Kincaid, but are just too coward to do anything about it? How you can look in the mirror every day is beyond me. Now you can stay out here and hold hands with this vein sucker if you want, but I'm going to go in there and put a stop to all of this."

"You know there were witnesses at the Crimson Madness that heard you say you would kill him," Victor said to Kansas. "If we have a murder on our hands, perhaps we should interrogate you on your whereabouts. With what you know about Kincaid, you have to admit, there is motive."

"Are you threatening me, Victor? At least have the guts to say what's on your mind."

"Kincaid is a very high profile man. We don't want to draw attention to his death in respect for his family. You know as well as I do that the press would eat something like this up. We plan on telling them after the body is taken away. The last thing we need is for the media to jump to conclusions like you are." Kansas was in full good cop/bad cop mode.

"Is it all worth it to you? Willing to see everyone that supports your dead ass dead, while you do nothing about it simply to save the bat district a little bad press? If you had done this the right way, chances are, there wouldn't have been but one victim. Now with each cover up, your lies have to get bigger and more complicated. I was told about this. Told about Kincaid's death so save all your lies for someone else."

"Another vampire informant I'm guessing."

"Let's just say a little bird told me about tonight." I looked around him to the inside of the mansion, then turned back to Kansas. "And another thing, how are you going to explain this when you supposedly have the killer locked up. Blows your cover sky high doesn't it?"

"Again, Paul, you are not needed here, so go home. I don't owe you or Asa anything. You can leave on your own, or I can have you taken out of here."

"If you're covering this murder up then it leads me to a very serious problem."

"And what's that, Isaac?" Kansas asked.

"What are you covering up with the Guzman girl? God don't tell me you know who did that and are doing nothing."

"You really think I'd turn the other cheek when a small child was killed?"

"All depends on what Quinn tells you to turn a cheek on. Lately, you've been turning your cheek on a lot of things. You're nothing more than his little whipping boy."

He swung at me, but I dodged the effort. "You go to hell, Isaac."

"If I ever find out that you had anything to do with covering up that kids death, I'll see to it that you're buried alive for it." I looked at the mansion. "His death will come as a blessing to most, but this town will never forgive you hiding the death of a child."

Detective Price joined us. "What seems to be the problem, boys?" My only sliver of truth was among us. I was surprised to see him here. Like he had said, this wasn't his case.

"Nothing. Paul and I were just talking about the weather."

"No, I'm accusing *you* of being a dirty cop." I remained focused.

"The head was already severed when we found him," Price answered softly.

"Jesus, Frank," Kansas huffed. "I can't believe you're doing this. Are you seriously going to kiss your retirement goodbye over this?" Kansas literally spun in circles holding his forehead in his hands. His façade world was instantly a pile of ruble at his feet.

Frank Price raised his hand to silence. "We need to find this vampire and we need to find him fast." He looked to the house and took a deep breath. "He was sleazy and sick, but that doesn't mean we don't find the one responsible. If I lose everything, so be it, but I'm not going to keep pretending that these things aren't happening. We have a killer on our hands and he's targeting certain people. I need Paul to find out who it is and why." Price stared into Kansas' eyes. "It's time we take our streets back from the monsters."

"You know Paul isn't going to be anything short of a deterrent in all of this," Victor snarled.

Price glanced at the blood junkie, then started, "Look Paul, we need to keep this as quiet as possible. At the request of the Vampire Council, we tried to keep it all to ourselves. It was the Council's request to hunt down and kill the rouge." He looked to Victor. "That's why he's here."

"They sent Victor to hunt down and kill this rouge? God, Frank, Victor's a cold blooded killer himself." I rolled my eyes. "Talk about the wolf watching the sheep." My train of thought was evaporating at the thought of Victor being involved. "I know you weren't born yesterday. We are talking about monsters. Cold blooded killers that look at us as nothing more than food. My guess is Quinn and his deadbeats are behind this. And now you cover up the killing of humans so they can help with the murders. Thanks to Kansas, other than Kincaid, we don't even have bodies to examine bite marks on."

"You're blowing it all out of proportion. We simply don't want the public to think they're not safe in the vampire district over this. This area lives and dies by tourism. If they don't feel safe, they don't come. If they don't come, people lose their livelihoods."

"You doing nothing is costing people to lose their livelihoods."

"We have most of the other members of the Knights of the Night in protection," Kansas added. "We've been doing our own investigation in cooperation with the Council."

"Well one thing that's working to your advantage, Kansas. There's fewer Knights to protect thanks to you and your bang up job around here."

"Here's something for you to chew on, Isaac. I'm in charge of this investigation and I decide who sees what's in that house. Guess what, you don't get in." He started to move away, heading back toward the house.

"He's the only one that can find him, Zeke," Price said.

Kansas turned again. "And I want you out of here too, old man. You've done nothing here tonight but undermine my authority. You'll be lucky if the department lets you work a crosswalk after all this."

"We have a vampire victim here, Zeke and we ain't any closer to catching him than we were a month ago. Besides, the cat's out of the bag on this one. Either he goes in, or I blow the whistle on the whole thing."

Kansas stared at me for what seemed an eternity. "I should have left you to die with Maximilian when I had the chance." With that, he walked away.

I started to say something when Price lifted his hand. "I need you to promise me you will keep your mouth shut on this."

"Jesus, Price…" another hand went up.

Price looked to me and whispered. "I want to show you something." He waited until Kansas was out of hearing range. "Like I told you before, we ain't getting any closer to the killer and keeping the lid on this for much longer just ain't going to be possible. I need you to help us find the killer before there's another death."

"Only if I have your word that I have free reign over the investigation. You turn over everything you have on this case and I question who I want and how I want."

Price gave me an evil grin. "I was hoping you'd see things my way."

CHAPTER NINETEEN

Bright lights blinded me as my eyes adjusted from the darkness outside to the high wattage illumination inside the home. I could hear the hushed voices inside, soft crying, and the shroud of silence that still prevailed over everything. I assumed it was some scantily clad skank gold digger. Even with the small sounds, the silence refused to go away. It only goes to show, even porn stars have feelings.

When my sight returned, I looked around the vast area in front of me. "It amazes me that anyone need this much room. There's no doubt in my mind two people could go days without seeing one another," I said in a hushed voice as I followed Kansas, Price and Victor through the large living room.

"I need to talk to you before you go up there," Kansas said, stopping me short of the staircase.

"About what?"

"Handling this professionally. Price might be giving you a break here, but I won't waste a second throwing you out if you say or do one thing out of line here. You disrespect one person in this house and I'll bury you. We want this to be as quiet of an investigation as we can make it. Before the media gets wind of this, we want to talk to the family and handle this the proper way. Being who this is, I don't have to tell you they will have a field day with it."

"Meaning you want to make sure everybody gives the same story," I finished for him.

"Don't start with me tonight, Paul." A combination of aggravation and fatigue filled his voice.

"If you'd've told me, I could've dress to impress too," I said as we walked up the wide staircase. "At least I could have shaven."

"You dressing up is like putting perfume on a pig."

I smiled. It was true. "And they say you're not a motivator."

"Look, Paul, I want you to tell us what you can about the body and room. This'll not be one of your rants and raves about vampires and how they should all be killed. I know you must be full of yourself tonight, knowing who this is, but there's a lot of people that are upset."

"I still could've worn a tie." Digging at Kansas was a growing hobby of mine. He was like a toy. All I had to do was wind him up and let him go. Instant entertainment.

"Are we clear?" Price interrupted, trying to defuse the argument.

"Crystal."

From the top of the staircase, the room below looked even more impressive. The deep burgundy walls in contrast with the golds and overall shine gave the room character and taste. The large chandelier hulked over the room like a bright star. Exploding light filled the house. A large painting hung on the wall, close to five feet tall of a cockroach holding the sun in the palm of his hand. Cherubs sat at his feet, eyes looking up at him. It was bazaar to say the least. Cockroaches and suns don't mix. And I haven't seen many cherubs at their feet either. But then again, what would you expect to find in the home of a cockroach activist. Something told me it wasn't a Dubro original. Too much class and talent.

"So I guess since we're keeping this hush hush, it explains the lack of help and cars out front," I said as we approached the room I guessed to be the crime scene. It was the only door open and there was a buzz of activity going in and coming out of it.

"We were told to make this as unobtrusive as possible. That meant no marked cars, no ambulances, nothing, until the family is ready," Price said. He was usually smiling, shaking hands, approachable even in the face of death. But tonight it was clear to me, he was nothing more than a puppet on a string. Simply going through the motions.

The monsters scared him. That was the best thing for him. In my opinion, if you couldn't hate them, at least fear them. It helps with the decision making process. Not to mention more times than not, it kept you alive.

"What do you really know about the killings?" I asked.

"They're old school. Very old school," Price answered, stretching his arms wide as if telling a fish story.

"What do you mean by that?"

"Promise me you won't go around doing anything until we get all our ducks in a row." This request from Kansas.

"Act as though nothing ever happened, is that it?" I asked.

"Something like that." He looked at Price. They were communicating something. I didn't have all the pieces. I was the only one not in on the full story. See, I'm not a true member of the police force. I get the crumbs of information that fall from the table.

"By morning, we plan to release what we find to the media. We just want a few hours for the family as well as the police to do their job," Price said. "Your job is to help us track down and kill the vampire responsible. Nothing more, nothing less. Leave the media and politics involved to us."

"And what are you going to tell the media that you found?"

"The truth," Kansas said.

"About all of it, or just this?"

Kansas dropped his eyes from mine and never spoke.

"Jesus, Kansas, I'm not saying shout it to on the highest mountain, but this isn't right. You're putting every man, woman, and child in greater danger by the second."

"No one's in danger because we don't leak this to the press."

"I'll bet if you told that to the members of the Knights of the Night they might disagree. When a certain group is targeted for murder the living members seem to freak out about it just a little."

"We just need time to present what we know before we open our mouths," Price said as he pushed on my shoulder. "Come on, let's get this over with. The sooner we finalize this, the sooner we can tell the world."

I didn't budge from the wall. I would drag this out as long as I could now. I pulled a wooden stake from my leather trench coat. Checked the Magnum for bullets.

"You won't need that," Victor said.

"You have a better way of staking him?"

"Someone has beaten you to the punch," Dieter's dead face opened into a cynical smile as he exited the room. Great, now I had two undead looking over the corpse with me.

I felt my stomach tighten. "Oh, this is just getting better by the minute. What in the hell are you doing here? I would've thought you'd still be licking your wounds."

"Funny, I was about to ask you the very same question." He glared at Kansas and Price.

I remained silent. My hands crossed over my chest. Wooden stake in my right hand.

"I have been called to represent the undead."

"It's good to see you haven't changed after your near death experience, Dieter. Still the same slimy snake you've always been."

"A human had lost his life, possibly at the hands of a vampire, which in itself should make you very angry." He smiled as he kept himself between me and the body. "But this is very different. We are looking at the body of a vampire activist . . . maybe more. So I am very curious. Will you be angry or euphoric?"

"And what's that supposed to mean?"

"Do you really want me to say it out loud in front of everyone?"

I froze. Damn it, did everyone know about Kincaid but me?

"Why don't you wait outside," Price said from behind me.

"On the contrary, Detective. I must be present while the examination takes place. You know that," Dieter returned. "Besides, I am very concerned our agreement has been breeched now that he is here. Curious as to his actions on this matter."

I looked to Kansas, back to Dieter. "What agreement is that?"

"Nothing that concerns you." This from Victor.

Dieter held his hand up. "My friend Victor is to lead this hunt, not you, Avenger. This is an agreement between the Orlando Police Department and the commercial vampires of Orlando. Nothing personal."

"That's about to change, Dieter. I'm the new lead dog on this hunt."

Dieter turned to Kansas and Price, "If one vampire turns up missing or dead because of him, we will hunt him down and kill him ourselves."

"And you think we'd care?" Kansas answered.

"Paul, take a look at this," Price said as he moved me inside the bedroom. "We will discuss which one of you kills the other after while."

I could see Albert Kincaid lying on the large sleigh bed. Dieter stood between me and the body but I saw everything I'd find. I could smell the copper-like odor of the blood. I could feel the death, so real I could have wrapped it around me. Like with most bat head attacks, there was very little blood. Simply a corpse, white and empty. Next to the bed was the severed head, looking up at us with hollow sunken eyes. The skin already drawn and dry as if carved from fresh clay. Most people think there is a lot of blood at the scene of a roach attack, but that's simply not true. In fact, it's the opposite. A full sized healthy plasma parasite can draw all the blood from a human body, leaving the remains with only small drips of blood around the bite. Much like a raisin.

"Dieter, please, at least move out of Paul's way so he can see the body," Price said.

"Yeah, Dieter, move," I repeated, more direct.

Dieter bowed and motioned me by. "As you wish."

I walked along the right side of the bed. It came up to my waist. "How anyone can get up into one of these things I still don't know. Simply rolling out of bed could be fatal," I said to no one in particular.

"Something beat gravity to the punch," Price said. He gave out a nervous laugh. No one took it as a joke. It was simply a way to keep from screaming.

The gold and maroon bedspread was peeled to the bottom near his feet. Albert Kincaid was still dressed in black slacks, and a white dress shirt. "Unless he had laid down for a nap, I can't see this making sense. I'm no expert on the sleeping habits of the rich and famous, but I'm guessing it doesn't include dress clothes."

"There are those of us that are more sophisticated than you, Avenger," Dieter said in my mind.

"This coming from a dead man that sleeps in a coffin. You're right Dieter, you are the epitome of sophistication." Like turning into bats, the coffin urban legend was just that. From what I knew, the leeches really never slept. Simply found refuge from the ultra violet rays.

I stood above the body. My heart pounded against my chest. Cockroach activist or not, my thoughts continued to beg for an out. I wanted him to be alive. I had so many questions. Perhaps Kincaid's death had a silver lining. For me it was better to never know if he was in fact my father.

A coldness ran through my body as I tried to breathe. "Price, you're right. This *is* old school. The roach that did this was making sure the victim never rose from the dead. Something the newer monsters never practice." I moved closer to Price so I could whisper. "Who found him?"

"He was found by his live-in lover or so-called wife earlier in the morning," Kansas said from behind.

So much for whispering. "How early?"

"About one," Price added.

I looked in all the usual places for a bite. I didn't have to look long. It was in the nape of the neck, or what was left of it. Two puncture wounds with red trails of where blood had run down the skin and fell in a small puddle on the bed, the size of a quarter.

"Tell me what I should be looking for," Price finished. "He's been oozing blood since we got here. That's normal . . . right?"

"Blood never coagulates around a cockroach wound. The bite was done with care and finesse. The older ones can make a bite almost invisible. Leaving only the smallest of wounds." This time I didn't attempt to whisper. "When was the last time the grieving widow saw him alive?"

"Actually she hadn't seen him since this evening. He had several appointments. Mrs. Kincaid had a dinner and function with a friend and was out for the evening. She found him like this when she returned."

"And who was this friend?"

Kansas looked at a piece of paper in his hand. "An Isabella Dunlawton and Dubro."

I looked back at Kansas. "The painter?"

"I think they prefer the term artist." This coming from Dieter.

"Artist would imply talent."

Dieter laughed and moved toward me. "And what would you know about talent, my friend?"

"Enough to know that Dubro has none." I looked back to Price, "Why was Mrs. Kincaid meeting with Dubro?"

"Mr. Kincaid and his wife had invested in Dubro's gallery downtown in the district. Planned to raise money for vampire awareness through vampire art. After the attacks there the other night, I think they were doing damage control and circling the wagons. From what I heard, the gallery was making money hand over fist until then."

"Why can't people invest in real world issues like global warming or saving the woodpeckers or something? Besides, I'm beginning to think Kincaid was simply laundering his freak porn profit through the gallery. I doubt he'd know about art if it bit him on the ass."

"Mr. Kincaid has done quite a large amount of charity for both the human and the vampire community, Avenger. You are just too blind to see that in anyone that associates with us. Do not allow his . . . other business ventures to cloud your judgment."

"And what about our lucky gentleman here, who did he meet with?" I asked, ignoring Dieter.

Kansas spoke, "He had two appointments. One with Sylvester and one with Sasha."

"Sasha?" I tried to keep my emotions in tact.

"He was trying to come to a truce with him and the pure blood vampires from what Mrs. Kincaid said. After what happened the other night, I think it was another issue of damage control. Nothing speaks as loud as lost money to these people," Price answered. "The violence the other night really hurt the profit margin."

"Then we need to talk to both daisy pushers and get a couple of fang impressions."

"Feeling bad about supporting your new found friends, Avenger?"

"No, Dieter, I don't give a damn about Asa or Sasha. I just want the police department to grow balls and go after the right cockroach."

"About the body, are we correct in believing it was a vampire?"

Price interrupted. He stopped short of Dieter and Victor and looked to me. It was a rhetorical question, but one he had to ask to make things official.

"Yeah, it was a roach, but I think you already knew that." I looked as close into Dieter's eyes as I could without getting caught. It's hard not to look someone in the eyes when you talk to them. I played on that edge and it was stupid of me. "Where's Mrs. Kincaid now?"

"Downstairs. I've taken her statement and she's talking with other officers. I want to get her out of here before the media gets a hold of this. As for you, Mrs. Kincaid is off limits. I don't want you accusing her of anything. I don't even want you and her to meet in the hallways, is that clear?"

I shook my head. "Does she know anyone that wanted her husband dead?"

"Meaning?" Price asked.

"Meaning other than the blood slurpers we know about. I'm sure a man like Kincaid must have dozens of enemies, dying to see him like this."

"Are you accusing anyone?" Victor asked.

"I think Kincaid knew his attacker. And I think Asa is right. This is made to look like a pure blood attack to throw us off the trail. I'm betting against it though." I moved into Victor's space. "My money is on one of you."

"What makes you say that?" Price asked.

"Look around you. Nothing is messed up. Nothing broken. My theory is Mr. Kincaid was very comfortable with the cockroach that did this. He had no cause for alarm. I'm not so sure he'd have been this comfortable around Sasha," I added. "Or any of the pure bloods for that matter."

"Perhaps Mr. Kincaid was caught in the Sasha's gaze," Price said. "He would never have fought back in that scenario."

"Perhaps it was you that killed him, Avenger. Rumors are, that you threatened Albert Kincaid not days ago," Dieter challenged. "After all, you do have vampire virus in your veins."

I ignored him and talked to the two detectives. "The cockroach that did this wanted to cut the head off of the Knights of the Night, not just Kincaid."

"So you think he was killed because of who he was?" Kansas asked.

"Who he was, what he knew, something. I'm just saying that the cockroach that killed Kincaid didn't do it to feed. There is a lot more to it. That's why I'm saying talk to the wife. Maybe she got tired of waiting on her inheritance."

"You think Mrs. Kincaid had something to do with this?" Price asked, disgust in his voice. "All this time you've been telling us that it was a vampire and accusing us of not saying anything and now you've only been here twenty minutes and you're accusing his wife? Even if she did do it, it makes no sense that she would have killed the other members does it?"

"That's what we are going to dig and find out. Porn stars do crazy things for money. Porn stars married to rich husbands maybe venture a little farther. Who knows?"

"But Mrs. Kincaid couldn't have done it," Price added.

"Don't let her fake implants sway you, you dirty old man. She's got all the bells and whistles to make any man or coffin sleeper kill for her. And the only thing bigger than Mrs. Kincaid's rack is her husband's bank account."

"So you think it has to do with money and love?" Kansas asked.

"Both do strange things to people, even if you have all you need in the world. I think a cockroach did the dirty work, but let's face it, with Kincaid out of the picture, there's a big hole in the power structure in the Knights not to mention his adult film business. Let's not forget where Kincaid met the plastic blonde bimbo downstairs. Chances are, she's been plotting with a blood leech. The other murders may all be to throw us off track."

"God, I can't believe what I'm hearing." Kansas looked at me peppered with anger.

"Perhaps it was to bring him over to the vampires," Price said as he moved close to me. "It would be a terrible waste to the vampires to have him be a mortal when he could aid a cause for eternity."

"If that was the case, Frank, they would have taken the body with them. They left it here for us to find. The body was never meant to rise again. Whoever did this wanted death to happen. Permanently. There was no afterlife in the cards for him."

"We'll get you a warrant for Sasha and Sylvester," Kansas added.

"I want one for Dubro too."

"He has an alibi."

"Kansas, his alibi was with Mrs. Kincaid. Find out where they went, what they did. Trusting in any of them is nothing short of stupid. I still say, sniff close to home."

"The family deserves their time to..." Dieter searched for the word, "grieve." He backed away from me, but I followed keeping the distance at a short range. "Allow the family this time, deny to the media that it was a vampire attack, and I'll sign the necessary paperwork. Open your mouth, and I'll make sure this is as complicated as it can get."

I looked back to Kansas and Price. "Are you hearing this? Tell me you're no longer in bed with the roaches and covering this up. You can't be serious about this."

"It was at the family's request that we are delaying the inevitable," Victor said.

"It's at my request, we are to handle this with sensitivity to keep any violence down," Kansas added.

I laughed. "Keep the violence down." I grabbed him by the neck and pushed him to the bed over Albert Kincaid's body. "Look at that. Look at that, Kansas. Doesn't it look to you as though violence might have already taken place? We have a dead man here, killed by a monster and you are siding with them. All the money and influence in the world won't change that. You can hide behind your lies of doing it for the family, but we both know this is cockroach driven from the beginning. Drag your feet on this all you want, but I'm telling you here and now, I won't back you up on your stories of what happened here. I don't care how hard the family is grieving, I won't watch you, the police and the cockroaches act like nothing happened here. The lies end here tonight."

Hands grabbed me and pulled both Kansas and me back up. "You're reading too much into this, Paul." This from Detective Price. "The family would simply prefer not to have cameras and microphones in their faces so soon after all this. This is going to be a media circus when it hits the fan."

"Maybe Mrs. Kincaid should look at this. Let her see what her cause is really about. Maybe if the pain sinks in, the reality will follow. Give these things all the rights to live you want, but it changes nothing. They are still cold blooded killers. Mark my words, she's not as innocent as you want her to be in this."

"It's not our place to judge her. Not now."

"Have a little bit of common sense, Paul," Kansas started. "How would you like it if you knew your spouse wasn't just killed in your bedroom, but beheaded as well? Let's show a little bit of compassion."

"I am showing compassion. Compassion for all of humanity. Now get those warrants put together now. For once in all of this, get your head out of Quinn's ass and help the people you serve."

"Get out!" Kansas yelled. His face showed the anger that always flowed near the surface. Hands twisted my shirt tight around my neck. "Get out now. I won't allow you to tell me or this investigation team what we will and will not do. You're a has been. A relic. And let's not forget the fact that you too have vampire virus running through your veins. Maybe we should be investigating you since you're all hell bound on this witch hunt."

"How dare you bring something like that up." I started to go for his throat when Price grabbed me. "You hate me right now because you know I'm right. I'm a constant reminder of how you sold out."

"I'd rather be a sellout than a cockroach," Kansas barked.

Price brought his elbow across Kansas' nose, breaking it. I know. I heard the damn thing snap. Did I mention how much I liked Price?

CHAPTER TWENTY

Kincaid had been dead two days now and he still consumed every waking minute and haunted every dream and nightmare. I should have been focused on finding not one, but two killer vampires, but instead, I wanted to just go and shake Kincaid until he woke up and ask him my million questions.

I got a call as I was driving along Orange Avenue. "Paul Isaac." It wasn't a question.

"Yeah?"

"Feel like saving a life?" The voice asked.

"Who is this?"

"Crimson Madness. Don't be late. Lives are now in your hands. And come alone."

The phone went dead. My body tensed.

Without hesitation I shifted the 'Cuda into high gear and allowed the engine to growl with excessive power. Time would tell if I was speeding towards saving a life or ending mine.

After paralleling the car next to the Crimson Madness, I put on the leather trench coat and loaded it with as much arsenal as I could. Chances were, I'd need it. There was no need to sneak or tip toe up to the door. The fang heads inside already knew I was here.

The Crimson Madness looked much different than it did the night of the killings. No longer was there red neon bathing the sky, glowing lights inside welcoming the tourists, or even the lines of well dressed patrons milling around. The Crimson Madness would still be closed for another two hours or so. Darkness draped over the already existing shadows. It stood out among the neon around it like a bruise.

After being happy with my firepower and other coffin crispy devices, I walked to the entrance and looked in circles, making sure there was nothing sneaking up on me. I pulled hard on the ten foot high glass doors. They were easily the heaviest doors I had ever come across. I was convinced there were people that had wanted to visit the gallery and had to walk away simply because they couldn't get inside.

As the large door shut behind me, I began to look around for hidden figures in the darkness, but found nothing more menacing than terribly bad art. There were no sounds. The limited light sources were the streetlights that soaked through the large panes of glass.

I walked over to the light switch and found it dead. By the empty sounds of the gallery, it was pretty clear that there was no electrical power.

In front of me, I saw a sign on a table. "Art to Die For, Featuring Paul Isaac." I slowly pulled the Magnum from its holster and eased a wooden stake from the trench coat. The signage said it all. Someone was about to die. The only question was who.

On the table were a large candle and a book of matches. My

paranoia shifted from a sneak attack to being set up as a game. One that would most definitely favored the monster hidden in the dark.

The only thing to do was play the game and see what happened. Announcing my arrival seemed trivial. Whatever wanted me here already knew my whereabouts and would make themselves known in due time. I returned the wooden stake to the trench coat and took a match from the book and lit it. The orange glow hit my eyes while the sulpher hit my nose. I lit the candle and had a small amount of flickering light.

Keeping my back as close to the walls as I could, I began to move down the hallway, in search of my future kill. At the end of the maze, I came to a new sign. "Want to keep Isabella alive?"

I looked at it and thought. I had a candle in one hand and the Magnum in the other. The last thing I wanted to do was compromise either one, but if there was a cockroach on the other side of the door, I'd fair much better with the Magnum than the candle. Looking around again, I sat the candle down and reached for the door knob and turned it.

The door gave way without a fight. Inside were hundreds more candles, glowing brightly. Heat hit me like opening an oven, but it was the power that caused me to stumble. It stung me like a swarm of bees, nearly bringing me to my knees.

Sylvester sat in an over sized velvet chair that made him appear almost noble. He sipped from a wine glass, but I had a bad feeling it wasn't fermented grapes in the liquid. Below him was a long and narrow table filled with countless candles and a man slumped over with a sack over his head. Dried blood stained his white shirt.

"So good to see you came with such haste," Sylvester said as he mocked a toast to me with the glass, then took a swig.

"Where is she?" I already had the Magnum on him. It was all I could do to keep my words from shaking as I spoke. Shadows hit the wall behind him and gave the illusion of others moving about in the room with us. I prayed they were no more than a distraction.

"Ahh, sweet Isabella. So young and so full of dreams. I would give anything to be that young and impressionable again, would not you, Avenger?"

"If you think I won't blow your head off right here, right now, you're sadly mistaken. Now if I were you I'd tell me where she is in order to stay alive."

"Not a fan of youth, Avenger?"

"One."

"Living forever is as close as you can get to it. You should try it one day."

"Two."

"I see." He motioned from a dark space to his left and held out his hand. Isabella walked to him and took his hand. She looked down. There was something about her that had changed. She looked pale in the limited light.

"Now let her go and we all leave with our heads," I finished.

He released her hand. "Here, you can take her. I've already fed tonight. She is of no use to me. She has done all I needed her to do."

Isabella refused to look me in the eyes. Tears welled and fell down her cheeks, but words didn't form and her feet never moved.

"Isabella, now would be a real good time to move toward me," I said as calmly as I could. She stood still. If it wasn't for the breathing, I wouldn't have known she was alive.

"You heard the Saint Avenger, Isabella. Do not keep him waiting." Sylvester gave her a light kick on the behind, sending her legs in motion towards me, but even then she stopped short.

Her eyes looked up to me for the first time, drowning in new tears. "I'm so sorry," she mouthed.

Heat sucked the air from my lungs as I looked around the room. It was filled with paintings from Dubro and candles every few inches, but it was the man at the table that my eyes kept coming back to. Keeping my eyes on Sylvester, I pulled Isabella to me. "Come on, we have to go now."

"He plans to kill you," she whispered.

"I kind of already figured that out. Why were you here?" I answered.

"To kill us. Surely you could have guessed that," this from Sylvester. So much for whispering. "Oh, come now, Avenger, do not look so surprised. You heard the beautiful, young woman yourself. Asking you to help her kill Dubro and myself." Sylvester threw the wine glass to the floor in a violent pitch. "You do not possibly think I or many of the powerful vampires did not know of her plans. She has tried to cut the throats of those that fed her. But it is you that I wanted to speak with, not some amateur vampire slayer."

"Now I'm here, so let her go safely."

He motioned her forward. "She is free to go. I have much larger bait."

"Couldn't pick up a phone like anyone else? Turned into a bat and flown over?"

"What? And miss your face?" In the shadows that played in the room I could see he was dressed in a burgundy silk suit with gold buttons. Long white hair flowed along his already pale face. They almost glowed against the dark clothing. Mirrored sunglasses caught the reflecting candlelight.

I pushed Isabella towards the hallway I had come up. Like a good little freak, she wasted no time in making her exit. I couldn't put my finger on it, but I didn't like Ms. Dunlawton. I didn't want her to become coffin bait, but I wasn't going to lose sleep over her either.

"Can I get you something to drink?" Sylvester asked as he looked at his own goblet.

I looked back to the man at the table. "What do you want?" His face was hidden. I kept an eye on him. For all I knew he was another blood muncher. "I'm sure you didn't bring me here to critique Dubro's art, so answer my question."

He looked back at me and gave me a boyish grin. "You are here for an opportunity to save human lives. I am surprised you have not figured that out yet."

"Really? And who's he?" Still looking at the man.

"Curiosity finally got to you. I'm surprised you do not recognize him." He stood and began to walk to the table where the man still sat silent and motionless.

"It's kind of hard when you've covered his head."

Sylvester pulled the man's head up and removed the burlap sack. I could see a gag in his mouth, dark with stains of blood. It was now that I felt everything in my body go numb.

"Kansas?" I said more than asked. His eyes were glassy and dilated. High on cockroach magic. In his current state, he couldn't hear me or see me. He was nothing more than a human rag doll.

"Ahh, it did not take you as long as I thought it might. You could say we were having lunch together. Now you know what is at stake." Sylvester flashed his big albino smile and released Kansas' head back down. It free fell with a violent thump.

I pulled the Magnum up on Sylvester and fired. My bullet missed him as he dashed behind Kansas and practically disappeared. Dead hands grabbed Kansas by the throat. Nails dug into skin.

"Perhaps you should listen to all I have to say before wasting all your bullets on something you can not kill. I do believe your friend's life will depend on you listening more than acting." He remained in my line of fire. I couldn't get the shot off.

I kept the Magnum up on Sylvester all the same. "I'm taking him with me. There'll be no negotiations or talks. One of us would be alive and the other dead. Simple as that.

"If you do as I say, he will be yours to do with as you like."

"I'm not at your beck and call, Sylvester. I'll take him and I'll take him now." I began to move toward Kansas with big steps. I wasn't going to wait for him to make the first move.

In a single leap he jumped over Kansas and was on me. His fist hit me like a ton of bricks. I could feel every bone in my body jar. Stinging strikes of pain dug into my bones. The second blow struck from behind. Knocking me the rest of the way to the floor. I opened my mouth to gasp for air, but I couldn't. It was as if invisible hands had clamped around my throat.

I saw his boots. I closed my eyes. I knew what was coming next. The boot caught me just under the chin and flipped me on my back after an extended amount of time flying through the air. I pulled the trigger on the Magnum again, only to hear it hit a hollow wall. Isabella screamed in the distance.

"Do you wish to listen to me, rather than to die?" he asked. "As you would say, it does not matter to me either way." His mouth was inches from my ear as I continued to lie on the floor. The smell of blood on his breath overwhelmed me.

I did my best to come to my feet. I could feel my face swell. I pulled a crucifix from my pocket and held it tight. If I got close enough, I'd ram it down his throat.

"Still believing you can defeat me with your trinkets, Avenger? You know those things do not work on us unless you truly believe." He moved just out of reach. "Here you are hell bent on dying and you are the only one that can save your friend. Such a shame."

"What do you want with him?"

"It's not really him I want. He is simply insurance."

I moved the Magnum on him again and was about to pull the trigger when out of the darkness came two other blood drinkers. I swallowed hard. This was about to get ugly . . . for me.

CHAPTER TWENTY-ONE

One was Sanguine and the other was Victor, the roach I had a run in with a few years back before the laws went into effect. He, along with a few of his disgusting friends, had fed on a woman when they unfortunately ran into me. After killing his accomplices, I began to interrogate Victor, hoping to find the rest of the coven. He refused to be a good informant and I proceeded to pour holy water laced with silver over his head until he gave me the answers I was satisfied with. He was able to break free, but not until I had disfigured his face so badly that there was nothing left but muscle and bone. Since a dirt napper cannot die from a loss of flesh or infection, and a wound produced from silver never heals, Victor now lives with the permanent open wounds of my destruction.

"We have brought you here to take advantage of your services," Sylvester responded.

I continued to look at the other cockroaches that had gathered in the room, filling it with far more power than I had ever felt at the Crimson Madness a few nights earlier. At least six now stood looking back at me. I could see Victor's cheekbone through the hole in his skin, red with wet blood that would never stop running. He stared at me like a wounded dog. "What about my services would ask of that would get you killed?"

"We have tried to be patient and come to a truce with Sasha and the pure bloods, but have found them to be non-sympathetic to our requests. So now it is up to you to bring about a resolution to all of this."

"You mean Asa."

He nodded. "Indeed."

"And what does that have to do with me? I didn't arrest him."

"I am quite aware of that, Avenger. But with Asa's arrest, a new door of opportunity and demise has been opened. Now it is up to you to settle all the debts the police have left unpaid."

"Seems to me that Quinn has the police department in his back pocket. You could have gone to him and saved us both a lot of time. Now your only option is me staking you."

"His motives and mine are distinctly different. Quinn is nothing short of a procrastinating coward. Now Asa and Sasha have declared war. As long as Asa remains under arrest, the pure bloods find hope in their cause to kill all commercial vampires and regain their non-human status."

"Don't worry about that, Sylvester. I plan to take away the hope for all of you, given the chance."

"We both find ourselves in a unique situation. If he is freed, the pure blood vampires will be at our throats and if he is to stay in custody, they will be at the humans' throats. Now we are on the brink of war and you have the power to stop it. Whether Asa is freed or not will determine who will hold the advantage in this city. I think you would agree, over all, we are the least vicious among the general public and the most law abiding. I am offering an alliance with you and the humans against the pure bloods if Asa is killed for the deaths of the Knights."

"I can't believe what I'm hearing. You seem to think I really care which side wins and which side loses. You're all cockroaches to me. Whether you die and rise as roaches or are spit out of their mother's womb makes no difference to me. As for the police, they don't get my sympathy either. They're just as much to blame for all the tension as anyone."

"We want you to make sure that Asa never leaves the jail alive. The pure blood vampires look to him for guidance and leadership. Without him, they will fall like a house of cards and the danger they pose to our kind will be lost. We plan to cut the head off of their existence as you might say. For your help, we will make sure the pure bloods do not start war with the humans."

"So you're doing it for humanity. Is that it?"

He smiled. "It is all about timing, Avenger. If done properly, the pure bloods will attack each other for power or possibly attack Quinn in retaliation. Either way, the distraction will buy my vampires much needed time."

I took a step toward Kansas. "So you're hoping that by having Asa killed, the pure bloods will assassinate Quinn and you will be the new healing leader."

He paused for effect. "Look at it this way, Avenger. You will have your revenge and save this man's life all in a single act. It is no secret that you would want nothing more than see Quinn dead after what he did to you."

I looked around the room trying to figure out how I was going to kill Sylvester and the other monsters in the room. Being out numbered was nothing new. Being out numbered and having to save Kansas was. Falling just below the gaze of Sylvester, I could see the soulless creature that hid behind that deadly smile.

"And if I don't go along?" I finally spoke.

Victor interrupted. "Simple. We kill him. Suck him dry while you helplessly watch. Think you can cut his head off, knowing you could have saved him?" The monster looked at me. "Do not think I have forgotten what you did to me," he said pointing to his oozing face.

"It's an improvement if you ask me."

He took a step toward Kansas.

Sylvester raised his hand. "Must we go through all this again? It seems it would be so much easier to do what we ask than have us kill both, you and the detective. You will save this man's life by simply doing nothing."

"That's where you're so wrong, Sylvester. Bringing me here only saved me a little time hunting you down."

He took another sip from the cup and ran a finger along the table next to Kansas as he strolled. "You know nothing of what you speak." He purposely turned his back on me. It almost looked like an act of boredom, but I knew better. His white hair sparkled in the candlelight, almost reflective catching all the other colors in the room. "All vampires, commercial or pure blood, are not the killers you try to portray. It is nothing more than silly superstitions humans have made up over the years."

"Bet your victims would disagree."

"We could say the same about you," Sanguine said as she stepped out of the shadows. She smiled as she moved next to Sylvester. "I told you I would kill you one night, and it looks like that night might have come sooner than I thought." With a swanky walk she moved to Kansas. I gripped my Magnum. She looked back to me. "And now, it looks like I get to kill your friend as a bonus." She played with Kansas' hair as she spoke. He breathed in deep. I had to find a way to get him out of here in one piece. Trouble was, I wasn't sure how to get myself out of here in one piece. Sanguine kissed Kansas on the cheek. Her body grew rigid as she now stood looking straight at me. "I can taste your fear, executioner. Death is near."

"I agree. Yours." It was growing hard to keep my back to all the bloodsuckers. "What do you know about Kincaid's death?" Time to see which fang freak blinked.

She laughed. "I know nothing of his death. But if the occasion has arisen, it is you that would come to mind first."

"How so?"

"It was you that threatened the life of Albert Kincaid and you know more about vampire attacks than any other human. You have more motive than anyone."

"Given the choice, I'd had him committed, not killed." I began to move forward, towards Kansas. Victor flanked my move. Out of the blood suckers before me, I wasn't sure which would make the first move. My gut told me it wouldn't be Sylvester. He had far too much to lose by attacking. He still counted on my alliance, not to mention becoming Orlando's newest master daisy pusher.

"Perhaps a certain priest has told you of your linage. One that had you so enraged that you killed Albert Kincaid. As I have heard said before, dead men tell no tales. A secret so well known in the vampire nation that it is almost comical that you have remained in the dark."

You know it to be true, do you not? Killed him to protect the honor of your pathetic father." Victor moved away from the puddle of infectious puss and blood at his feet.

Again, a laugh escaped Sanguine's mouth. "I think your father, or should I say the man you thought was your father, was the only one left in the dark. I think the vampires killed him out of pity, not revenge."

I moved the Magnum on her. She quickly had her fingernails dug in the side of Kansas' neck. Half moon cuts instantly began to bleed. "Be careful, Avenger, or you may find yourself in a condition worse than the detective. He is temporarily under my magic. I assure you that he is fine for now. Anytime after that depends upon you. His well being will be your motivation to act intelligently."

"He appears to be bleeding. Most people that are bleeding aren't fine."

"We got hungry," Victor said. "Tasted like chicken."

I shot the Magnum at him, catching just enough of his shoulder that it brought about blood, but not enough to kill him. He lunged over the candle lit table, nails drawn, looking more like a rabid tiger than a coffin muncher.

The puss head landed on me, his face only inches from mine. Long, sharp fangs appeared near my throat. I forced my arm against his chest, trying to hold off the attack. A single drop of blood fell from his facial wound and landed on my forehead. I got instant willies as I felt it run to the back of my head. The large hole in his right cheek exposed his teeth and jawbone as saliva trickled from the opening.

Before his jaws could latch onto my throat, I lifted him up and pushed as hard as I could, upward. Razor sharp fingernails missed me by the thinnest of margins. He crashed hard on the floor behind me and slid to the wall.

I wasted no time in bringing out a crucifix and wrapped it around his neck. He screamed as it sizzled against his skin in instant blisters. Those same razor sharp fingernails reached for the chain. I kept it pulled tight, keeping him under control. Pulling the crucifix to his skin.

While he was still on his knees, I kicked him with everything I had and catapulted him onto a table filled with candles. Hot wax poured over his already open wounds. Caked globs of hotness stuck to his skin like grotesque blisters. Flames lit on his skin for a second, before burning out. The smell of burnt hair filled the room. Puking was a possibility now. I put the Magnum back in its holster and pulled a wooden stake from my trench coat. Tonight, I was going to kill him old school. From my experiences, it was far more painful. Just the way I liked it. I moved over top of him. Both hands gripped to the stake.

Victor's eyes were still wide with anticipated death. He remained still. Both undead and living hands wrapped tight around the wood. Not knowing if I would be able to get the stake to his heart or not.

"Now what was it you were saying about killing me?" I said to Victor. He never answered back. Verbally, that is. A swift kick to my groin shot me backwards.

Sylvester was on top of me, now with the stake in his own hands, pointed at my chest. "If you do not mind, Avenger, I would like to finish our conversation as civil as possible. I do not wish to kill you tonight, but I will if it is warranted. I have already wasted too much time with you. You either do as I say, or we kill detective Kansas. It really is that simple."

I started to laugh. "You think you're really smart don't you? You're telling me you want Asa to stay behind bars knowing I will do everything I can to do the exact opposite."

"I do not do mind games or Freudian exercises. Met the man, not a big fan. Now, if you don't mind, you need to talk to the police and make sure my demands are met or prepare for Mr. Kansas' funeral."

"I want to know that he's all right."

"You can take my word for it."

"I don't think so." For a change, I was hoping the wolf in me kicked in. Being hit and kicked this many times in the face and between the legs was starting to hurt. A lot.

Sylvester yanked the stake from my hands and threw it to the floor. He turned away and moved back to the far side of the table. "You presume to think that you are in charge here, Mr. Isaac but I assure you, you are not. There is a human life in the balance and you seem to only toy with it. You only have the illusion of choice in this matter."

"That's where you're wrong Sylvester. It's you that's playing with life." I looked back to Kansas, then trying to watch the other vampires as well. "You've kidnapped a police officer and fed from him. This time tomorrow, I'll have all your heads on a stick. Even if your twisted plan of becoming a master vampire are fulfilled, you will be a hunted maggot muncher." I smiled wide. "And killing you will be inside the human laws."

"You are wasting time, Avenger. Vampire word travels fast. Especially when it involves a master vampire such as Asa. Detective Kansas' life depends on your haste. Others wishing to aspire to master vampire will not be as accommodating to you and the humans."

"I'm not leaving without him."

"It is non-negotiable." Candlelight bloomed in the room far brighter than it had been. At second glance, it wasn't more candlelight, it was fire. The exit was now an orange glow of heat. Some son of a bitch had set the Crimson Madness on fire!

CHAPTER TWENTY-TWO

I instantly searched for Kansas. Even in the glow of the fire, things just out of its reach remained pitch black. Confusion instantly took over. Not only from me, but from the solar crispies as well. Keep in mind, cockroaches can catch fire too. Sylvester was far more twisted than I had thought. Not only had he frolicked through the city killing members of the Knights of the Night, he was going to burn the vampires, Kansas and myself, as well as the gallery of his lover.

I looked at the table where Kansas had been. Yes, that's right. Had been. He was gone. I looked among the scrambling monsters as the heat and smoke continued to engulf the gallery.

A large cockroach landed on me from somewhere in the blackness. Fangs ready to sink into skin. I pulled the Magnum up and put it against his throat. Without hesitation, I pulled the trigger. I felt him lift off of me as the bullet plowed through his chest.

As he fell beside me, I continued to move back toward the table that had suddenly been overturned by coffin heads trying to escape the fire. I couldn't find Kansas. I found myself with no clear sense of thought or direction.

Another fang freak came at me. I pulled the Magnum up on him and was about to pull the trigger. A shot caught him in the ribs. He fell to the floor in a series of screams. The shot wasn't fatal. Whoever had delivered the bullet wasn't using the right firepower. Before the monster could come back to his feet, I put him out of his misery.

From my right, I saw the source of the extra firepower. Isabella. She shot as quickly as she could and had been fairly accurate, but without the right bullets, she was going to do nothing short of getting herself killed.

I pulled the 9mm from my hip holster. It had silver nitrate bullets. Not lethal to a night dweller, but it would cause enough pain that it bought time. I began to shoot anything that moved. Magnum in my right hand, 9mm in the left.

With as much speed as I could manage, I began to move toward Isabella. There was only seconds before the coffin munchers would realize that she was no threat to them. Sure she meant well, I guess, but give me a break. I had already gotten her out of here once and that was usually my limit. Call me ungrateful if you want, but face it, this chick has her own agenda of killing the daisy pushers. I'm sure she's not here for me. Coincidence at best.

Her eyes met mine. The fear in our eyes reflected on our faces as we moved toward the exit of the room. "Here take this," I said as I shoved the 9mm in her left hand.

"I have a gun," she said.

I grabbed the gun and threw it. "It won't do anything except get you killed. Regular bullets don't kill vampires. Don't you know anything?"

I pulled a vial of holy water from my pocket and sprayed it in the eyes of the approaching vampires. I dowsed the second vial on

Isabella and myself. It would be a deterrent at best, but when you're out numbered like we were, you improvise the best you can.

She took the gun and we continued to move down the hallway dodging biting flames. The vampires moved with us. Being equally combustible, they were simply trying to escape the fire as well.

A vampire landed on Isabella's back and attempted to bite. The barrel of my Magnum met his skull. "Say goodnight." I pulled the trigger and he evaporated like a good little batboy.

Isabella jumped to her feet and brushed away the fallen ash from the dead vein licker. She looked at me and started to say something but I interrupted her. "What are you doing here? I thought I told you to get out of here."

"Killing vampires, same as you."

"No, the only thing you're doing is getting yourself killed." I pulled her down the long hallway toward the outside of the Crimson Madness. She looked up at me. "Where's Dubro?"

"Dead I hope." I looked down at the 9mm still in her hand. "Give me that," I finished as I took it and stuck it back in my hip holster.

"He wasn't here? Do you know where he is?"

"We didn't exactly get that far in the conversation. I was trying to save the life of a friend, not help you cash in on an opportunity."

She remained silent. I didn't have time to worry about her and her flamboyant boss. I had to find Sylvester. I led her outside and let go of her hand. I heard the first sounds of the sirens moving in the night. They wouldn't be able to save much of the gallery, but I didn't see all the harm in that. I had been inside the Crimson Madness twice and both times I had to fight my way back out. Let it fall to ashes for all I cared.

I felt the fist hit me before I saw the monster. It was all I could do to keep from falling to the ground. It was the most wonderful sneak attack ever. With all the strength I had, I fought back. I hit it in the ribs followed by a swift kick to his knee. It buckled it the wrong way. He hit the sidewalk with a scream of pain. His hands went for the knee, my hands went for the 9mm. Again, I didn't want him dead just yet.

I stuck the barrel of the 9mm in his back. Placed my body weight on him. Knee firmly in his spine. I could have tried threats first before pulling the trigger, but what was the fun in that? I had a good friend in the hands of monsters. Being politically correct or law abiding wasn't going to save him.

The bullet hit in his kidney. More screams filled the night. Harmonizing with the sirens. Growing closer. Black and green fluid poured from the wound. "Now where did they take Kansas?"

My victim never answered. He tried to roll away from me, but with my new strength, I was able to hold him solid to the concrete. "You'll be too late to save him."

"Kill him," Isabella screamed from above. I hoped she was talking to me, but who knew with that crazy woman.

I pulled the cockroach from the ground by the collar. Rage didn't allow me to think clearly. Truth be told, I used it as an excuse. I put the gun against his head and spoke. "This is your last chance, before I do something really nasty to you. Now I want to know where Sylvester took Detective Kansas."

Red lights flashed against the white building that now was in a full blaze. I began to drag him to a more secluded area to finish my interrogation with as few of witnesses as possible. To help in my lack of time, I pulled the silver bladed knife from its sheath and drove it into the mangled knee. Ahh, the screams of pure pain.

"Forget the detective, ask him where's Dubro?" Isabella asked as she followed me into the semi-dark alley.

I looked up at her and nearly threw her back in the street. "You inconsiderate bitch. A man's life hangs in the balance. Think about doing more than making money off a dead artist. Get out of my sight before I put the next bullet in you."

Her face showed that I wasn't kidding. It was enough of a

distraction that the overgrown bat I had by the collar was able to break free. His long fingernails dug deep into my skin. Fangs only a breath away from breaking skin of their own. I brought the 9mm up and fired. He fell to the ground at my feet, writhing in pain as the silver slowly worked its magic. I stood over him as he bled silver nitrate and whatever else made up these things. "I'll not ask you again. Where did they take him?"

The coffin muncher knew I wasn't kidding. They may be soulless and evil, but they didn't like to face death anymore than we did. And he was naïve enough to think if he gave me the answer I wanted I would let him live. Gullible monster, no chance.

He looked at the gun and tried to decide how much he would have to divulge to stay alive. Answer? All of it. And even then he wasn't going to make it out alive. I shoved the gun into his cheek. "Live or die, you miserable vein weasel, it doesn't matter to me. I'll find him either way. The only difference is you have one option that will keep you alive and one that will get you killed so make a good choice."

Isabella began to run.

A part of me wanted her to go down in flames. Another liked her way of thinking. I had made my mind up on one thing. The next person to save her from the coffin bags wouldn't be me. I had done that enough.

The cockroach tried to use the diversion to make his move. His hands grabbed for the gun. A knee went into my stomach. His fangs snapped close to my skin. I shoved the gun deeper into his cheek. "Did you forget I had a gun still on you, you idiot?"

He laughed. "Like you said, Avenger, silver can't kill me."

I moved the 9mm to his chest over his heart and pulled the trigger. Blood shot from the wound. I was lucky enough to catch most of it. His eyes went hollow. His knees folded under him. "Shoot you in the heart and you die anyway," I said as he went limp.

I came back to my feet, only to see a well-dressed daisy pusher in front of me. Next to him, a small puddle of blood grew with each added drop. With all the speed I could muster, I brought the Magnum up on my next victim. My eyes followed the frame to the face. "Dieter." I stopped and stared at his hand.

He held the head of a blood muncher, eyes and mouth wide with the last drop of fear. Muscle and veins still twitched and dripped. It was enough of a distraction I forgot to pull the trigger.

"I see you got some head tonight," I said as I backed up a few feet.

"I hope you find yourself amusing, Avenger. I, on the other hand, do not."

I put the 9mm away, pulled the Magnum and placed it on his chest. "Unless you can tell me where to find Sylvester and Sanguine, you're a dead man. And even then, I may kill you for the hell of it."

He placed his hand on the Magnum and moved it away from his chest. His power slithered along my skin. It gave me the creeps. "Perhaps before shooting me, you should pay your gratitude."

He moved just enough that I could see a slumped figure bathed in the bright lights of an ambulance. Rescue workers feverishly worked on the scene.

I jumped to my feet and started to run to it. It was Kansas. He was bloody and unconscious. Dieter's pale dead hand reached out and stopped me, keeping me in the shadows. I looked back to Dieter.

"The detective is in capable hands. Keeping in the shadows will allow you your time for revenge. I assure you he will live." He looked down at the head of the dead maggot taxi. "I have taken care of the vampire that had him in dire straights. This shall allow you time for matters closer at hand."

"Thank you." I couldn't believe the words had spewed from my mouth. I had actually thanked a cockroach. Note to self: Wash my mouth out with soap. "Dieter, I hope you don't think this changes things between us. I will still kill you one day."

He smiled wide and nodded. "I will be looking forward to it, Avenger." So much for our budding friendship. The cockroach head fell to the ground with a hollow thump, dead eyes looking up at me. "But there is more."

"With you, there always is."

"I have already informed Detective Price, but wished to inform you as well." He gave a dramatic pause. A storm brewed in his dead eyes. "I am afraid there has been another child killed in the city."

I felt my body started to implode. I did the only thing that came natural. I grabbed Dieter by the collar. "Funny how every time there's another body, you're the first to know about it." I let him go and paced as I tried to collect my thoughts. Firemen and police began to move into the area to fight the flames and do crowd control. I'm not even sure anyone noticed the piles of ash that had been fang heads at one time. I wasn't going to confess to it. "As you can see, I don't have time for wild goose chases right now." I began to move from the alley as the fire continued to eat away at the Crimson Madness.

"I do not do wild goose chases. I simply came here to retrieve you from…" he looked at the flames that were licking their way out of the lower floor windows of the Crimson Madness and then back to me. "From this place. The sun will rise in under an hour and I will not be able to be there. I trust in you to make the best of decisions until nightfall."

I continued to watch the action around Kansas. I wanted to make sure he was okay, but I knew my advantage was keeping anyone from seeing me. Dead roaches and a burning roach gallery would raise a lot of questions for one, and two, I wanted to handle Sylvester and Sanguine all on my own with no authority any the wiser. Revenge would be sweet and secretive. No rules, all justice.

"There is more if you care to know." Dieter flanked my steps in the shadows. Like me, he didn't want to answer questions about his whereabouts tonight. His voice grew cold and matter-of-fact. "The small child may have links to both sets of killings."

My knees buckled and my head spun. I instinctively squeezed the butt of the Magnum. Why, I wasn't sure. Perhaps it was nothing more than my security blanket. Perhaps it was because I knew death had picked up speed and was knocking on my door. "Meaning not only the child killer but also the Knights of the Night?"

Dieter nodded.

"What makes you think that?"

"The child is the son of John Luvara."

"Attorney for the Knights."

Again, nothing more than a nod.

I started to speak when my cell phone rang. It was Price. The message was brief, but made Dieter's story a little more believable. The senior detective was crying and very upset. Like anyone else down here, finding a child is the ultimate nightmare.

I started to tell him about Kansas, only to find he wasn't really there. Besides, the last thing I wanted to do was add to his stress and give him a second heart attack. Let sleeping dogs lie is my motto. His voice was there, but the man itself was somewhere far away. I had a dilemma. Go after Sylvester or help with another murder involving a small child. This town was truly going to hell in a hand basket.

I turned to face Dieter. "How did you know where to find me?"

He looked at what was left of the Crimson Madness and the remains of dead daisy pushers, now nothing more than ash. "As I have told you so many times before, Avenger, all one needs to do is follow the dead bodies."

CHAPTER TWENTY-THREE

I arrived at the house just as the sun rose. To the outside world it was a nice normal day. But there was a family nearby that was grieving the loss of their child. Unlike the last crime scene I attended, there were plenty of patrol cars and unmarked vehicles in the area. One lone ambulance. For once, the crime scene was not being treated like a secret.

Getting out of the car was something I dreaded. Not that I doubted my feelings when seeing the dead body, but instead that I wouldn't have any feelings when seeing it. I had been around death for so long that I feared growing jaded by the scene.

I saw Price sitting on the hood of one of the patrol cars. He looked over at me, but never made a move to meet me or even acknowledge I was there. Even from a distance I could see the redness in his eyes. He had been crying and was visibly upset. Usually even in the coldness of death, he was a warm spot. Not today.

I did the only thing I knew to do. I went to him and put my arm around his shoulder and gave him a hug. He looked at me and began to cry again. "He was just a baby. How could anyone do that to a baby? I have a grandson about that age."

"How old?"

"Five."

My heart sank. Even the most ruthless cockroaches stayed away from small children. It was almost like a code among the monsters. Kids were off limits, no matter what. And now, I was about to be face to face with the second victim of an attack.

"You have to get this guy Paul," Price finished. His voice was so distant it didn't sound real.

"I will." I lit a cigar to calm my bucket of nerves. I paced in front of the yard as I watched the officers and medics move in and out of the home. "Anything you can tell me before I go in there?"

"The vampire didn't feed off the boy."

I turned to face Price as I let out the first lung full of smoke. "What did you say?"

"The vampire. He didn't feed off the boy. Simply drained his blood in the tub."

My mouth moved but nothing came out at first. I must have heard it wrong. "What do you mean the cockroach drained the blood?"

"The boy was bitten on the jugular and laid down in the bathtub to bleed to death. I've never seen anything like it in all my years on the force. There are signs that whoever did it, bathed with the dead body and blood." He took his glasses off and wiped his eyes. "What kind of monster would do this kind of thing to a child?" He looked down at the cigar. "Finish smoking that thing and get in there. I want this over as soon as possible." I took a drag from the cigar, placed it on the driveway, and walked toward the house.

No one had to tell me there had been a brutal murder in the house. I could smell it. Blood had an unmistakable odor as recognizable as frying bacon. Everything in the house seemed to have a covering of death on it. Like a spider web, it wrapped around you and stayed there.

Usually when I came to a crime scene, there was conversation about everything from sports to politics going on. Either the officers and paramedics were so jaded that nothing shocked them anymore, or they were trying to keep the scene from haunting them in their dreams. This morning, things were different. No one spoke a word. It was as if this one life had stopped all life from going on.

I moved down the hall behind Price and through the bathroom door, trying to think of anything that might help me from either puking or screaming.

"This is what we've got," Price said as he hitched up his pants and played with his tie. I could see the horror written on his face and couldn't blame him. He turned to hide the tears that instantly welled in his eyes.

Like Price said, the boy was lying in a pool of his own blood, eyes hollow and staring toward the ceiling. His little mouth was wide open as if screaming in silence. There was no innocence in his face anymore. Death had come slow and painfully. His body looked stiff. The skin slimy and unreal.

"How long has he been dead?" I asked.

"We're thinking over twelve hours."

"Twelve hours! Where were his parents when all of this happened?"

"They don't remember anything. Just woke up this morning and this is what they found. According to them, they think they were induced with vampire magic."

"They *think* that's what happened? They don't know?"

"I guess not."

"You buy their story?" I didn't yet.

"I don't know. Can something like that really happen?"

I shrugged. "I'm not sure. Cockroach magic is real, but they should've had some recollection as to who put them under. Usually the victim will remember who they were with before the magic hits them. It's just the time while under the magic they don't recall."

"This doesn't seem to have a lot in common with the other death. Nothing about the two bodies are the same. Including how they died and how the body was left."

"I can tell there's a 'but' coming."

Price's eyes darted around the room as if looking for a place to escape. Finally, he shook his head. "Yeah, there's a 'but'. The Crimson Madness burned to the ground this morning."

I tried to look surprised and was smart enough not to divulge any more information than I would have to. With any luck, no one had told him about Kansas or me being there. "I'm not following."

There was a new look in his eyes. One that left me with an uncomfortable feeling. "We've connected a few dots that are a bit disturbing and damning." His voice fell to a whisper. "Remember the Guzman kid?"

I shook my head. "Of course. The other child that was murdered." Still, I was having a hard time following Price's logic.

"Seems as though Mr. Guzman was in a skin flick with under aged girls and vampires not long ago. The film company was Kincaid's." He stopped long enough for it to sink in. "Now, on top of that, somebody burned down one of the safe houses that does some of the filming, killed a few vampires and threatened the lives of a few young actresses."

I began to shake. All the evidence was shifting to yours truly. I slapped my forehead. "That's why Guzman was so hell bent on finding Kincaid and killing him beside all the blood suckers. He was tying up loose ends just like the daisy pushers are." I looked back to Price. "But Price...I...I never..."

He threw up a hand. "I don't think you had anything to do with the deaths of the kids. No way. I'm just telling you all this because people are starting to talk. We have a couple of girls that say you were at the safe house going ballistic, not to mention killing. Quinn

Rubio has told us that Albert Kincaid might have been linked to your mother's death and someone may have told you." I opened my mouth to speak, but again, he put up a hand. "I know, I know, you didn't kill him. Just telling you how all this looks. Now I'm going to tell you something else that you can trust I'll take to the grave. Dieter says he found you not far from the Crimson Madness shortly after it burned to the ground and the gallery might have been funded by Kincaid. Tell me you didn't have anything to do with it."

I was having fantasies of killing Dieter. He had done his part of setting me up for this. "Frank, I was there, but I didn't burn it to the ground. It was Sylvester and Sanguine that did that honor. I didn't kill Kincaid and killing those roaches at the safe house was justified. They were feeding and having sex with under aged girls on film. The law is very clear on that."

"So you have proof that that was what was going on? The girls say otherwise."

"It's on film." I stopped, knowing that all my evidence was now nothing more than melted debris. "Let's look at this differently. We have someone that killed the Guzman girl because her dad was playing around in under aged porn, a man that was making a lot of money off of it, and now a lawyer's son that is dead perhaps because he is the lawyer representing NecroPussy. Sounds to me as though our killer is a little disgruntled. This isn't about cockroach rights or the Knights at all. It's about keeping dirty secrets quiet."

Price shook his head. "You don't have much time. I can't keep the lid on what I know forever. You have to get me the real killer or I'll have two in my jail that are innocent in this. I can only give you twenty-four hours."

I reluctantly shook my head and looked along the walls and floor for any signs of prints. Nothing. It was as if the monster had floated out of the room. I needed undisputable hard evidence that Sylvester and Sanguine were in on these killings or I'd be making license plates for the rest of my pathetic life. "Thank you, Frank. I'll find those responsible for this. You know that." I looked at the bathtub full of blood. I could smell it and it didn't repulse me. In fact, I could taste the extra saliva form in my mouth as though I had smelled a well prepared steak. But this was no steak. I closed my eyes tight. It was the undead virus running through my veins. I would never become a blood bank, but I would always be a carrier of the disease. I could feel the sweat run down my scalp. My hands were gripped tight to the towel bar above the toilet, aching to let go and dip a finger in the red liquid. I refused to give in to the temptation. I was too human for that. I looked out the window to distract myself. "The sun's up. I'll be able to move through the city without any problems. Keep the police off my back and I'll make sure the bastards talk." I began to walk away from the bathroom. "I need to go. There's a special monster I need to see right away. I think he might know something about this."

"Paul," I heard from behind me as I began to walk out of the bathroom. I turned to face Price. "Please, no more dead bodies without a warrant. I don't like doing this, even if they deserved it. I need everything to be on the up and up. Got it?"

"Then I need a warrant for Sylvester and Sanguine. If I don't find them today, I'll sure as hell need it tonight."

"What about the boy?" Price asked as he followed me.

"What about him?" I turned to see an uneasy look on Price's face.

"Don't you need to do something?"

"Meaning cut his head off?"

He shook his head.

"No. He didn't die from a cockroach bite. He died from a loss of blood. He won't rise as the undead."

CHAPTER TWENTY-FOUR

As I moved down a block off of the famed coffin condo high rises on Orange Avenue, just north of the hospital, I could see the emergency vehicles. Traffic in the area had come to a standstill as officers and medical staff directed cars down alternate streets. I popped the clutch on the 'Cuda and parked it along the sidewalk. I would easily be able to walk to the condo building quicker than wait through the traffic.

I had been on the phone with Stephanie, Zeke Kansas' wife, checking on his condition. Seems as though he was going to pull through, but it didn't make my anxiety and less. I was being pulled in two directions. To my right, was the condo of the finger painter Dubro and his soon to be dead lover, Sylvester. Every part of my being said to take care of business, that Kansas was in good hands, but I kept hearing Price in my head and saw those squinting eyes. No more dead vampires! And he was right. I had to be patient and wait for the timing to come to me.

I saw several officers move in and out of the parking lot like ants as they tried to secure the area the best they could. The fifteen-story condo sat on top of the garage like a large mother hen, looking out over the city. It stood out like a sore thumb. There were no windows. Something about sunlight and burning the occupants, I don't know. The condo association called it an added precaution, I called it a missed opportunity. My steps quickened as I approached. For this much activity in front of a roach condo building in the afternoon, something was big. My pace slowed as I took all the activity in.

A hundred feet ahead of me, I saw Officer Rook. I had known her for about two years. She usually worked the monster beat involving a homicide. Rook had been an active member of the Tortured Skin case. Again, things looked grim for someone. I kept my fingers crossed it was a monster that had bit the big one.

"Paul, thank God you're here. I can't get a hold of Price," Terry Rook said as she walked to me. I could see a hint of panic in her face. Another sign that things were not good for someone or something. "You seen him?"

I shook my head no simply because I didn't want to get into the questions that would follow. I watched as the police and lab workers moved into the garage. "What's going on here?"

"Like you haven't heard?"

Should I? I thought. I simply shook my head as I scanned the area.

"Someone attacked and killed Dubro. Shot his limo to hell," she said. "Burned his gallery to the ground. Both the building and body are now nothing more than piles of ash. Way too convenient to be a coincidence."

I tried to speak but the words lodged in my throat. I wanted to follow her, but my legs wouldn't move. "Dubro's dead?" *Isabella,* I thought again. All this time I thought she was nothing more than words, but now...

Rook looked back at me still standing in the same spot she had left me. "Come on, Paul," she said as she held up the yellow tape that separated the crime scene from the media whores and onlook-ers. "You can't tell me this is all that big of a surprise to you. I know what happened to Kansas and know you were there."

I shook my head and let sleeping dogs lie. I knew the more I tried to convince her I was innocent, the guiltier it would make me look. Besides, I wanted to see this for myself. I forced my legs to move. My heart raced with excitement and anxiety.

As we made our way to the first floor garage, the officers and paramedics grew thicker, but through an opening I could see the long black limo, mortally wounded with several bullet holes. I could see my own reflection in the carefully waxed paint and I didn't like what I saw. Sounds echoed loudly against the smooth concrete, caused me to jump needlessly from time to time.

"Who would kill him like this? I mean, my God, he was just an artist." Rook looked at the carnage ahead of her. I still wasn't sure if she embraced the monsters or hated them. She was so politically correct around them it sucked. I could tell she was waiting for a confession. I simply shook my head.

"Just because he dabbles in finger paints doesn't mean he's not a monster."

"Seriously, Paul, only an angry person would do something like this. Anyone come to mind?" Again, camouflaged accusations.

"He was a vein freak, self indulged, self centered, rich and greedy." I looked at Rook. "Nope, no one comes to mind." I smiled and pointed to a camera mounted high on the garage wall. "Any witnesses?"

"No. Whoever did this, knew the building and the security cameras pretty well. The whole thing happened in a small sliver of area where the cameras don't get. We could see the limo getting shot up, but the shooter was out of range. Pretty convenient, don't you think. "

I stopped just short of the limo and looked at the bullet holes. I counted four. "Dubro the only one that was killed in this?" I gingerly stepped over the nuggets of glass that littered the ground.

Rook shook her head. "Dubro and his driver. Whoever did it knew what it took to bring down a vampire. Someone that knew their weapons and how to use them." She cleared her throat and peeked up at me and blocked the sun from her eyes with her right hand. "Whoever it was, was using ultra violet bullets. There's nothing left of Dubro other than ash on the back seat."

"What about the driver?"

"He's human. Or I should say *was* human. Shot in the head. You know as well as I do that ultra violet bullets will kill us just as easily as a traditional bullet."

"So there's your answer Rook. I didn't do this. All your investigating and questions can rest. I don't smoke humans." Might as well let her know I saw through her carefully worded interrogation.

Rook remained at attention and shook her head. "I have two young girls that filled out statements that say otherwise." She shrugged and began to move closer to the limo.

I stopped her with my hand. "Big difference between that and this. I was trying to scare those girls into making better judgments. In the end, they and their parents will thank me for it and you know it. Besides, unless you know something I don't, they don't have bullet holes in the side of their heads." I looked ahead to the crime scene. "This I had nothing to do with. My hands are clean." Rook shook her head as she took everything in. "Anyone talk to Sylvester?" I asked for my personal agenda, but it made me appear the concerned and thorough man I never was. I hoped he was still at large. If he was in custody, it would make it a bit more awkward to torture and kill him.

"We have people working on it, but so far nothing." She stopped and gave me that same look Price had given me earlier. I immediately grew tense. "Paul, I need to ask you a difficult question. We will find him won't we?"

"No, I didn't kill him. I'd been a lot more thorough than this."

"I have to ask." She gave a fake smile and we both pretended to believe one another. I wanted to move closer to the scene. Rook remained planted. "Then how did you know about this? You know what they say about a killer returning to the scene of a crime."

"Proven false. Saw it on *Myth Busters.* I was actually going to see Kansas at the hospital. Ran up on this by accident." Her face remained unchanged. "Then I was going to come here and ask Sylvester a few questions about Kincaid's death. Seems he and Kincaid were supposed to have a meeting the night he died." I looked toward the limo again. Anxiety was building in me. I wanted to see for myself that the daisy pusher was truly dead. "And now I'm not convinced he's not covering all his tracks. Dead cock-roaches tell no tales."

"That's it?" Still a non-believer.

I shook my head. "No. Then I was going to kill him."

She simply stared at me while the wheels turned in her head. "I just think this is more than a lover's quarrel. This was violent and ugly. I just don't see it."

"I wouldn't rule it out. He is a blood sucker after all. Loyalty isn't their strongest trait. And he did try to kill Kansas for Christ's sake. So don't put him up on some pedestal like a choirboy." I swam with my own thoughts of Isabella. I felt guilty not saying anything, but I wanted to talk to her first. For the life of me though, I wasn't sure how she could pull something like this off by herself. She didn't have a clue on killing blood bats. "With any luck, maybe whoever killed Dubro, wasted Sylvester too. Fang head nearly got us all killed the other night at the Crimson Madness."

"That's why when I saw this, I immediately thought of you. There's been a few rumors circulating and your name comes up a lot." She gave a nervous laugh. "The department, Quinn and the Council have asked us to follow you." She stopped. "Off the record."

I didn't laugh back. It was a sensitive subject at the moment. I was losing allies faster than I wanted to think about. "So you do think I had something to do with all this don't you?" I took a deep breath and tried not to allow my emotions to take over. I felt as though every pair of eyes at the crime scene were focused on me.

She shrugged. "I'm not pointing any fingers. I'm simply asking so I know what not to do and what questions not to ask. I don't want to find any evidence that might link you to this. From what I hear you've made some big threats." Rook looked at the other officers still in the distance. "I don't think you did this, but if you did, you have to help me dispose of anything that I might find."

I couldn't believe what I was hearing. "Rook, you know me. Yes, I'm a bastard from time to time, stretch the rules a lot, shoot off at the mouth, but straight up murder? Come on, you know better than that."

"I want to believe it. I just need to hear it from you, so I know where I stand."

I tried to read her face. I couldn't. I never realized how guilty I sounded until I ran it back in my head. Now, even I was doubting myself. I looked at the bullet holes in the limo again. The best way of clearing my name was to find the real killer. Isabella was becoming more than a pain in the rear. She had stepped into murder. Cockroach murder, mind you, but murder all the same. And the trail of dead vein weasels were becoming an albatross around my neck.

Something about this didn't look like her work. She would have been able to get closer to him than start shooting through a limo's window. I shoved the thoughts out of my mind. First things first. "Can I look inside?"

"I'm not supposed to let you, but unless someone gets antsy, go ahead. Just don't touch anything yet. The photographer and forensics still have work to do." Rook opened the door with a gloved hand and ushered me in. I looked at the freckled woman in front of me and smiled. She always seemed in a good mood even in the middle of things like this. Unlike me, she wasn't jaded, cynical, and angry. I nodded back as I stuck my head in.

Inside the back of the limo was filled with dried blood and ash. Two bullet holes were found in the back of the seat. The two bullets I was assuming had killed Dubro. I moved my head back out of the car. "You did get those bullets didn't you?"

She shook her head. "They won't be a match with your bullets will they?"

I started to speak, feeling anger and hurt battling inside. I balled my fists tight in frustration. Rook had already judged me and nothing short of a confession by the real killer would change her mind. And I wasn't convinced that would do it.

Again she shook her head and this time, touched my arm. "The press and the vampire community will jump to the same conclusions and you know it. I don't mind sticking my neck out for you, but if I do, don't make me look like a fool." Nice recovery even if it was nothing more than lip service.

I had to give her this. She was a good liar. "I'll bring it by the station later."

She continued to stare at me.

"What?" I asked.

"Did you burn the Crimson Madness down this morning?"

I snapped to attention. "No. Sylvester did that. He's the one that took the chunk out of Kansas' neck. I was there to save him. Seems Dubro's partner is not only a killer, but also a pretty thorough pyromaniac."

"Why would he burn down his lover's gallery? That doesn't make any sense."

I looked back to the camera for a better angle on where the shooter might have been. "Common sense and fangs aren't the best of bedfellows. Seems he had Kansas as insurance that the police would make Asa go away. He plans to be the new big Kahuna in these parts. Things got a little out of control and Sylvester lit the place up and took Kansas with him."

"How'd you get him back, then?" For the first time, I saw nothing more than the simple question. No accusations or threats.

I stalled as I thought about every lie I could muster. "Dieter killed the vein leech that was holding Kansas. Without Dieter's help, we might have lost him." I shrugged. "Simple as that." I didn't feel like taking the conversation any further and simply shut up. I tend to do that when I get cornered with someone that has more intelligence than me, which is why I talk to as few people as possible. I looked back at the limo. "And you're saying with all the gunfire, no one saw any of this."

"No. That's the beauty of the killing. It happened sometime in the night. It wasn't even discovered until a human maid found him."

"You say the driver was human?"

"Yeah, Mike Conboy. He had been Dubro's limo driver for the past two years."

"Does he check out?"

"Yeah. We think he was simply killed to hush everything. We are pretty sure Dubro was the main target." She placed a hand on my shoulder. "But you still think our killer is Sylvester don't you?"

I took a step back and allowed her hand to fall from my shoulder. Nothing personal, I just didn't like to be touched. "He's my obvious choice, but I'm not ruling out anything just yet. Why he would kill the other Knights of the Night members is what's throwing me." I moved back to Rook. Close enough that I was sure no one would hear us. "Any connections with the driver or Dubro involving porn?"

Rook jumped. "Excuse me?"

I smiled with embarrassment. "I'm sure it's no secret to you that Kincaid was distributing the stuff, the girls that you were talking about were involved in a cockroach porn house and stars of his latest skin flick, the monsters I killed that night were into it, the

Guzman daughter's dad was a star in one of the movies, and now Mike Luvara's son has been killed, and he's not only the lawyer for Asa, but also NecroPussy."

"Kincaid's company."

I laughed. "Ahh, Ms. Rook, you know your fang porn."

She gave me a playful slap on the chest. "I'll look into it. Nothing about this job surprises me." The smile remained. "But now I have a question for you."

Her smile was infectious. It caused me to smile. "Since all the evidence is pointing to you, that leads me to a very big question. Maybe you're doing a movie or two you don't want anyone to know about."

My smile bloomed into a belly laugh. "The only blow job from a daisy pusher I'm interested in involves wind and ash. Now get those naked images of me out of your dirty mind and bring me the head of Sylvester. I want it hanging from my rear view mirror."

CHAPTER TWENTY-FIVE

I arrived at the hospital after what seemed like a hundred more phone calls to both the nurses' desk and Kansas' wife, Stephanie, trying to find out as much information as I could about his condition. If there was any encouraging news to be found, it was in the fact that Kansas was alive and expected to make a full recovery. It was good to know I wasn't going to have to cut his head off to keep him from rising as a coffin crunch. In that alone, I counted my blessings. I felt responsible for what happened. I should have been able to do more than I did.

No, that wasn't it. The truth was, it wasn't me that saved his life, but instead a damn cockroach. I had always considered them to be soulless creatures and still do, but now they were giving me vibes that they could be rehabilitated like an alcoholic or something. I hoped I was wrong. For me, it was a lot more fun to cut out their heart than to imagine they had one.

I already knew the room number and that made things easier. I wouldn't have to talk to any of the candy stripers. Point for me. Still, it didn't do anything about the butterflies in my stomach. I wasn't sure what I would say, how Kansas or his wife would react to seeing me, or how I would react when seeing them.

My take on hospitals is a lot lower than most people. When I visited them it was usually to see a fanged victim and that meant cutting off the head along with cutting out the heart. It's hard to have good memories of the place based on that.

I came to the door and took a deep breath. There was no turning back now. My feet had other ideas and stayed put, kept me just out of sight. Still, I could hear the beeping of machines and other sounds that left me a little unsettled. Two officers flanked each side of the door like gargoyles.

"Hey Paul," a voice from behind said. It was fatigued and hollow.

I jumped as it shoved me back into reality. "Stephanie," I said to Ezekiel Kansas' wife. She looked pale and tired and I couldn't blame her. "How is he?"

"The doctors gave him something for the pain and he's been sleeping all day. Just coming in and out from time to time. He hasn't said much, but I think he's having nightmares." I looked at her hands. They trembled as they held a bottle of juice and a bag of peanuts.

"Can't say I blame him if he is." I moved aside and gave her an opportunity to go ahead of me to the room. I wasn't sure about her, but I needed a buddy system for this.

She was petite and looked younger than I guessed she truly was. The bangs of her brown hair played with her eyelashes. She and Kansas made a perfect couple. Sugar coated love story with a white picket fence. "You've got to talk to him."

I could tell she meant it differently than I thought by the way she said it. "Talk to him about what?"

"Getting out of doing this stuff. I nearly lost him." She began to cry. I was having an anxiety attack. The last thing I was good at was being a shoulder to cry on.

"I understand." It was simple, but it got the point across to her. I think.

"There's more to lose now than ever. I'm pregnant and the thought of raising this baby without its father scares me to death. Being a cop is one thing, but working the monster district is something all together different."

I missed the whole second part of the conversation. "You're pregnant?" It came out sounding like I had just heard she had cancer.

"God, Paul don't make it sound so bad."

"What's to be so excited about? They poop and eat, then grow up to hate and disrespect you." I smiled and gave her a hug. "Seriously, I couldn't be happier for you. You'll make great parents."

She shook her head. "He doesn't know. Unfortunately, I didn't find out until yesterday. I was going to tell him tonight, but then all this happened. Please promise me you'll talk to him."

"Stephanie, I've known you two for a long time, and would do anything for either one of you, but let's be real here. This is your territory not mine."

"So you'd rather see our child raised without a father? Those bastards nearly killed him last night."

Her big brown eyes looked at me full of tears and fear. She was right. Maybe we could compromise and talk to Kansas about a transfer or something. "I'll see what I can do, but I'm not going to say anything about the baby until you tell him. If he knew I knew about it before him, he'd kill us both right here."

She gave her best fake smile and hugged me. "Just plant the seed in his head about leaving the force." She grabbed my hand and began to pull me forward. "Come on in, I'm sure he'd love to see you."

Like an obedient dog, I followed. Kansas was lying on the bed, bandages along his neck and shoulders. Blue marks spotted his face, inflated by swelling. There was no doubt he was in a lot of pain.

With all his strength, he opened his eyes slowly and tried to smile. "Paul, what are you doing here?"

"I heard tonight was turkey and mashed potato night and I thought if you weren't going to eat yours, someone should." I found stupid remarks helped me cope with things like this. Appropriate? Probably not, but it keeps me from screaming. "Besides, I think what they did to your face is an improvement."

He smiled, then winced as the pain reminded him of why he was in a hospital. "You always did know how to kick a good man when he was down."

"Who said anything about a good man?"

He lifted his middle finger groggily.

"How are you feeling?" I asked.

"I'm on good drugs, so I'm not real sure. I just wish I knew who it was that did this. Knew what happened."

"You don't remember?" I looked to Stephanie and then back to Kansas. The last thing I wanted to do was tell him everything I knew with his pregnant wife standing there. She was a basket of nerves as it was. "Let's just say you had an off night."

"You were there?" he whispered.

"Yeah." I could feel Stephanie Kansas looking at me, but I refused to look back.

"The police want to question anyone that saw anything," Stephanie added. "Did you see who did this to Zeke?"

I finally turned to meet her eyes. "Yeah."

"Who?" she snapped.

"Steph, can you give us a minute?" Kansas asked.

She looked at him for a second, then to me. I could tell by her gaze that she blamed me for having to take a walk. But at the same time she gave me the "talk to him" look. I couldn't win for losing today. "I'll notify the doctors," she simply said and walked out, closing the door behind her.

"Who did this?" Kansas asked.

"You really don't know?"

"I remember. I just wanted you to tell me all over again," he said laced with sarcasm. Well at least his personality was healing at a rapid rate. "Start from the beginning."

I cleared my throat. "I got a call from Isabella Dunlawton. She told me that she was being held hostage. When I got to the Crimson Madness that's when I found you. They told me that they were going to kill you if the police allowed Asa to go free."

"Who's they?"

"Sylvester and Sanguine mostly." I let that sink in for a minute. "You were already beaten up pretty bad when I got there. All I know for sure is they planned on killing you if Asa took a single step out of the police headquarters."

He rolled his eyes in my direction. "What do we do? We don't have anything to hold him on. His attorney has been on our back about that for some time now. Especially with Albert Kincaid being killed while he was locked up." He hit the bed in frustration. "I really stepped in it this time, didn't I?" He looked over to me best he could. "Go ahead with the 'I told you so speech'."

I shook my head, but said nothing.

"What is it?"

"It's about Mike Luvara."

"I'm listening."

"His son was killed last night."

Kansas closed his eyes. I wasn't sure if it was from the pain or from hearing of the killing. "My God, what has this world come to? They killed his son? He was only about five or six."

I thought about what Stephanie had told me and it was hitting home. "That's the scary thing about dealing with the roaches. They will use and kill anyone or anything in order to get their way. I'm living proof of that. Working the monster district is not something a family man should find himself in." God I was smooth.

"I can't even imagine something like that. How soulless do you have to be to kill someone's child just because he's representing a client?"

"They saw it as a way of controlling him."

"Did Mike see who done it?"

"No. Like you, they were under magic, or at least claim to have been, but we have reason to believe that Sylvester had something to do with it."

Kansas went into a deep thought. "I do remember something about last night."

I looked at the door to the room as if Kansas was about to reveal a big secret. "What's that?"

"I had gone to the Crimson Madness on my way back from Albert Kincaid's house. You had said something that made me think."

"First time for everything, I guess."

He tried to laugh again, but couldn't. A hand went to the wound on his neck. "I'm serious. You said someone had something to lose in all this. I went to talk to Dubro and Sylvester about the deaths. I never told you, but I looked through phone records, Blackberry's, notes, everything and one thing continuously popped out."

"What's that?"

"Each of them had some sort of financial obligation to the Crimson Madness Gallery and Sylvester was on the list of vampires they all talked to just before losing their heads." He pushed the button on the bed that raised him up to more of a sitting position. I could see on his face, it wasn't a pleasant experience. "I don't think the killings are political at all. They're financial. Sylvester is like the strong arm part of the partnership, squeezing money out of the Knights."

"Have you told Price or anyone else about this?"

"Not yet. The next thing I knew I was waking up and seeing your ugly mug. And another thing, I think Dubro is just as guilty. He's the brains."

"I don't think we'll have to worry too much about Dubro anymore either. Someone shot and killed him just before dawn this morning."

I could see the shock run through him. "Did you do it?"

"Not you too! No matter who I talk too, they all think I killed Dubro."

"Well you look to the obvious ones first."

"You've been talking to Price haven't you?"

He tried to laugh again, then it melted into pain and serious thoughts. "Do you know who did it?"

"Not yet, but based on what you've just said and what my gut tells me, it has to do with Sylvester too." Yeah, I know, I really thought Isabella had something to do with it, but I just didn't think she'd be able to pull something like that off by herself. Perhaps they were a partnership.

"Get him for us, Paul. Get him for me," Kansas said as he moved toward the white Styrofoam pitcher of water on the night-stand next to him. I moved to get it for him, but he brushed me off. He was a stubborn man that didn't want to appear helpless.

"I will." I hoped I wasn't lying to myself. I wasn't sure if Kansas knew how powerful Sylvester and Sanguine were, but I did and it scared the shit out of me. I looked at Kansas as he melted back into the bed.

"This has all been my fault hasn't it?"

I wasn't sure how to answer it. I had told him at one time, it was, but now, obviously, things had changed. "You did what you thought was right." It was the worst lie I had ever said. Simply letting him off the hook.

"If I wasn't lying here in a hospital bed, would you still be saying that?"

I smiled but said nothing.

"My point exactly. You were right. I allowed them to cloud my judgment. I'm not like you."

"Meaning?"

"I'm not able to tell them what I really think without wondering every time the sun goes down they aren't waiting for me in the shadows to harm me or my wife. I'm scared of them."

I understood what he was saying. It was the same reason there was never a Mrs. Isaac in the picture. I knew the bat heads well enough to know that if there was anything they could use against you, they would. I had lost people in my life because of it. "There's nothing to be ashamed of, Kansas. Being afraid of them is only human. And having a family only gives them an edge. No one with a family should be doing this line of work."

"So what do I do?"

Just as I was about to say something, Stephanie came back into the room, along with a nurse. She looked at me, then to her husband. She had said a lot with her eyes, but I had nothing to set her fears to ease. Her news would change her husband's mind far easier than anything I could ever say or do. I simply knew if he was going to still play with the monsters, having a kid was the last thing he wanted to bring into the world. It was sad to say it that way, but with a child-killing coffin creeper already loose in the city, I couldn't think of it any other way. I thought about his question. What should he do? "Think about what you have to lose and make your decision based on that." I gave a quick glance to Stephanie. "Sometimes things come along that change your mind for you."

With that, I left Kansas in the care of his loving wife and the nursing staff. Sleep was calling me. I would go home and get as much as I could before the sun set again.

CHAPTER TWENTY-SIX

A s I pulled into the driveway, it became very clear, I wasn't going to get much sleep today. Isabella stood at the end of the driveway. I rolled down the window, already knowing I was about to be drawn into another predicament I didn't want to be a part of.

"I thought you'd never get here," she said as she leaned in. I could tell by her eyes that she had been crying. They were red and tired. Her voice shook as she spoke. Even though I knew why she was scared and why she was here, there was a dash of innocence about her.

"How long have you been here?"

"Shortly after I heard the news."

"About Dubro." I said it as a statement, not a question.

"I didn't do it. I know what you're thinking, but I didn't kill him. Sylvester will be looking for me. You know that as well as I do."

I shut the engine off and opened the door. The act moved her back a few feet. "Forgive me if I'm not among your supporters on this. It's been the only thing you've talked about since I met you. In fact, you nearly got us both killed because of it. Now the deal's been done and you come to me to proclaim your innocence. I haven't figured out if you really are this crazy or simply a manipulator." I started to walk toward the house. "Either way, I'm not getting involved."

She looked to the house. "Can we just go inside for a few minutes and talk? I don't like standing out here where anyone can see us."

I never looked back. I raised my hand, protesting another word from her pie hole. "Not getting involved."

"Just hear my side of the story. I have nowhere else to go."

I turned and opened my mouth to say no, but there was something that made me second-guess myself. I knew what it was. Fatigue. There was enough swimming in my head without adding Isabella's problems to the mix, to fill an ocean. Still, like a good Boy Scout, I let her inside.

My home was usually my sanctuary. A place where the monsters and humans alike, were at bay even if only for a few hours. Now, I had to baby sit and listen to a woman that I'd bet my right nut, was guilty as hell.

"Nice place," she started.

"How did you know where I lived?"

"Like I've told you before, Mr. Isaac, I know you better than you probably know yourself. I have lived and breathed you for the last five years."

"I know a therapist that would love to get her hands on you." I wanted to get some sleep and I wasn't going to accomplish that goal until we got to the bottom of this. "Now the only advice I can give you is use what's left of the sunlight to get the hell out of Dodge."

"After we left the Crimson Madness, I thought about everything you said and you were right. The only thing I was going to do was get myself killed if I tried to go after Dubro. I was thinking all wrong." She looked out the window again. It wouldn't do me any good to tell her that she was safe until the sun went down. "I know now that Dubro's not the vampire I should have been going after."

"Where did you go after we parted ways?"

"I went to my apartment and started to pack. I was going to go back home to Wisconsin. Get away from all the vampire hell down here and do my best to live a normal life. But I don't think I can. Sylvester and Sanguine know what I planned on doing. Running away won't do anything but by a few extra days. They'll find me. You know that."

"You have a bigger dilemma than the blood drinkers right now. It's just a matter of time before the police connect the dots that lead them to you."

"The police? Why the police? I've already told you, I didn't kill anything."

"Did anyone see you go back to your apartment?"

"I don't know. I was tired and scared and the last thing I thought I would need was an alibi." She wiped away tears as she began to pace around the room. I wanted to sit, wanted to ask her to sit, but I knew better. When you ask people to sit, they tend to believe you want them to stay. And that was not the case.

"You need to go to the police. Tell them everything you told me. Worst case scenario, you'll have protection."

"Protection? From who?"

"Not who, what. The guys with the fangs. If they think you killed Dubro, they will come after you. If not out of revenge, greed."

"So now you know why I'm so desperate." She tried to smile, but it just wasn't happening. She continued to pace around the room. Her nerves not allowing her to stand still. Then the unthinkable happened. She fell to the couch and hunched over, her hands holding her head. Game over. She wasn't going anywhere for a while now.

I walked to the couch but refused to sit down, no matter how tired I got. "Do you still have the paintings?"

"Yeah, they're locked away in a secured area, why?"

"If everything you say about the paintings is true. They'll sky rocket in value now that Dubro is dead. They will come for them. Blood's not the only thing they're addicted to. Give them to the police. At least it will take the greed out of the fang equation."

"Meaning, you think Sylvester will try and kill me to get the paintings for himself."

I shook my head. "Wouldn't you? I mean, if he thinks you killed his boyfriend, stole paintings that will be worth a small fortune, I have very little doubt that he will come calling. Maybe not today or tomorrow, but someday he will come collecting what he feels is his."

"You have to help me get them to a buyer before Sylvester finds them."

I laughed as I heard her response. "I have enough on my plate as it is without helping you make a profit off of a dead porn artist and sail into the sunset. Not to mention, the paintings aren't yours to sell."

She stood and went to the window, peaking out of the corner of the curtain then turned back to me. "It's not what you think. I don't want to make a dime off of those paintings for myself and go sailing into a sunset like you think. It's for my brother."

"Your brother? Quite the philanthropist aren't you."

"You know nothing." She slumped into the couch, as if she melted.

"Enlighten me. I'd love to know," I lied.

Now she stood and started the pacing again. I wasn't sure if I was getting closer to getting her out of my home or not. Her long blonde hair fell across her pale face. It was the first time I had ever seen her so casual. She had been prim and proper in the past. I guess murder and the assault of the undead can do that to the best of them.

"My brother needs my help." Large sad eyes looked into mine. There was very little doubt that she had used her beauty and those eyes to manipulate men to do her bidding. I still didn't trust her any further than I could throw her, but something told me what she was about to say was from the bottom of her heart. Confessions of a cockroach killer. "The money was going to be for him."

"I've already told you. All the money in the world isn't going to save him. Best thing is to detach from those ideas and come to terms with the fact that he's a dead man."

She nodded and laughed nervously. "Well, do you want to know why he's in trouble?" Her eyes looked into me like laser beams. Cold and icy, yet something soft.

"Why would I care?" Equally cold and icy, minus the soft.

"He's a vampire." Again, those eyes hooked me in. "I know you really don't care, but I want to save him."

"Save him from what?"

"I've been helping him hide for the last couple of years in safe houses, paying off vampire hunters like yourself, to keep him alive. Vampire hunters are always calling and harassing me about his whereabouts. I thought if I could make enough off of the paintings, I could help him get somewhere safe. Somewhere the police and executioners would leave him alone. He was killed on film."

Now she had my attention. "Killed on film? Gotta here this one."

She looked away and rubbed her hands together. "He got into the wrong crowd. Starting making movies." Eyes returned to me. "Adult movies."

I grew instantly cold. I wasn't sure I wanted to hear anymore.

"Vampire adult movies. The vampire that killed him was Sanguine. She's the vampire I should have tried to kill, but I don't have to tell you how dangerous she is. Instead I chose the soft underbelly of the operation."

I wanted to walk toward her, but couldn't. I took a deep breath and thought. No matter what I said, it would either be a lie or sound like one. "Your brother is in fact a fugitive of the law and there's nothing I or the profits of the paintings could do about that. They will find him and kill him. The money will run out eventually, and you'll find yourself either dead or in jail. If what you say about Sanguine and your brother is true, you need to let the police know. At least we can legally kill her that way." I planned on doing it, legally or not, but why tell her all my dirty laundry. I had an uneasy feeling. Isabella now had a reason to kill Kincaid and Dubro and possibly had a hand in the deaths of the Guzman's and Luvara's kids. I shivered at the thought. The woman in front of me was delusional, but to think she might have killed kids made me shut down. I wouldn't even consider it. "Go to the police." I fought to keep my voice from breaking. "Turn your brother in and do both of you a favor." I felt for the Magnum. Just in case. Isabella had suddenly gotten a lot more dangerous.

"He didn't have a choice in the matter. It's not his fault and it's not fair."

And she was right. "I know, but the law is still the law. Show them the film. At least you will know they will go after Sanguine. It's the most you can hope for. Otherwise, both you and your brother will be pushing daisies with nothing to show for it."

"I bet you wouldn't think so if it were your parents." Her voice finally changed from the trembling little girl to the angry woman I better knew her as.

I walked to her and grabbed her by the arms. "You leave my parents out of this. Whatever happened to them had nothing to do with you and your brother. And just like my parents, your brother is dead. What he is now, is something very dangerous. He will kill you one day if you're not careful no matter how much you love him or how much you do for him. End it now and give yourself some peace."

She broke free from my grasp. "Peace? You think you can

lecture me on peace? You are nothing more than an angry man unwilling to find peace for yourself. You're afraid of finding it and afraid of not. Not to mention the fact that I know about your mother and Kincaid. Don't forget how hell bent you were on talking to him the other night. I, along with everyone else, heard your threats. For all we know, Sylvester and Sanguine might be the killers of your parents as well. Wouldn't you like to stake them just on that possibility alone?"

I was being baited and I knew it. If I grew angry, it played into her hands. I had to stay focused on what I had to do. If this bitch was guilty of killing Dubro, she had rid the world of a non-talented artist, but it wouldn't buy sympathy from me. "Well thank you for that observation. I guess you're right. You really do know me better than I know myself. Now if you will excuse me, I need to get a few hours of sleep before I go back into that hell hole world and hunt down a serial killing monster not much different from the brother of yours that you're willing to kill and be killed for. I wish you well, but I'm not going to help you."

She began to cry. God, why is it that anytime you try and have an argument with a woman, she always pulls the crying card. They have to know men have no defense against that shit.

"I told you, I'm innocent. I didn't kill anybody. You have to believe me." Before I knew it she had her arms wrapped tight around me and her head against my chest. All I needed now was for her to blow her nose on my shirt and we'd be complete. "I'm begging you to just keep Sylvester from killing me. I'll take the paintings to the police first thing tomorrow. You have my word."

Awkwardly, I put my arms around her. Why, I wasn't really sure other than until I calmed her down, she wasn't going anywhere. "It's going to be okay. Have you told anyone else of your plans to kill Dubro?" Personally, I didn't care, but if I could calm her down enough to make a run for it, I'd take a hug for the team.

She looked up at me. "No, no one but you."

"Good. You have that on your side." Then I said the one thing that to this day I wasn't sure why. Note to self: Cut out my tongue the first chance I get. "Stay here until we can figure something out." I winced as I said it.

At least it stopped the gushes of tears as she loosened her grip and looked up at me. "Are you sure?"

"Yeah." I turned her loose, expecting her to do the same, but she still held tight. I tensed as I saw the tears replaced with a sweet smile.

She leaned up on her toes and kissed me gently on the lips. "Your secret is safe with me too."

I leaned my head and shoulders as far back, away from her as I could, but still those arms were wrapped tight. "What secret?"

"That you're a real tough as nails kind of guy with a heart."

I started to speak when the second kiss came at me all stealth like. If I had tried to talk now, I'd have bit her tongue. Finger tips ran along the skin on the back of my shaven head, nails threatening to scratch. I could smell her. The sweet scent of perfume filled my nose as her body began to mold against mine like never before.

I suddenly realized why I chose killing cockroaches over dating. At least with the dead heads, I knew what to expect.

CHAPTER TWENTY-SEVEN

A part of me wanted to push her away and end this as quickly as it started, but there was always that other part that seems to deny reasonability and accountability. The part that leaves you quivering for days just thinking about what you did the night before and how it would impact your life from that point on.

This was that part.

I put my arms back around her and slowly opened my mouth more, allowing her tongue to not only run along the edge of my mouth but also explore every detail. I could feel my temperature heating up. Fatigue and desire mixed to give me a euphoric concoction of lust. My hands ran along her shoulder blades, feeling the Achilles heel of make out sessions. The dreaded bra strap.

Without warning, her tongue exited my mouth and we were able to breathe again. I hadn't realized I had been holding my breath until that moment. I looked down into her eyes expecting to see shock and dismay, but instead saw the tiny sparkles of reflected light.

"I'm sorry. We probably shouldn't be doing this," I said, more to see what she was thinking than anything.

"I know." Her lips once again clamped down on mine, pulling my head to her. She let out a soft groan as she pulled me down to the couch on top of her. Then she began her assault again. I kept most of my weight on my arms. I was nearly twice as big as she was and the last thing I wanted to do was suffocate her.

With me like a bridge over top of her, she began to run her hands under my shirt, freeing it from my pants. I could feel the shivers run across my back as her fingers moved up and down my torso. Those same hands began to lift the shirt from my body, edging it up over my head, exposing me from the waist up.

I looked down at her, trying to see in her eyes again, but they were busy scanning my chest and abs. I wasn't the most fit of men, so part of me waited to see if laughter would be the next sound. To my relief, there was nothing.

As the shirt fell to the floor, I lifted back up and sat across her knees and pulled her up with my free hand. She fell against my chest, lips retraced the path her eyes had just taken. I pulled her shirt up over her head in a quick move, exposing her ample breast, still hidden behind that damn black lace bra. I stared at it like an impregnable wall, hiding a great treasure guarded by an evil monster. A monster that would deny me of what I sought if I wasn't smooth and precise.

My hands reached around to her back and grabbed the clasp. With a simple squeeze and pull, I was amazed at how easily it came apart. I brought both ends around to the front and pulled it free from her body, exposing the prize beneath them.

Her breasts were slightly larger than average, with large erect nipples. My hands discarded the bra to the floor as she melted gently back to the couch and reached for the buckle to my belt. I breathed in to allow her more access to do her work, and in no time at all the belt was free and I found my jeans held together only by the zipper.

There was no romantic way to get past the next part. I don't care what you say or see in the movies on the big screen. Getting your pants off is comical when you're trying to set a mood like this. I stood up briefly, unzipped and let them fall to my ankles and stepped out.

I reached for her pants undoing them in great haste. She reared up to allow me to pull them free of her bottom. She had an amazing beauty to her now. Her straight golden hair fell across her face and body. A black thong that matched the bra only remained. I had to laugh to myself looking at her. To know her, you'd never think that the prim and proper lady had a bad side. A true case of leather and lace.

She looked at me, still standing above her and smiled. "Come here." Her hands pulled at the waistband of my briefs, causing me to move forward into her grasp. I expected to find my underwear shredded to the floor in a blinding move, but instead, she ran her fingers inside, grasping me tightly.

I tried not to groan too loudly as she pulled me down to her. Her mouth opened wide, waiting for my lips to join hers. This time when my arms braced my weight above hers, I could feel them tremble with desire, making them uncontrollably weak.

Her mouth let go of mine. Her tongue licked across my neck and upper shoulder, biting gently at first, then hard enough that it made me wince. I wanted more.

Again, she shoved me upward and this time the briefs were gone as if she were a magician. "Much better don't you think?" she purred.

I simply smiled and reached for her panties, pulling them off slowly, watching them trail down her silky white legs. The contrast of the black lace against the white skin was amazing. I ran them through my hands for a few seconds, looking at her looking back at me, before dropping them to the floor.

"Do you like what you see, Mr. Isaac?" she said as she ran her fingers across her own breasts, eyes doing the smiling.

"Indeed," I responded as I ran the tip of my finger along her leg as lightly as I could. I could feel her shiver with the sensation. As my finger moved upward, I lowered myself over her breasts. My hand reached for the left one, squeezing it gently into my mouth. I sucked on it, rolling my tongue across her nipple as I felt her hands reach for the back of my head and push me further against it.

Her body began to hunch slightly. I heard her breathing increase. I continued to suck lightly against the breast as I reached for the other with my free hand. Her skin was hot to the touch, smooth like rose petals. I could smell her scent increasing. Neither of us would wait much longer.

I looked in her eyes yet again, trying to make sure we were both on the same page. Without saying a word, I felt her legs open like butterfly wings, giving me my answer. She smiled and traced my face with her fingers as beads of sweat began to form across her stomach and forehead.

I entered her with finesse and care as her next breath seemed to have been taken from her. I waited for it to return, only to find her hips already moving up and down, pulling me further inside. Now it was my turn to find breathing a difficult task as I felt the pleasure run through me like a bolt of lightning. I kissed her deeply to keep the throaty groan from escaping my mouth.

Her legs wrapped tightly around my body giving me no chance of escape even if I wanted it. The rhythm continued to increase as she held me tighter and tighter. Nails drove their way inside my skin, allowing the pain to mix with the pleasure. The deeper the nails dug, the harder I made the thrusts, matching her sensation to sensation. Her head rolled upward as her back arched, pushing upward with her feet, now dug into the couch.

Like an explosion deep inside her, I felt the rush of completion roll through her. She became rigid and trembled as I met her in the act. I wasn't sure, but I think it was me that screamed the loudest as I collapsed on top of her, wet sweaty skin meeting with the other. Deep breaths from both our bodies pushed against the other. I tried to regain control of my body. I felt her melt from the rigid response to nothing more than mush. Fingernails that only a few seconds ago had been lethal weapon were now gently scratching my back in lazy circles.

With everything I had, I raised up to see if she was okay, seeing the content smile under me. "I needed that," she said with a giggle. "I'm not nearly as stressed now."

I rose up further. "There's nothing we just did that will make your situation go away. You're still in a lot of trouble. The question is, whether that trouble is from police or cockroach."

She moved, allowing me to spoon behind her. It worked for both of us. Isabella thought I was being a thoughtful man, but in truth, I was just dead tired. "You don't think I'm innocent in Dubro's death do you?"

I thought about it. "No. But I hope I'm wrong."

If she responded, I didn't hear her. I was taken in a deep sleep.

CHAPTER TWENTY-EIGHT

I wasn't sure how long I had been asleep, but when I woke, I knew it had been too long. Everything in the house was dark, which could mean only one thing. The sun had set and time was wasting. Again, I heard the doorbell ring three quick times followed by an echo of knocks.

It took a few seconds to remember where I was and the identity of the naked woman still fast asleep next to me. It didn't take long for me to regret the act, but that would have to wait for another time. I rose from the couch as easily as I could. I'd rather she stayed asleep than answer questions or experience that uneasy feeling that came with one-night stands.

I bounced on one leg as I slipped on my jeans, minus the underwear. The knocks on the door happened again. I looked back to Isabella and hoped to see those big eyes still shut. She grunted lightly and turned away from me, but to my benefit, she never woke. I wasn't sure who was at the door, but they were about to get an ear full.

Looking out the window, I didn't see a car in the driveway other than the 'Cuda. There wasn't anyone standing on the porch area either. If this was a Girl Scout selling cookies, she was relentless. I grabbed the Magnum just in case. After all, I made my living by killing monsters and they stayed alive by trying to kill me.

As the door opened, I knew I had made a huge mistake. I wanted to shut it and go back to sleep, marking the whole thing up as a bad nightmare. But truth be told, she stood there, large as life and there wasn't a damn thing I could do about it.

She was dressed in snakeskin leather pants and a mesh tank top. Of course there wasn't a bra. That would just not be her. "Angie, what are you doing here?"

"It's good to see you too." She gave me a reserved smile. I couldn't be sure, but I think we were both wishing I hadn't answered the door now.

I dropped my defenses as I eased out the door, trying to keep Isabella hidden. "I didn't mean it that way. What's wrong?"

"There's a lot going down in Bat Town right now, and I thought you'd want to know. I think they're going to burn the police station down."

The police station is at the end of Bat Town, so if anything goes down in the monster district it affects both the good and the evil. I looked at my watch. Nine o'clock. "What's going on?"

"There's two mobs around the police station. One that's pro Asa and one that's con. Each threatening to do violence if they don't get their way. You know as well as I do that with the added firepower of Dubro's death, it won't take much to send both ends over the edge. People, as well as the vampires, are angry and scared."

"Meaning whether they let Asa go or not, someone's going to be pissed." I needed to go to Bat Town, and needed to get there now, but I had to get dressed and ready first. I could kick myself. Not that I overslept, but instead for the predicament that I had put myself in. If I went in, Angie would want to come with me. And I knew I couldn't just invite her inside to wait for me to get ready. I had a naked woman sleeping on the couch. Somehow I just knew that would bring up a question or two. "Asa and Sasha will see this as an opportunity to even some scores."

"Yeah, so come on, we have to get going now, or things are going to get out of control."

"Where are you getting this 'we' from? You stay out of it. I've done enough saving over the last few nights to last a life-time. I've gotten myself in a no win situation and the best thing for you to do is stay out of it and stay alive. Going to the hospital to see what's left of your friends is starting to be a real pain in the ass."

"And that's all that will be left if you do nothing. Asa isn't the type of vampire that believes in forgiveness. He will kill Kansas, his wife, and anyone else that's had lunch with him in the last few days," Angie shouted. She was right. Asa would do everything she said he would and more.

"I think Asa will have enough of a distraction from the commercial undead if he's set free tonight. Price is supposed to have extra men at the hospital as a precaution. Sylvester is the one that will be looking for an opportunity to spill blood."

"We're talking about Asa. He'll go on a killing spree for what's happened to him and he won't just go after vampires. For once in your life, don't be a knucklehead."

"You think he'll come after Kansas and the police?"

"Don't you?" Her eyes grew as large as saucers. There was no fear, but excitement. "He's been a vampire all his life. He doesn't follow the rules of life as we know them. He will stop at nothing to kill Quinn, Sylvester, you, Kansas, anything that he sees as a threat or pumps blood. Now you can either work with me and we can kill him together, or we can do it separately and probably attend each other's funeral. I'm going to stop this with or without you." She went for the door. I stopped her. She looked up at me with a puzzled look. "What?"

"I'll meet you there. I need to get ready. Tonight there's no such thing as being over prepared."

"Or hesitation, now hurry up." She reached for the door again.

Again, I stopped her. "I told you, I'll be there as soon as I get everything I need. As you can see I still have to get dressed."

I caught her scanning my exposed chest. "I want to watch."

"I don't think now is the time to explore fetishes."

"Still, it could be fun." She went to hug me, but I stopped her. Sort of. She quickly laced her fingers in mine. It was like some sort of Chinese puzzle box. I couldn't break free. "Are you sure? I promise to keep my hands to myself."

"I don't think so. You go ahead and I'll meet you there," I tried again.

She smiled as she watched me sink in my situation. "What? You got another girl in there?"

I laughed back, feeling the blood rush to my head to the point I was afraid it might explode. "No, nothing like that, I just need to get some things ready before I get going."

"You seem a little nervous? What's up?"

I hated the fact that I was so transparent. "Nothing, it's just been a stressful few days. Kansas nearly got killed last night by Sylvester, Dubro is dead, and now Asa is going to shred this town like it's never seen before."

"Nothing a little sex couldn't cure. You know, take the edge off things." Fingernails traced along my chest.

"Not everything can be cured with sex, Angie."

"Then the woman you have on your couch isn't doing it right."

I nearly jumped out of the shoes I didn't have on. "What do you mean by that?"

She howled with laughter. "I'm just saying maybe you need to get laid. Properly." She licked her lips. "You can't bottle up all that stress forever, you know. Besides, Romeo, I'm a werewolf. I can hear and smell far better than you can, and I smell slut." She sniffed the air. "And it's close."

I was about to say something. What? I don't remember now, just as the door opened, exposing Isabella dressed in her black thong and my shirt. I could feel my world spinning out of control and there was nothing I could do about it but hold on for the ride.

Angie looked at me with those same wide eyes, along with a wide mouth. It was the first time I had ever known her to be speech-less and I wasn't sure if it was a good thing or not. Then it was over. "Ahh, there it is. I told you I smelled slut." She walked around Isabella, scanning her from her head to her toes. "She's the one I nearly tore the head off of at the gallery the other night. Too bad I didn't." Then her assault turned to me. "So when were you going to tell me about this?"

"I didn't see where it involved you."

Isabella volleyed her stare between the two of us. She clutched the shirt close to her. If it had been me in her situation, I'd have closed the door, locked it and never came out again. But that wasn't Isabella. She stood there like a damn neon sign. "Am I interrupting something here?"

"Yes," Angie snapped.

"No," I followed.

"You come into my club the other night all pissy that I was kissing some guy and then you go and bang her? Maybe you should make things a little clearer on the rules of our relationship."

"Relationship?" Poor Isabella. I'll bet she was wondering what she had gotten herself in.

"That's just it, Angie. You and I don't have a relationship," I said.

"Then what was that scene last night about? It sure seemed as though something was going on that had you all up in arms. You nearly bit my head off for simply kissing with some guy." She looked over to Isabella. "Is this what you want? Some vampire loving whore? You know as well as I do that she's in bed with the vampires and now I guess so are you. That's the real reason you're hesitating coming with me to fight against Asa isn't it. I knew you had low morals, but to be something like this, is a new low even for you."

With that Isabella attempted to slap her, but the werewolf in Angie was too quick for the move. She held Isabella's wrist tight and brought her to the floor. "That's enough," I shouted. "Right now, I just wish I could shoot both of you. I used to tell myself I didn't want a relationship because it gave the daisy pushers an advantage, but now I see that's a lie. The truth is, I don't have the patience to put up with crap like this. If you don't like the way I run my personal life, stay out of it."

Angie let go of Isabella and looked at me with a look that I knew I didn't want. I had seen her have that look with people before and it usually ended with someone bleeding. "Fine. Stay here and fuck her all you want. I'm going to keep the vampires from turning this city into a smorgasbord."

She turned to leave, stepping down the two stairs to the front yard. I went after her. "Wait in the car. I'll be there in a few minutes. You're right. It'll take both of us to take on the blood lappers we'll be up against. The police will be nothing more than casualties and you know it."

The sexy shifter stared at me. "Do you love her?"

"Just wait in the car. I'll be out in a few minutes. We'll talk about this on the way."

She looked past me to Isabella. "You've proving my point."

"What's that?"

"I told you, you wouldn't trust your heart to me simply because I was a monster. No matter what I say or do, no matter how attracted you are to me, no matter how much I prove that I love you, you will only see one thing. The monster. Pity." Yikes, those last words were soaked in scorned bitterness.

"It's not like that and you know it. Things just happened. I'm sorry. It was a mistake to even do what I did." Again, I felt as though I needed to explain myself. I was being forced into a relationship that I didn't even have. Go figure.

"A mistake? Which part? Screwing her or hurting me?"

I remained silent. I couldn't think of anything to say that I knew I wouldn't regret later.

"I can't make you love me or trust in me unless you chose to do so yourself. You're right, I have no say so in who you screw around with, but the same goes with me. Don't come around me making a scene every time you catch me with someone. It's just best if we leave our personal lives alone and separate. Keep in mind, I'm doing this to kill a vampire, not for you. And you can thank me later."

"For what?" I asked.

"Me allowing you to watch my ass, knowing you want this body, and still allowing you the opportunity to have it." With Angie, things came back to a sexual nature. It was something I honestly didn't think she could help. But as always, she was right. Watching her walk away was as titillating as watching her approach.

The wolf moved to the 'Cuda with the patent stripper strut. She was right in the fact I had gotten angry with her for a lot less than what I had been caught doing, but the truth was, we weren't an item, so it shouldn't matter. So why did it?

She was addictive.

She was dangerous.

Far more dangerous than the cockroaches I was about to lose my life to.

CHAPTER TWENTY-NINE

Anger does one of two things. Either makes you spew at the mouth with hurtful words that can never be taken back, or cause an uneasy silence that is so thick it actually can take shape. I was lucky. Angie and I had taken the second option on our way to the police station. I knew it would only be a matter of time before it all came up again, but for now, we both agreed to let sleeping dogs lie.

Church Street was clogged with people protesting one way or the other over Asa's arrest and roaches in general. Most of the mob didn't realize it, but they were playing right into the hands of the pure bloods and their secret agenda.

Angie and I snaked our way through the growing crowd and tried to find Price, who according to a quick phone call I had with him, was supposed to be near the steps of the police station. Still, finding him would be like finding a needle in a hay stack.

The heat from the blast hit me before I ever saw the light of the explosion. One minute I was standing and the next, I was airborne and came to a stop on my back. As I tried to bounce back to my feet, I could hear the screaming. See the running. With the air knocked out of my lungs I looked along the ground in search of Angie.

I caught a glimpse of her through the webbing of running people, coming back to her feet and looking to me for answers. Answers I wasn't sure I had.

"Find Price," I shouted to her. I started to run toward the police station, now blazing along the east side of the building.

"No, I'm going with you," she shouted back.

"Angie, I'm not even going to argue the point with you. Find him and let him know to be ready for a cockroach feeding frenzy."

She cursed me out with those seductive eyes, but never responded verbally. See, women can be taught.

I reached out my hand. "Come on, I'll get you through as much of this as I can." I pulled her through the stampeding crowd. There was no time to check and see if either of us were wounded. Our adrenalin had already kicked in anyway. The one common thought was to get out from under the running feet around us. I felt like a fish trying to swim upstream. Gaining a little ground, then getting knocked backwards and having to start again.

I looked toward the area where Price was supposed to be. The crowd was still too heavy to see anything other than a sea of faceless figures. All running in a direction thought to be safe. Tonight, I wasn't sure that direction existed. "Find Price and tell him to meet me inside with as many men vampire trained as he has."

"But I…" she started.

"No buts, just do it," I said as I ran along the sidewalk as fast as I could. If I was really lucky, one or more of the coffin maggots would already be dead.

Black smoke poured from the open wound in the side of the police station, as personnel from inside were being evacuated. They ran from the flames, but I knew there was something far more sinister still inside.

Luckily for me, I knew the station fairly well and worked my way past the exodus of officers and to the holding area where bad little vampires were kept. With a gaping whole in the wall, going through security doors wasn't going to be all that necessary. But I knew what lay on the other side of the damaged wall was anything but dead.

My head was slammed hard into the concrete wall as I entered. Buckling my knees and blinding my sight. Before I could regain my composure, I ran into a powerful fist with my face.

On my back I looked up to see Sasha. He was dressed in black from head to toe. Dark sunglasses covered his eyes as he exposed his fangs.

"Sorry, I didn't come here to feed the vein weasels," I said as I kicked my leg out, meeting with his knee. It spun him around, nearly dumping him on top of me. I tried to reach for the Magnum, but there wasn't time.

"Who said anything about feeding off of you? I plan on killing you," he added as he brought his fist down on my chest. I could feel every vital organ in my body instantly bruise. The second blow missed as I rolled out of the way. Sasha growled in pain and held the fist close.

It gave me enough time to come back to my feet and land a punch to his ribs. I could feel my strength grow with each hit. Shifter and undead blood fed my muscles. I heard the rib crack, but wasted no time in delivering a twin blow in the same spot.

Sasha spun away from me and practically climbed along the wall like a spider and landed behind me. I turned to keep my focus on him, only to be met with another powerful punch to the head. It was followed by another, then another, then another.

I knew he was true to his word. Sasha planned on killing me, making it as brutal and bloody as he could. Why, I wasn't sure. And truthfully it didn't matter. Whether you know why a roach wants to kill you or not, the results are the same. Dead.

With everything I had in me, I pulled a punch under his chin that lifted him off his feet. It catapulted him to the wall. As he bounced back, I hit him again, across the face. A trail of blood and saliva flew from his face like a popped zit. But still the monster came at me.

I pulled the Magnum from the shoulder holster and brought my aim down on Sasha. His speed was incredible. It was as if he was in front of me one second and gone the next. I pulled the trigger anyway and caught just enough of him that it drilled a hole through his shoulder blade. Blood welled from the open wound at first followed by a small flame. He quickly covered the wound with his opposite hand, as pain and flames began to mix. With a vein junkie as powerful as Sasha was, sometimes unless you get the ultra violet bullet lodged just right, they won't go down with one shot. Which was alright with me. I had plenty more where that came from.

I lowered the Magnum on him again and smelt the burning flesh and fresh blood. His eyes were wild like a Bengal tiger. Razor sharp fangs willing to slice me like paper. The shot went off. Hands gripped my throat. Inertia lifted us both upward until gravity caught.

We slammed to the floor and slid on spilt blood. Some mine. Some his. I wasn't sure if the bullet caught him or not, but one thing was for sure. He was still alive.

His body was now on top of mine. Fingers laced tight around my throat. I couldn't breathe. He lifted my head, then slammed it back down. His knee dug into my wrist that had the Magnum. I wasn't sure if the bullets were going to kill him or not. I had never seen anything like this.

"That will suffice," I heard from above me. Somehow I didn't think it was God, and I knew it wasn't someone that aligned them-selves with him. I felt the power and recognized the voice.

Fingers still gripped tight around my neck, but at least the slam-ming had stopped. Win the little battles, I always say. Sasha's weight shifted slightly from my wrist and I instantly brought the

Magnum to his temple. I could see him looking above to the dark giant. Moving only his eyes.

Ahh, Sasha thought I was here to kill Asa. Wish he'd asked. It could have saved us both a lot of blood and bruises.

"Mr. Isaac, it is so good to see you again," Asa said as his face now towered over me. From the floor he looked ten feet tall.

I could see the wetness of the blood still trickling from Sasha's shoulder. The bullet had passed clean through the shoulder. The ultra violet never had time to do its trick. Burned flesh filled the room. He held it close and grunted with pain.

"Rise," Asa said to Sasha.

Sasha's stare moved to my hand holding the Magnum.

"Mr. Isaac, will you please allow Sasha to stand without violence?"

I thought about my options. I didn't like any of them.

"I said please," Asa patronized.

I lowered the gun, but not my defenses.

The Russian dirt napper looked down at me with an evil grin. Like a deadly viper, his fangs were at my throat, but never got the chance to dig in. I was too slick for that. He rose from me slowly, eyes large and empty as he pulled my silver knife from his throat. Sasha tried to remain standing, but stumbled backwards to the floor. Fresh blood trailed him to the floor.

I crab walked to the other wall. If there was one thing I didn't want to happen, it was having another blood lover sneak from behind. I tried to keep my focus on Asa and Sasha. One towered above. The other slumped on the floor.

"I am an innocent man, Mr. Isaac. There is nothing the police can do to bind me to this place. Never could. I simply waited until the enemy made their move. Exposing them."

I looked around at the growing smoke from the remnants of the explosion. I could still hear people screaming and moving in the distance. Sirens wailed and got closer. For me, they might be too late.

"Do you call having your minions bomb the police station to get you out, innocent?" I asked.

Asa walked slowly toward me. I gripped the Magnum tight. "Is that what you think, Avenger? Do you think it was I that caused this chaos?"

"I don't know, but if you take another step forward, you're going to look a lot like Sasha."

For some reason that made him laugh. "Tell me, have you found the killer that we both seek yet?"

"I'm close," I said as I continued to watch Sasha. He was no longer moving. His eyes were glassy like doll's eyes, yet I knew he wasn't dead. At any second, he could be at my throat again. Between the ultra violet bullets and the sting of the silver blade, I had a few seconds to ponder my next move. Every once in a while, I'd hear a gurgle of labored breath. Unlike the undead, the pure bloods breathed.

"And you have a name to this killer?"

"Sylvester." I slowly stood, ignoring the pounding headache I had, thanks to Sasha. I allowed Asa to see the Magnum in my hand as he inched forward. I planned on putting the next bullet in him, but I wanted to see if my killer would show up to the smell of fresh meat. If Sylvester knew Asa was dead, he might be a no show.

"Ahh, the cat. He is powerful and should prove to be quite an adversary for you. And how did you come to the conclusion that Sylvester is your killer?"

"Circumstantial evidence, but all the money to be made at the Crimson Madness was linked to Dubro and Sylvester. Every one of the dead members of the Knights of the Night had a meeting set up with Sylvester on the night they died. And now Dubro is dead too. My theory is he plans on taking the money and running."

"I hear the Crimson Madness has burned to the ground as well."

I wasn't about to tell him I might have had something to do with that. "Yeah, insurance money on top of everything else. Bonus."

"All this leads me to one question. Why are you here? Shouldn't you be hunting down your dangerous killer instead of pandering into my affairs?"

"I had a hunch Sylvester would show up here to kill you. He plans on taking over all the blood activity down here. But now that your guys caused this explosion, I'm not sure he'll show."

"As I have told you before, Avenger, none of my vampires caused the explosion. And as for Sylvester, he is far from being powerful enough to be more than an annoyance."

"Maybe if you looked past your own self indulgence, you would see a third scenario. I'm here to kill Sylvester if he shows up. If he kills you, well then, we all win."

"Then you have missed the opportunity altogether."

I knew we were about to play another mind game and now wasn't the time for it, but he knew me too well. I had to ask. "Missed what opportunity?"

Asa shook his head. "You see, you know nothing about vampire logic and the game of cat and mouse."

Sasha began to stand again, grimacing in pain. His face showed the hatred he had for me. His long brown hair raked across his bloody face. No longer the dapper bat head with the cool shades. I hadn't won the fight, but thank God, I didn't lose it either. My gut told me to go ahead and hammer him again with the Magnum, this time making my shot selection more precise, but I held off. For now. I wanted to know everything they knew before I "accidentally" killed them.

"And I assume you will indulge me with this plasmatic logic and cat and mouse game. Please ole wise one, share with me your ultimate wisdom."

He grinned as he followed my eyes to Sasha. "Diversion is the key to success. Master it and you are more likely to gain your prize." I simply stared back. "Meaning Sylvester will attempt to kill the one he will gain the most from by this diversion."

I heard the footsteps move up what remained of the hallway. I could hear Price's huffing and could smell Angie's perfume. Back up had arrived. "Diversion? What diversion?" Price asked.

"While you and the police are here attacking me, looking for a killer, Sylvester is readying himself for the real prize," Asa said to Price.

"What the hell happened to him," Angie asked as she approached what was left of Sasha.

"He got something stuck in his throat," I said to her, but never lost sight of Asa.

Angie took her left elbow and crushed Sasha's nose. I could hear the cartilage splinter and could feel the pain as the leech fell back to the floor, now unconscious. It was rare when I was the rational one, but God I loved her technique.

Asa looked at her with a demonic stare, but remained rigid. "My dear Angela. I see you have still not learned to control your anger."

"What's he mean by this is a diversion, Paul?" Price asked.

"You think Sylvester is going to use this time to kill Quinn," I finished.

Asa smiled and nodded. "Not as stupid as I feared, Avenger."

I started to speak again when Asa put that large hand out in front of my face. "Enough with your interrogations. I think I will leave now. Leave you to your killer and the blood you all shed." With that he began to walk away.

"I didn't say you could go anywhere," Price snapped, pulling his gun on the master cockroach. I looked behind the detective to see about six more officers in full cockroach fight gear, complete with neck covering, crucifixes and ultra violet lights.

"My dear good man, I did not ask you. Your laws will never bind me or my kind. I have indulged in your game for the last few days, but it is becoming far too taxing to bow to such petty grievances." Asa's eyes returned to me. I dropped just below his glare. "As for you, Mr. Isaac, remember that diversion is the key to the game."

I tried to stop him, but like a misty fog he was gone. Practically evaporated into thin air, leaving Sasha on the floor to bleed and possibly die. I didn't find it all that appalling. Like Asa had said, cockroaches beat to their own drum and what we, as civilized humans, might consider to be cruel, is just a way of life to them.

I turned to see Price staring back at me, his mouth wide as his eyes. "What the hell was that all about?"

I returned the Magnum to my shoulder holster and looked at Price and Angie. "Where's Quinn?"

"In the vampire district I presume," Price answered.

"Asa was right. The bombing wasn't to get him out or kill him, but instead keep us away from Quinn."

CHAPTER THIRTY

The police had evacuated most of Bat Town by the time we got there. They had sided with precaution and shut the entire district down. It wasn't unusual since the legalization of the maggot taxis for radical groups to set off explosives in hopes of killing or at the very least discouraging their coming out party. A part of me got giddy when I heard of such things, but truth be told, it was usually humans that were hurt or killed when the bombs went off.

Now it was happening here, in Orlando, but I had reason to believe our little terrorist had fangs and a different agenda.

The Coffin sat at the far end of Bat Town, near Orange Avenue, nestled under the towering bank buildings that made up the skyline. On any other night, it would be one of the most happening restaurants in the entire city. Filled with eager patrons, live soft jazz, and a creepiness you just had to feel for yourself. There was something about eating at a table hosted by a master blood tick. Of course the cockroach never ate anything, but he or she would give the guests all they wanted in conversation.

But now, there was nothing but a silent building. Dark and presumably deserted. Police officers in full riot gear ran and directed the last of the tourists out of the district. All vein lovers were told to take cover until the area was secured.

It wasn't the first time I had been in the Coffin Restaurant, so I sort of knew my way around. Which was good. The inside was pitch black except for a number of candles flickering on a few tables in the main room. The illumination was just enough to see shadows but not enough that I could see all the creepy crawlies hidden in the corners. Dieter stood just inside, staring into space. If he were human, I'd have said it was shock. But with the undead, I wasn't sure if it was a state that could be achieved. Personally, I didn't care one way or the other.

"Dieter, where's Quinn?"

The dead man turned to me. His face showed absolutely no emotions what so ever. "I fear I do not have that answer, Avenger. I fear Sylvester may have committed an act of treason upon the nation."

"We need to find him now. Get up here and lead the way," I said as I pushed him forward.

"What are we looking for?" Price asked me.

"I don't know yet. All I know is if it moves, it probably needs to be killed." I pulled out my Magnum and all the officers with us did the same with their weapons of choice. Ready or not, we all moved forward inside a place ironically named The Coffin.

We began to fan out in the restaurant, yet trying to stay as close together as possible. I wasn't sure what we were going to find in here, but so far I hadn't found or seen either Quinn or Sylvester. There was a chance I had been wrong about my hunch. I wasn't sure how I felt about that. A part of me came here to kick cockroach ass and a part of me saw it as a chance to walk away, let someone else take on Sylvester.

Dieter turned to me slowly. I could see there was something

about him I had never seen before. Call it reluctance, but I saw it as fear. It made me rethink my being here. If he was scared of something in here that might be a threat, then I really needed to be scared. Unlike me, he was among his kind and in a familiar surroundings.

"What?" I asked in my best caring voice. Not.

"I do not know if I can do this."

I stopped and looked at him, trying to read the new emotion in him. "What's up with your dead ass?"

"There are things I cannot explain."

"Are we talking about your ugliness or your bad sense of style?"

He looked at me with those huge black dead eyes. "This is not a time to practice your sarcasm. I find myself between unexplainable fear and uncontrollable revenge."

"Well choose an emotion and get going," Angie added. I looked at her and tried not to smile. There was no way that we could ever make it as a couple. We were far too much alike.

"I appreciate your enthusiasm, wolf, but this is nothing that concerns you. There is a history with Sylvester that you will never understand." He peered into the darkness with reluctance.

I suddenly had doubts about Dieter and what he was going to do if and when we found Quinn and Sylvester. After all, I had him here against his own will. And I didn't trust him to begin with, but now that he was acting a little psycho, I wondered if I shouldn't just kill him now and get it over with. In the back of my mind, I knew I would probably have to kill him when push came to shove anyway. I pulled a crucifix from my pocket and put it up to him. "Now tell me what you're talking about or I'll cook you right here."

He looked at the crucifix, spinning on the chain. "Why do you think that you would need to threaten me with such things? I am here to save the master vampire of Orlando. I do not see how I am a threat to you at this time?"

"Because you're acting like a damn idiot. Not to mention I don't trust you any farther than I can throw you. You have two choices. Either you are with us or you're dead. Make up your mind and make it up now. I don't have time to hold your hand."

"Remember at the Guzman's home I told you about my son being killed by a vampire."

I shook my head.

"You later asked me how I had become a vampire, myself."

"It was Sylvester?" I asked.

He shook his head. "I had nothing left in my life. I had lost my family to the vampires. My wife, my son. I became angry like you and tried to kill all the vampires I could find. Death was the only gift God could give me at that point. But instead, I am cursed to walk the earth forever."

"Sounds like we're kindred spirits, Dieter, how beautiful," I snapped. "Now let's get going."

"I was hunting three vampires down one night and they ambushed me. I still remember the fangs going deep into my skin, the blood draining me to white. He tortured me for hours before killing me. Drinking just enough blood to keep me weak, not enough to bring death to me. It wasn't for days before he finally ended it."

"If you're looking for sympathy from me, Dieter, you're not going to get it. I don't care what happened to you, only what I can do to end it. Sounds like you know what it's like to kill and be killed, yet you do the very same thing to others. If anything I see you as less of a cockroach than before the story. If you really want me to see you as something but the monster you are, let me use you as target practice."

"I only ask you to allow me to see Sylvester die. Allow us to put our differences away for the night and work together for a common goal. If I am to die tonight, so be it, but I ask you to kill him so that I can see the life fall from his eyes. Do this and I will let you kill me as well."

I wasn't sure what to say to the last part of that. I mean, sure, I wanted to kill him, but I didn't want it to be his idea. Kind of takes all the fun out of it.

From behind, I heard the door shut and lock. I spun to see what had either locked us in, or was now locked inside with us. In the compromised darkness I could hear motion. Better put, speed. It echoed throughout the room, encompassing us in something that I knew we'd have to kill to survive.

We all hit the ground in a crouched position, weapons pointed along the walls. The candlelight vanished and we were now in total darkness. It is amazing how sounds are amplified when you are in the dark with things that are going to be at your throat in only a moment.

I followed one of the sounds moving behind me and shot. In the flash caused by the gun, I saw the most horrific thing I had ever seen. It was a child! A roach, but a child as well.

"Price, you there?" I asked.

"They're children!"

I couldn't see his face, but in my mind's eye I could see his reaction. His firepower came to a stop. "No, no, they're coffin bits, keep shooting," I shouted.

From my left, I heard the little snappers attack the officers with Price. Blood curdling screams, followed by ripped flesh and then eerie silence. I grew more and more hesitant as the people with me began to break rank and look for any source of safety. The last thing I wanted to do was shoot at sounds only to find I was shooting at the good guys. Or worse yet, take a bullet from one of them.

I heard Angie turn next to me. A burst of power showered over me as the wolf in her began to emerge, followed by a deep growl. Where Dieter was, I couldn't say, but I knew he wouldn't be of any help in the fight.

I was hit hard by a cockroach. Followed by a second one. It drove me down with tremendous inertia. My natural reaction had my hands around the throat of one of the mini killers. Even though I knew it was either kill it or be killed, the thought of it being a child made me sick to my stomach.

With a quick snap, I broke its neck. I felt the grasp loosen immediately. The second blood sucker remained tight on my back. Claws dug deep into my skin. I drove my body back towards the wall, crushing it with my weight. I could feel the hands release from me. I wasted no time in turning and firing a shot into its chest. It didn't take me as long as I thought to get over the fact that they were small children. Like the adult monsters, I had to remember they were now nothing more than living dead. I wasn't killing a child, I was killing a blood leech. Period.

Above me I could hear the shots still being fired by Price and his officers. There seemed to be far more screaming and silence happening than I wanted to believe. I could kick myself for having the old man here. I had been protecting his heart and now I had him in the coven of mini munchers that would kill not only him, but all of us.

Across the room I could hear someone or something run. Furniture spilled along the floor. It was followed by a second flurry of speed. There was a pursuit taking place. The optimist in me wanted to believe it was one of the officers chasing one of the little creeps down, but the pessimist in me new better.

"Dieter!" I shouted.

"Yes."

I was surprised to find how close to me he still was. "Can you do anything to stop them?"

"I am afraid I cannot. They are not of our coven. I have no control over them." It was amazing to me just how cool and collect he was. Either he had nerves of steel or knew he wouldn't be killed by the little demons.

Then I did something I never thought I would ever do. "Come here."

I felt him move close to me before he was there.

"Can you see them?" I asked.

"I can."

"Take this," I said as I handed him the Magnum. "Kill them or we'll all die."

I felt his hands reach around the gun, taking it from my grasp. A dumb move no matter how I tried to defend it, but there was no other way to end this with our throats still intact. "Double cross me and I will make sure I kill you before I fade to black."

I heard the Magnum fire again and again. In the flashes that split through the darkness, I could see things falling to the floor. I hoped it was fang heads, but there wasn't enough time between the flashes to tell. The only thing I could say for sure was the power in the room was fading. Just because the daisy pushers had been small didn't mean they were short on power. One thing I had learned in my profession was evil came in an assortment of packages.

Then the shooting stopped. I remained still for a number of seconds listening to the darkness for any signs of movement. My heart was beating so hard I couldn't hear. I hadn't realized just how scared I had been until now.

"Dieter, are they all dead?"

"Yes, they are all deceased."

"Where's the Magnum?"

"It is still in my hands."

"Price, you okay?" I asked as I fumbled in the dark, searching for the Magnum in Dieter's hands.

"I'm alive if that's what you're asking," he responded.

"Not for long," a new voice said. I knew who it was.

"Sanguine, so nice of you to stop by. Now I won't have to hunt you down and kill you."

That was followed by a deep laugh. I didn't find anything all that amusing.

CHAPTER THIRTY-ONE

As if by magic, the candles on the tables in the room grew a small flame and gave us just enough light to see the carnage on the floor. Both human and undead. I took a deep breath and tried to force the images from my mind. Around me I saw dead and dying officers that I had known for years, even though we had probably never said more than five words to each other. Then there was the other. Small children, mostly between the ages of six and ten, finally truly dead.

Now with a trace of sight, I looked to Dieter to regain the Magnum, only to find it pointed at Sanguine. "What do you think you're doing?"

Price immediately had his weapon on Dieter. "My God, what have we gotten ourselves into?"

He took quick glances around him. "What do we do Paul? I ain't never broken up a vampire fight."

"Easy, we kill the winner." I eased closer to Dieter, my hand out. "Give me that, Dieter. I really don't care who kills Sanguine as long as when we leave here, she's dead." I just wanted the Magnum back in my hands. I knew we were about to go face to face with a really powerful roach and I wouldn't be able to kill it without an advantage.

"You are God here. It is up to you to decide who lives and who dies." Sanguine slithered toward Dieter. "You can either kill me and be killed by Master Sylvester with nothing gained or kill the humans and their wolf and be a hero among all the vampires." She gave a deep growling laugh. "Kill them and we will drink to your success."

Angie returned to human form and drew close to the necro porn star. "If you want us dead, you'll have to go through me." Her naked body flickered in the light, exposing lights and shadows as they danced on her skin.

Sanguine turned to meet Angie and showed her fangs. "I do believe we have some unfinished business of our own, do we not?"

"Bring it on, bitch," Angie said as she stopped just out of Sanguine's reach. "There's nothing I like better than tying up loose ends. Getting my nails dirty is just icing on the cake."

"Kill her, Dieter. Do not be the bumbling idiot you've been your entire life," Sanguine barked. "Kill them all."

"You do it and you know the police will hunt you down and turn you to ash." I tried to remain calm and not let him see just how enraged I was. I wanted the Magnum back in a bad way. "We all lose and the only one that wins is Sylvester. After what you've told me, I'm sure you don't want that." I moved with caution. "Besides, Sanguine will be dead soon enough. I know a big secret about you, sweetheart."

"You cannot fathom killing me, human."

"You killed Isabella Dunlawton's brother in one of Kincaid's movies. That alone will have you separated from your sick head. Make it easy on all of us and just take the bullet. Trust me, no one will shed a tear over it."

"Here to save your damsel in distress. How sweet, Avenger.

First greed, then revenge. It matters not, Avenger. Isabella will die at our discretion. We are simply biding time." She grew confident as she stared me down. "I suppose she has told you about her part in the Crimson Films hasn't she?"

The shock that went through me left me paralyzed. How many skeletons were in this chick's closet?

Sanguine laughed. "You do not have to answer. Your face tells me all I need to know." I could feel her power grow. "She used to be Albert's bookkeeper and got caught in a very bad predicament. Seems she was taking more than her share. She was given the choice of allowing me to feed from her or handing over fresh meat. First she brought us the young virgin Mr. Guzman was filmed with. Poor man didn't know what he was sticking it in at the time, but when he found out, he grew quite upset and threatened to go to the police."

"That's why Guzman was going to kill Isabella and Kincaid that night."

Sanguine smiled. "Now you know. But then to make herself appear innocent, she tried to go to the authorities. I stopped her. Planned on killing her really, when she offered me something I couldn't refuse."

"She gave you her brother," Price answered.

Another evil smile. "That's right, detective. But before doing so, she tried to double cross me and bring in a vampire executioner to kill me. Let's just say, it didn't go as planned. I killed the man and her brother as punishment. Now she is out to save her brother and even the score. Two objectives that will never be reached."

I opened my mouth, but it was Dieter that beat me to the next question. "Where is Sylvester? He is the one that shall die tonight by my hands. Isabella shall be addressed at a later time."

Sanguine laughed. "Why would you kill Sylvester and myself, Dieter? Those with you have been your true enemy. We are your family. Your lifeline. Your power. And very soon your masters."

"He's the one that made me like this. The one that made me live forever. I want my revenge for what he's taken away from me."

"Taken away? He has given you life. Nothing short of being a true god. We control life, death and the after life." She began to walk behind him, watching me all the time. "Besides, could you really kill your true master?" She floated along the room like a demented kite. "Soon he will rule the entire city. Knowing you killed the executioner will gain you much power and prestige. Something Quinn never allowed you to taste." She became motionless. It is the scariest thing roaches do. They don't breathe, they don't move, they are practically standing dead. "Sylvester *will* kill Quinn Rubio. Do not follow his fate. We will join forces with the pure blood vampires and kill all the humans." She looked back to Dieter. "Remember all the lives the humans have taken something away from us. This one in particular," she said pointing to yours truly. "You hold the only thing he has that can kill you. Pull the trigger and vindicate all the loss in your life."

"It will do me no good. No matter how many times I kill, it will never ease the pain of losing my son on that night. It simply reminds me of what I am. Over the centuries I have tried such methods. Death does not bring about retribution or solace. Only nightmares and more hatred."

She rolled her eyes. "You will never be more than a servant vampire earning no more respect than," she turned to Angie, "a common wolf." Back to Dieter. "Without our preying on them, they would overgrow like weeds, bringing about more disease than they already carry. We thin the herd. Indulge in the hunt. Relish the kill."

Angie continued to hold her tongue, but like a bomb, I knew it would go off at any moment. I counted my lucky stars she had shown restraint. If anyone made any sudden moves, I was sure Dieter would put a bullet in me.

"Your son was more of a man than you ever were. And now you have a chance to kill the one that would destroy you if it were not for human law, yet you hesitate? Why?" She was now inches from Dieter.

"What do you know about my son?" Pale Boy looked more dead and hollow than I had ever seen him before.

"I'm the one that killed him. Then killed your beautiful wife."

I saw the hurt and anger mix in those dead eyes of his. He HI steadied myself for the move that would either save or take my life. I looked to Sanguine, who stood only feet away from us, on a stage where the jazz bands would have been. She was dressed in dark red suede, thigh high riding boots of black. There was a smell of fresh cut roses in the air. Perfume on a pig if you ask me.

Her finger traced the barrel of the Magnum, still pointed at her. "Dieter, for once I am proud of you. You are suddenly showing signs of a spine." Sanguine moved even closer. "But do you have the guts to pull the trigger. Turn on your own kind. You know the humans next to you will kill you either way. I, on the other hand, had given your son life, as I have all the others I have tasted. I made him one of my children. Took their blood, gave them life. It was you that brought him death."

"It was you," I said as I moved closer to Sanguine, yet trying to stay clear of where the bullet may go if it was released. "You killed the Guzman girl."

She smiled back at me. "So it was. They are the only ones that have the true pure blood. Some even say it is the fountain of eternal youth." She licked her lips. "I knew you would draw conclusions about her father and Kincaid's business and I would remain out of your focus. How predictable. To the point of disappointment."

"And the Lavara boy?"

Sanguine gave out an evil laugh. "Nothing more than keeping you and the police chasing your tails. I knew such acts would have Dieter trembling in his pants. Sooner or later he would come for your involvement. Oh, how predictable you all are."

"God, give me the gun, Dieter."

"Kill them, Dieter, or I kill you." Sanguine lunged for Dieter, mouth open, fangs exposed. He pulled the trigger. Questioning eyes looked back at us filled quickly with betrayal. Her head exploded throughout the room. Flesh fell over all of us in a flurry of gray matter and cold blood. I heaved twice and swallowed my guts each time.

The body, minus the head stood at attention for about a minute before crumbling to the floor. What remained of her turned to ash. The smell of burnt skin filled the room. I felt like Dorothy at the end of The Wizard of Oz. We had just killed the Wicked Witch.

I looked to Dieter who stared down at what had been one of the most evil women I had ever come across. It was closure for him. Call it sympathy or apathy, but for now, I'd grant him his moment of peace.

Moving with great caution, I came up behind him and took the Magnum out of his hand. I wasn't sure he even knew I had done it, still in that mannequin like state.

Still looking at what was left of Sanguine, he spoke, "End it now, Avenger."

"I'm not going to kill you, Dieter. I'm all out of ugly bullets. Besides, we still need to find Sylvester before he kills Quinn and jumps into bed with the Asa and Sasha."

"I would have thought you would want Quinn dead," Dieter replied.

"I do, but if Sylvester kills him, there will really be a power struggle in this city. It will cause more blood shed not less. Asa and Sasha will not play nice and share like he thinks. And now that Sanguine is dust, he's a little outnumbered and out powered. And that will give rival commercial roaches hope of gaining power."

"Spread out and look for him. We still have a blood sucker to find," I added. We began to cautiously fan out across the floor. I was willing to use Dieter as my bloodhound. He would be drawn to his master a lot easier than I would. Plus, if anything was booby trapped, it should get him instead of us.

"He is this way," Dieter said as he stepped over the dead body of one of the fallen officers.

"This had better not be a trap, Dieter," Price said as he followed in line behind the coffin liter and myself.

"There is no trap, detective. If I wanted to kill you, I would have done it when I had the weapon."

Price looked at me with scared eyes. Dieter was telling the truth. He might have been a real snake in the grass, but he was as blunt as it came when he needed to be.

We worked our way past the main room of the restaurant and down a narrow hall to the kitchen. Dieter stopped short of the freezer door.

"Can you feel Sylvester here?" Price asked.

"No," Dieter simply replied as he reached for the handle. I wanted more time to prepare myself for what was on the other side, but I was thrown into a commitment before I had time to argue. I regressed to my back up plan. Have Magnum ready to fire at anything that moved. "Sylvester sold me to Quinn many years ago. My alliance and pull to him no longer exists."

I opened the door with little fanfare. There were no creepy crawlies slithering along the floor or lunging for our throats. Only darkness, our overworked imaginations and a wave of Arctic air. A crucifix hung overhead as a deterrent for anything undead to attempt escape.

Dieter stopped short of entering the room. I instinctively reached for the light switch and turned it on. In front of us stood the master undead of Orlando, decorated in ice, his dead skin a light shade of blue. He had been tortured quite a bit by the looks of him.

He turned in our direction. It was all I could do not to continue the torture.

"Master, you are safe now," Dieter explained.

"I wouldn't say that." I moved past the skinny monster.

He tried to speak, but the ice made it impossible for him to communicate. "'Sup, buttercup? Ready for a little payback?" I asked as I pulled the crucifix down. It tends to make vein hogs a little nervous when they see it. And when they're nervous, they tend to cooperate a little easier. Especially when they know death can come at any second. "Where's Sylvester?" I screamed as I held it up to his face.

"Look," Angie said, picking up a cell phone next to Quinn. There was a small note attached to it that simply read, 'Call me'.

"He said to tell you to call it if you were still alive. Otherwise, Sanguine was to call after she killed you," Quinn said behind a film of pain.

I took the phone from Angie and opened it. A single number was already programmed and ready to call. I attempted to keep my shaking hands from view as I pressed the green button. The coldness of the phone snapped at my ear. There was only one ring before a voice answered. A voice I knew well.

"With whom am I speaking?"

"What's this about, Sylvester?"

"Avenger? Such a shame. I had so much faith in Sanguine. Does not change things in the least though." His voice showed the sick humor behind it. "I take it you found my little package. I left him just for you. Consider him a gift of alliance. Kill him and we both get what we want."

"And that is?"

"For you, it is not what I want as it is important where I am."

Question. Why is it that a cockroach can never just give you a straight answer? They are as filled with riddles as a Twinkie is with filling. I did my best to remain calm. The more agitated my voice got, the more Sylvester would think he was winning.

"Okay, I'll bite. Where are you?"

"I have come to check on our friend Detective Kansas and his beautiful wife. We have some unfinished business to take care of. All as a favor to Asa. Kill Quinn and I will allow him and his family to live. No tricks, Avenger, we both know Mrs. Kansas is in a delicate way."

"What's he saying?" Angie whispered. I held up a hand to keep her quite.

"You touch any of them and I swear to God, no one will find a flake of ash when I'm done with you." My whole body was now convulsing out of control. I wanted to throw the phone against the wall.

"Just do what you're told and I will keep my end of the bargain. You have my word."

"And what is that, Sylvester. You're nothing more than a serial killer. I know about you and the Knights."

"I killed none of the Knights as you have presumed. And if you do not meet with me, I will bleed one person at the hospital every minute starting with Stephanie Kansas." There was a moment of silence. "And I want Isabella as well. Tick tock, my friend."

Cold chills cascaded down every vertebra in my spine. I knew this cold-blooded hellion would kill a mother and unborn child without thinking about it. I didn't have a lot of time, so I did the only thing I could. I tried to stall. "What do you want with Isabella?"

"It is not what you think. It is not to gain revenge for killing Dubro. I hated the arrogant filth. No, I want the paintings that rightfully belong to me. I am the one that had to cater to his needs and handle his affairs, not her. She can get away with the murder, I do not care, but if she or you defy me the paintings I will hunt her down for all eternity. She will never be able to enjoy her profits. Always looking over her shoulder. Wondering if tonight will be her fateful night."

"So it's about money and greed."

"Five minutes is all you have, Avenger. I wouldn't waste it with further questions. Produce Isabella. Double cross me or try to be a hero and I assure you, there will be blood."

I had to continue to stall and I knew it. There was no way I could get to the hospital in five minutes, even if I wanted to. Negotiating with vein weasels never gave you a winning result, and I wasn't going to let him call the shots tonight. This was going to end tonight one way or the other.

"Where do you think you're going?" Price asked.

"This is personal, Frank. Take care of things here. If I'm lucky, I'll see you in the morning." I started to leave when Angie caught up with me.

"I'm coming with you."

"Not this time, Angie. I need you to stay here and help with Price. I don't like leaving him alone with two fang heads. They will kill him just to spite me and you know it."

"I'm not a baby sitter, Paul."

"And I don't need one." This from Price. "Now you tell me what's going on here. You look like you've seen a ghost."

"Sylvester is going to die tonight. I have to go."

"Where is he?" Price asked.

"At the hospital. I'll explain when I get back. I only have five minutes to get there before he starts his little execution. I don't want to be late." I thought about what Stephanie had told me. "I have just added another reason to kill the monster responsible for all this."

CHAPTER THIRTY-TWO

I entered the hospital filled with fear and apprehension. Inside, I felt as though I had brought this upon the Kansas' for who I was and what I did. My mind was very focused. I had to reach Kansas' room. Logic told me Sylvester would be close by. I sprinted up the four flights of stairs, knowing the elevators would be clogged with people and take far too long. The hallways weren't much better. I could hear voices and machines all around me. Life still existed here, but for how long I wasn't sure.

The dark shadow stepped out of one of the rooms with confidence. He blocked all the light in the hallway like an eclipse of the sun. "Asa," I said.

He gave me a half smile, but it wasn't friendly. "So nice of you to join us, Avenger."

"What are you doing here?"

"Revenge, my friend. Bittersweet revenge." He walked in my direction, his boots squeaked along the well waxed floor. "Detective Kansas has tried to take away my life, now I will take away something of his."

I put my hand on the Magnum. "Where's Sylvester?"

"Do you really think that weapon will kill me? I am far more powerful than anything you have on you."

"Take another step and we'll see." I pulled the gun into position. "I understand you might be a little ticked off at Kansas, but it's not worth losing your life over. Now where's Sylvester?"

"Close. We both want him dead, but for very different reasons. Do not worry of him. It is me that you will have to deal with if you chose to be the hero." He stopped about fifteen feet from me. "I will give you Sylvester, but Detective Kansas is mine."

"I don't negotiate with cockroaches. Now I'm only going to ask you once more to either walk away, or let me by. I *am* going to go to Kansas' room and get him and his wife out of here safely. The only thing still in doubt is if you leave on your own or in a body bag. Choose wisely."

"You will not find them in the room you seek."

I knew this wasn't good. "Where are they?"

"That is why we must talk before we start the killing."

"Funny, I have nothing to say that I haven't already said. Now walk away like a good little blood sucker." I took a step forward, keeping my eyes glued on him.

"Perhaps there is a way we both can get what we want out of this without bloodshed."

"Such as?"

"You look for a killer of your kind and to protect the ones you love, is this not true?"

"Yes."

"I seek the same for my kind."

"As I always seem to say when we talk, Asa, get to a point."

"I will help you kill Sylvester if you allow me to feed upon your power. Both vampire and wolf virus running through your veins, making you far more powerful than you know, yet human enough to walk in the sunlight. I wish to feel it in my own veins. Do this and I will allow you to walk out of here with the humans you seek. I can smell your blood." He sniffed the air. "Intoxicating. Delicious."

"You seem to think I need your help in killing Sylvester." I remained still. I wanted enough space between us in case he decided to do something. If I were right up on him, he'd be able to overpower me with both strength and speed. "And as for the Big Gulp, answer's no."

"And you, Avenger, seem to think you have a choice."

I didn't allow enough room. He was on top of me in a blur of speed, knocking me backwards on the waxed floor. I slid for what seemed to be forever. His black hands wrapped tight around my throat. I brought the Magnum around best I could and fired it into his side. The vice grip like hands released my throat as he howled in pain. I could see the blood ooze from the wound between two ribs.

His large fist came back down on me, crushing into my jaw. It felt as though my eye socket was now in the back of my head. Before I had time to think, a second blast came across the same spot and sent my sight into a world of dark colors mixing with the unimaginable pain. I waited for the bullet to take its toll on him, turning him into nothing more than a glorified ashtray. But instead, he continued to pound away at my face and body.

I had to get out from under him. If I didn't, I was as good as dead. The Magnum pushed against his skin, but this time he moved with speed that caught me off guard yet again. The bullet missed, but when he moved, I was able to roll out from under him.

I jumped to my feet and wiped away the endless flow of blood from my eyes. Staring at the face of an ancient master coffin critter is not something that usually ends well, but I was there like it or not.

The blood continued to flow from the wound in Asa's side. "Why aren't you dead yet," I said as I pulled the trigger on the Magnum again. The recoil pushed me backwards as the bullet found its mark in Asa's chest. He dropped to his knees but came at me all the same. I backed away from his advance and fired again. Even with two bullets in him, he moved toward me. I could see the death in his face, but the revenge and hatred was still there. Growing and unstoppable.

A final push from the monster had him on me again. His large hands pinned me to the floor. I was unable to lift the Magnum up enough to get another bullet in him. Large droplets of blood fell on me as it escaped the wound in his chest. I could smell the sulpher of his burning skin.

Large fangs gleamed as he opened his mouth. Syrup-like saliva dripped from his lips. He had plans of feeding off of me, like it or not.

I mustered up all the strength I had and began to lift my pinned arm. It was the only way I was going to be able to save my own life.

"Once I feed from you, I shall be the most powerful vampire alive." His face lowered to the nape of my neck. I felt the razor-like fangs break my skin. My arms continued to lift but there wouldn't be enough time. Even if I could overpower him, with the blood loss, I would begin to weaken rather quickly. I screamed in both pain and rebellion, calling on all the hatred I had in me. Putting as much pressure on my elbow as I could, I began to lift from under him. I could feel the life in me being sucked away. I began to panic. I closed my eyes and head butted him as hard as I could. Nothing. Again I hit him in the head with my own. I felt the grip loosen this time. There was hope. A third time. I rammed my skull into his and felt the fangs retreat from the deep wound in my neck.

I brought the butt of the Magnum along the side of his head and repeated the action until he was face down next to me. Blood filled the wounds. It dropped to the floor around us. I stood as quick as I could. The hall spun from the loss of my own fluids. I stumbled as if drunk.

The Magnum was about to attack again when he pulled my leg out from under me. The bullet was wasted in the wall behind him. Fangs stuck in my boot like a snake. I kicked him hard with the free foot, knocking him off of me. I pulled the trigger several more times, out of fear more than anything. Hitting walls and ceiling and bat dung.

From my side, I removed a wooden stake and came at him again. He tried to come to his feet, but fell under his own weight to the floor. I wasted no time in burying the wooden stake deep into his back, driving it through his heart. Asa was dead.

Blood swelled from the wounds, but the fire I expected never happened. He was stronger than the light. Possibly just more evil.

I'd be back to cut his head off in a minute. Right now I had to get the blood flow to stop. I cautiously moved past Asa's dead body. There was something about those horror movies that always got to me. The bad guy always reached up and grabbed the good guy one last time. It didn't happen here.

I moved down the hallway, holding my neck as blood oozed between my fingers. Roaches have non-coagulating saliva that keeps the flow of blood moving and that wasn't going to work well for me. Bleeding to death wasn't on my agenda.

On the wall was a cockroach first aid kit. Standard in all public places since the new laws came down. They might be legal, but old habits died harder than the fang heads. And now that bloodsuckers were allowed in all public places without question, the chances of an attack were increased ten fold.

I opened the kit and pulled out the coagulating serum and needle. Did I mention I hated needles? With the amount of blood that poured from the wound I knew I didn't have much of a choice. I was already unsteady on my legs, weak, and sick to my stomach.

Thinking as many happy thoughts as I could, I broke the plastic packaging from the syringe and stuck it in the small glass bottle. Once I had the adequate amount, I went into the bathroom where I could see my handy work in the mirror and know where to shoot the serum.

My first reaction when I saw the wound was, I'm going to bleed to death before I can get this needle in my neck. As ironic as it sounds, I panic at the sight of blood. My blood anyway. I took a deep breath and jabbed the needle into the wound and pushed the serum in as quickly as possible, ignoring the burning sensation. Next, I cleaned as much blood away from the bite as I could with cold water until there was nothing but the small marks. New blood bubbled up immediately. Before it could run down my neck, I took a large piece of gauze and taped it to the wound. I didn't look pretty, but I would live. And that was important.

I returned to the hallway and found a note on the wall written in blood. "Follow the dead people". The only thing to do was play Sylvester's game of demented hide and seek. He had the hostages. He made the rules.

I found myself nearly falling to my knees in fear. Asa was no longer in the hallway. Either someone came and got him or he wasn't as dead as I thought. It would have to wait for now. If it was the latter, I was sure I'd see him again before this was all over.

I moved further down the hallway, past the nurses' station and began to understand what the note meant. On the floor in front of me was a young nurse, covered in blood. Her throat had been ripped completely out. A large pool of thick reddish black fluid formed a small lake in the middle of the floor. Her stomach had been ripped in half, exposing intestines and things I was sure I didn't want to know.

The trail of blood led me to the stairs on the opposite end of the hospital. Holding my breath and expecting the worst, I opened the door and looked in all directions including up. The more powerful vein high jackers can defy gravity and just hang in the air at ease. I didn't find a fang head, but I found the results of his work again. Another body draped across the stairs, his clothing stained with his own blood. Sylvester wasn't feeding. He was simply taking life. That made him even more dangerous than the typical cockroach.

Following the blood and bodies littered along the way, I snaked my way to a very fitting end. The morgue. I had been in every morgue in every hospital in Central Florida at one time or another and this one was no exception.

My finger reached for the buzzer, when the door automatically opened. I saw this as a bad sign. Sylvester already knew I was here. I took a moment to pray. Something I normally never did, but it seemed like the thing to do at the time. I opened the door, Magnum drawn.

I saw the albino vein junkie. He stood on the far end of the room. Below him, I saw Zeke and Stephanie Kansas, bound and gagged. Kansas looked at me, helpless and still a bit pale. Hopelessness was taking root. Stephanie looked at me with pure fear and she had good reason. She stood the chance of dying and never being able to tell her husband about their good fortune. I wasn't about to let that happen.

"So good you could make it," Sylvester said.

"And now I'm here to kill you." I pointed the Magnum at Sylvester and pulled the trigger to the worst sound I could hear. Nothing. Then it hit me. In all the excitement upstairs with Asa, my bite, and following the trail of corpses, it never dawned on me to refill the Magnum. I had suddenly gone from advantage to screwed.

Sylvester remained still for a few seconds before busting out in laughter. "The great executioner has come here to be the hero cowboy and forgot to load his gun. How typical."

He literally flew through the air and landed on me with the force of a small hurricane. Claws reached for my face, held my jaw. Fingernails pierced skin, threatening to break through to my mouth. "I see you have already been someone's meal," he said.

I reached for the 9mm on my hip and stuck it in his neck and pulled the trigger. This time I had better results. It was filled with silver nitrate bullets, but I was willing to take any advantage back that I could. Sylvester immediately retracted his hand from my face and held the wound. I shifted my weight, knocking him to the ground next to me.

I could hear the gurgling sounds coming from his throat as he choked on his own blood. From my coat, I pulled out a bottle of holy water and poured it in the wound and across his face. While distracted, I began to pummel his face with my fist. The sound of frying skin filled my ears. The smells of it went to my nose.

Sylvester began to lift from the floor, but I sent him right back with another bullet to the chest. He screamed and rolled along the floor several times before rising next to me.

I stepped back and tried to swallow my growing fear. The cockroach shed his vest as blood continued to flow from the neck wound. "You didn't think I'd be that easy to kill did you?" It was then, I saw the reason. "That's right," he started, "Kevlar. I know everything there is to know about you and your weapons and I am prepared to bring you and all the others to the grave." With anther quick move he slapped the 9mm from my hand. It slid across the floor. I wasn't sure where. Sylvester was on the attack again before I could see it stop. "I will kill them in front of you for denying my wishes."

I reached for the other wooden stake I had on me and moved toward him. My arm swung forward with the stake, only to be met by Sylvester's. My muscles burned against the strain. Pain blossomed in the wound at my neck. I could feel the traces of monster in me grow with each push. Still, I was no match for Sylvester one on one. I'd have to do the same thing I always did in this type of situation. Cheat.

I shoved my knee between his legs with everything I had. Sylvester dropped to the ground. I brought the stake down on him, catching him in the shoulder. It wasn't a fatal blow, but it kept him on the defensive. I pulled it from the wound. "End this now, Sylvester. Confess to the murders and I'll kill you as fast as I can." I took the blunt end of the large stake and began to hit him in the back of the head with everything I had. Again and again and again. Skin broke free into islands surrounded by blood. It showed up a lot better against his white hair and skin than most of the dirt nappers I had killed, making the wounds appear far worse than they probably were.

With each hit, he fell farther and farther onto the floor. I wanted him dead, but I wanted him to suffer too. I wanted to hear from his own lips that he had killed the man that might have been my father. Hear him confess to the deaths of the members of the Knights of the Night. I needed to hear it for myself.

I rolled him over and saw the dazed look in his stare. Close enough to death, he wouldn't be able to rise, but alive enough to give me my fix. "Tell me why you killed them." He stared back up at me. I could feel the power leaking from his body. There was no emotion in his face. I began to think maybe I had hit him one time too many to get my answers. I placed my foot on his throat and allowed more blood to leave the wound in the neck. "I won't ask you again. Confession is good for the soul." I pulled at the Kevlar vest, opened it and exposed his pale chest.

"I…never…killed…" The light faded into darkness. He wasn't dead, but I was willing to let him suffer for a few more minutes. Sylvester was going to struggle for his last few minutes of being undead.

I looked over to Kansas and Stephanie. A new look of horror filled Stephanie's eyes. Feeling I needed to get them out of here as soon as possible, I ran to Stephanie and began to cut the bindings from her hands and feet.

I heard her scream behind the gag in her mouth. The weak power gave him away. Sylvester stood behind me, blood dripped from his head and neck. Chunks of his skull were missing along with the clumps of white hair, revealing the brain underneath. One eye dangled from its socket like a pendulum on a clock. He looked like an egg that had been dropped.

My elbow met with his chest. Unlike his head, it was still quite solid, but it gave me the result I was looking for. Sylvester stumbled backwards. I moved toward him with all the power and speed I had. The cockroach dodged my attack. I fell to the floor empty handed. He stood above me and was about to do one of two things. Either say something or attempt to drive his fangs in me. Neither happened.

Stephanie fired the 9mm into his chest cavity three times, pushing dead flesh and pieces of his heart out of the wounds. He looked at me in helpless surprise, and then fell to the floor next to me.

I looked up at Stephanie, then to her husband. "He teach you that?" I tried to catch my breath.

She shook her head and gave out a nervous laugh. "Yeah. Says there are too many vampires in the world not to know how to use a gun."

I looked to Kansas and met his smile as I came back to my feet. "Let's get him out of here before something else comes through the door." I meant Asa. If he was still alive, there was no telling what he was thinking or when he might do it.

"Is it really over?" Stephanie asked.

I turned to see Sylvester bleeding on the floor. There was no power. No life. "Yeah, it's over."

CHAPTER THIRTY-THREE

I found a saw in the morgue and cut Sylvester's head off. The last thing I wanted was for him to get up and walk away like Asa apparently did. That scared the crap out of me. There is nothing worse than a master daisy pusher with a vendetta against you.

After the expected hugs and thank you's from Kansas and Stephanie, and after the paramedics began to check out my friends and make sure they were still in working shape, I did the only thing I knew to do. I disappeared into the night. I was covered head to toe with blood. Some mine, some not. I had been bitten, nearly bled to death, and battled with more blood lovers than I could remember. I was dead tired. Bad choice of words, I know, but it was the truth. My muscles were shaking and sore. My neck was throbbing and sensitive.

Knowing we had our true killer, I could now relax a little and sleep well. No longer was there the threat that tonight, another member of the Knights might bite the dust. Again, bad choice of words, but deal with it. And for icing on the cake, it looked like we might have killed the child killer that had plagued generations for centuries. All in all, it had been a good night.

I pulled into my driveway and closed my eyes for a few seconds, enjoying the nothingness I heard. If I was lucky, Isabella would be safely tucked away in bed, the threat on her life now gone. That was key. Now that it was over, she could leave, giving me back my home and my solitude. Yeah, there was that other thing, but I think it was for the best if I remained unattached for a while. It just worked out best for me that way.

Inside my home, I felt it. Something was very different. Isabella would not be able to put off this amount of energy. I stopped to listen to the sounds. Afraid to move or breathe. Somewhere in the darkness another cockroach roamed.

Asa. He wasn't dead. He had come here to settle a score and probably kill Isabella. After all, whoever ended up with the paintings, stood a good chance of landing a lot of money. And money spent just as easily for a thousand year old blood lapper as it did the rest of us.

I took a large step forward and turned on the light leading into the living room. Initially, I was blinded, but as the light filtered in, I was able to see anything that might have been hiding in the darkness.

Moving as smooth as I could, I pulled out the Magnum, now filled with ultraviolet bullets. "Isabella," I called out.

"Paul?" she asked, as she entered the room. There was something about her demeanor that told me she hadn't expected me back so soon. Or at all. "What are you doing here?"

"I kind of live here."

She gave a nervous laugh. We were both anxiously nervous, but I guessed it was about two different things. Isabella looked as though she had seen a ghost.

"You alright?" I asked.

"Yeah, shouldn't I be? Did you kill Sylvester?"

I shook my head as I began to move toward her, but looked in all directions for the vein head that I knew was still in my house. Where, I wasn't sure. "Is there anyone else here with you?"

"No, why?"

Now it was up to me to decide whether she was lying or didn't know about Asa being in the house. I continued to move through the room, looking in every corner. "I need you to walk toward me as easy as you can. We have to go."

"What's wrong, Paul?"

I took her hand and began to pull her toward the door. "I don't think you're alone in here."

"What do you mean I'm not alone? Of course I'm alone. Who else is here?" There was a slight resistance. I pulled anyway.

"I don't know, but I feel power. You happen to be real popular among the daisy pushers right now. They are just as big of whores when it comes to money as the humans are. Sylvester might be dead, but that's not the end of your problems."

She pulled away from my grasp. "Hold on and I'll get my pistol." Before I could tell her not to worry about it, she had it out. Pointed at me. "I can't tell if you're this stupid or smart."

I stood still. "Being at this end of a gun, I'm guessing stupid. I just don't know why yet."

"If you had just died, things wouldn't have had to be this complicated."

"So you killed Dubro didn't you?"

She smiled. "You could say that, I guess. We are business partners. I save my brother, he profits from the investments of the Knights. It's a shame I'll have to kill you, especially after last night."

Now I had changed gears. If Asa was here to kill the little princess, so be it. So much for gratitude. I had saved her life, given her a place to stay and killed the monster that was hot on her trail. What did I get in return? A gun stuck in my face. "How do you expect him to gain from anything in his current condition?"

Cascading down my stairs, I saw my answer. I wasn't sure whether to be freaked out or just pissed off. "So good to see you again, Avenger," Dubro said, wearing a shiny gold suit and sparking sunglasses. He stopped and looked at me as he hit the bottom stair. "You look as though you have just seen a ghost."

I looked to Isabella, back to Dubro. "You faked your own death?"

"Quite simple really. The police never check the ashes for forensics of any kind. They simply assumed. And you know what they say about people that assume."

"I don't suppose you can enlighten me on all of this."

"I do not see the harm in it. After all, Isabella will put a bullet in your brain as a final act to all of this anyway." He came to stand by Isabella. "You see, if people and vampires alike think you are dead, you can get away with so much more, do you not think?"

"And exactly what is it that you think you're getting away with?"

"Murder."

"How so?"

"You, as well as the police think Sylvester was your killer, correct?"

I nodded.

"So wrong, Avenger. It was me all the time. You see the Knights of the Night financed my art business. Every cent of it. Investing in their future they called it. They all agreed to invest in Crimson Madness in exchange, they would reap the reward of the profits it produced. I never intended for the gallery to make a single dime. In fact I did everything I could to ensure of its failure. That is why you were invited that night. I knew it would go horribly wrong. You cannot seem to leave a place without something bleeding and crawling in a corner to die. In the environment of that night, you were played like a song. In fact, I'm the one that tipped Sasha of the occasion."

"In order to run off with the money you killed them?"

"That is correct. It was much easier than I had ever dreamed. Sending Sylvester to be my bait. He might have been beautiful, but there was nothing going on upstairs. Simply powerful and power hungry. I had him set up meetings with each of them. Let those that would talk know of such things. Allow Sylvester to be caught with the fingerprints and other wonderfully horrible things. All I had to do after that was wait for you and the police to find it."

I looked to Isabella. "And you think he's just going to let you leave here with all those paintings? They are just as valuable to him as they are to you. You won't live through the night before he kills you."

"I'll take my chances. You see, this gun has ultraviolet bullets in it. If he tries anything foolish, he will be ash for real."

"This all explains why you didn't kill anyone at the Crimson last night. It was all a set up wasn't it?"

She laughed. "Guilty as charged."

"The fire at the Madness, you set it deliberately didn't you?"

Dubro broke in. "Not only will I be able to sail away with the Knight's money, but insurance money as well. You have to admit, it is quite flawless. I have left Isabella as the trustee to my accounts. She will be able to get everything for me."

"And you think you can trust her?"

"I know I can. I have her brother in my possession. One wrong move on her part, one sign of betrayal and I will turn him in to the authorities."

I glanced back to Isabella. "And I guess all those theatrics last night set me up to kill Sylvester for you didn't it."

"You catch on a little too late," Isabella started. "Now if you don't mind, I have a plane to catch and paintings to sell."

I moved the Magnum on her. It made her small pistol look like a water gun. "Drop the gun, or I swear, I'll blow your blond brains all over this room."

"Isabella, we must go," Dubro said softly. "Shoot him."

I kept my Magnum and eyes on Isabella, but talked to Dubro. I began to replant myself so I could keep my sight on both of them. There was no doubt that Dubro was far more dangerous than Isabella, but she had the gun pointing at me. That gave her a bit more respect. "What's wrong Dubro? Didn't you plan on me coming back alive and killing your little slave here? If I kill her, you have nothing."

"Quite the opposite, Avenger. At most it will be a delay. I have the Knights investment money, the key to the storage for the paintings, and no one on my trail. At most, I will lose a small amount from the insurance. Simply trivial in the long run."

"And if I kill you instead?" I asked, still talking to Dubro.

"Then you've helped me out. If he's really dead, I don't share anything with anybody," Isabella broke in. She took a step back and pointed the gun now on both me and Dubro. "In fact, I think I'll save myself a little trouble and kill you both."

Dubro laughed, but I could tell there was a hint of nervousness in it. "My dear Isabella, if you do such a thing, you are writing your brother's death warrant. We must learn to share and trust one another. There is so much to gain and lose in all of this for both of us."

"Isabella, you know as well as I do, he will kill you like he did the other humans he's used. Once he has all the money coming to him from your help, he will waste no time in sinking his fangs in you."

Dubro tried to move behind me, further away from Isabella. "Move back over here where I can see you or I'll turn you into a real flaming cockroach."

He stopped as he thought it through. Here we were. All together in my snuggly little home and none of us trusted the other. Kind of reminded me of an intense version of Thanksgivings I'd heard people talk about. "Kill him, Isabella. The sun will be up in only two hours and we have much to do."

Isabella looked at me. "Will you help me find my brother if I kill him?"

I shook my head. "No, not in the way you think. He's a fugitive and there's nothing I can do to help him."

I could see the hurt in her eyes and there was nothing I could do about it. Sure, I could've lied and gotten myself out of this situation a little easier, but then again, I never liked taking the easy road. It just wasn't me.

Before I had a chance to react, Dubro was on me, attacking with lethal power. "Looks as though Asa has beaten me to your throat, Avenger."

I refused to allow him to kill me. I brought the Magnum up to his chest and pulled the trigger. His fingers remained tight around my neck even though I could smell him start to burn from the inside out. I couldn't get my breath. Suffocating as I looked into his eyes. It was all I could do to keep my wits about me. His power was strong and pulled me in. *"If I die, you will die with me,"* he said in my mind.

I could now feel his pain as I continued to fight his power to destroy me. In doing so, he channeled his pain and hate into me. I could feel the bullet in my side as if I had shot myself. My muscles burned with the ultraviolet madness. Against my will, I began to buckle under the power and pain and fall to the floor. I wanted to shoot him again, but I wasn't sure if I could take the pain, as funny as that sounds to say it. But when you're fighting for your life, you do what you have to do. No matter the price it costs.

The Magnum now set against his chest. I took a deep breath and screamed. It was going to hurt like a son of a bitch. I pulled the trigger for the second time. The bullet found its mark and Dubro's heart exploded in his chest.

My hands held my own chest as the pain nearly tore me in two. I could feel Dubro's hands instantly release my throat, but it did nothing to help with my own pain. I wasn't sure how he was able to do it, but he was actually killing me with my own bullet.

I found myself face down on the floor, writhing in torture. My own muscles felt as though they were on fire. Was it all in my head? I couldn't straighten up enough to be sure. Then it ended as violently as it started. I knew Dubro was dead.

Still holding my chest, I rose to see what was left of Dubro glowing in orange ash. My breath remained shallow, but at least I was breathing again. The pain had eased like a retreating tide against the beach. I looked around for Isabella only to find the front door open.

I moved outside and searched in the darkness for any signs of her. There was nothing. She wouldn't get far. No one survived on their own long when coffin crispies were looking for you. She had the two things all roaches craved. Money and blood. They *would* find her. They had the time and the patience to do it. I would be doing her a favor by telling the police. Then again, the little bitch pulled a gun on me. I might get over it one day, but in the meantime, let her look over her shoulder every night and wonder when the attack would come. Let her become the hunted for a while. She wasn't my problem anymore. I hunted and killed fang heads and fang heads only. She made her bed, now she had to sleep in it. I hoped she would turn herself in one day, knowing how hopeless her situation was.

For me, I would try to get a good night of sleep and try to, once again, do some soul searching. Would I, or even could I, forgive my mother for something I wasn't even sure was true? Would I be able to give Price the respect he deserved and not simply think about what I thought was best for him? With Kansas becoming a father, would I be able to pull him into my dangerous world without thought? And then there was Angie. Could I ever see her as anything other than a monster? Had I made any progress on my own issues?

Screw it all. I was tired, the sun was rising and all good little vein weasels would be snug in their coffins. I needed sleep. Like it or not the darkness would return like a lost friend and it would all start over again.

ACKNOWLEDGMENTS

Since the time my first novel, *Tortured Skin* was published, I have realized a very big truth. Writing the book is only the beginning of the blood, sweat and tears of becoming a published author. And anyone that has put pen to paper knows that the author isn't the only person that has made the book a reality. There are people of every walk of life that have given time, effort, and sometimes financial support to make my dream come true. And for the belief in me and the Paul Isaac Vampire Series, I would like to thank the following for simply being who they are:

My original #1 fan, my grandmother. My mom and dad, who have given me every ounce of support by simply being there. My number two biggest fan, Lura. Allan Gilbreath for taking a chance on me even after meeting me! To my friend Dave, for buying the very first copy of *Tortured Skin*, Julie, for the free advertisement on the back of her car with the slogan, "Don't make me go Paul Isaac on you!". Great authors I've met along the way such as Lori Strongin for kicking my behind in gear to become a better writer, everyone with the Orlando Writer's League, the Florida Writer's

Conference, Allison Cassatta (who will be the next big name in vampire writing), Brian G. Murray and Terrie Relf for being good friends.

A big thank you to all the book festivals, shows, stores and web sites that have supported me. Dena of B&L books in Altamonte Springs, Fl., Sharon with Chapters Book Store in Galax, Va., David Price with Cold Coffee Magazine, Selene and Paula at Borders, Savannah Book Festival, Spooky Empire, Authors on Grayson, Writer's Chai, PopSyndicate, The Wiccan Community of Orlando and the Witches' Ball, Todd Martin of www.horrornews.net, www.usabooknews.com and Scarlett with www.vampirelibrarian.com.

And best of all, thank you to everyone that has read *Tortured Skin* and become a part of the Vampire Nation and James C. Gillen Fan Club. You are awesome. Now get over your bad self and start reading!

ABOUT THE AUTHOR

James C. Gillen is creative mind behind the award winning Paul Isaac Vampire Series, including Tortured Skin, Crimson Madness, and Sins of Retribution from Hydra Publications. He has won the Florida Writers Royal Palm Award for Best in Horror, Best in Horror at Imaginarium, Finalist with Book USA's Best in Horror.

James lives in Orlando, Florida with his American bulldog, Pursey. He's also a graphic artist and bass player for a couple of local jazz big bands. He enjoys riding motorcycles and spending quality time with his family.

ALSO BY JAMES C. GILLEN

The Paul Isaac Vampire Series

Tortured Skin

Sins of Retribution